MARSHAL OF SNOWDONIA

Frank Marshal Crime Thriller Book 1

SIMON MCCLEAVE

STAMFORD

MARSHAL OF SNOWDONIA

by Simon McCleave

A Frank Marshal Crime Thriller
Book 1

First published by Stamford Publishing Ltd in 2025

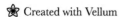 Created with Vellum

BOOKS BY SIMON McCLEAVE

THE DI RUTH HUNTER SERIES

#1. The Snowdonia Killings

#2. The Harlech Beach Killings

#3. The Dee Valley Killings

#4. The Devil's Cliff Killings

#5. The Berwyn River Killings

#6. The White Forest Killings

#7. The Solace Farm Killings

#8. The Menai Bridge Killings

#9. The Conway Harbour Killings

#10. The River Seine Killings

#11. The Lake Vyrnwy Killings

#12. The Chirk Castle Killings

#13. The Portmeirion Killings

#14. The Llandudno Pier Killings

#15. The Denbigh Asylum Killings

#16. The Wrexham Killings

#17. The Colwyn Bay Killings

#18. The Chester Killings

#19. The Llangollen Killings

#20. The Wirral Killings

#21. The Abersoch Killings

THE DC RUTH HUNTER MURDER CASE SERIES

#1. Diary of a War Crime

#2. The Razor Gang Murder

#3. An Imitation of Darkness

#4. This is London, SE15

THE ANGLESEY SERIES - DI LAURA HART

#1. The Dark Tide

#2. In Too Deep

#3. Blood on the Shore

#4. The Drowning Isle

#5. Dead in the Water

PSYCHOLOGICAL THRILLER

Last Night at Villa Lucia (Storm Publishing)

Your FREE book is waiting for you now!

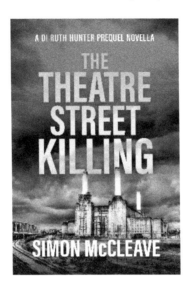

Get your FREE copy of the prequel to
the DI Ruth Hunter Series NOW
http://www.simonmccleave.com/vip-email-club
and join my VIP Email Club

Prologue

Consciousness returns to her in steady waves. Then a desperate gasping breath as she tries to suck in air. A rising panic as the air in her lungs seems to be running out of oxygen. And then, finally, a deep gasp of relief.

An odd mixture of scents drifts slowly to her nostrils. Musty and damp, but also acrid chemicals. Thick, like that of smelling salts from the old-fashioned first aid kits in the 70s. Or maybe a hairdressing salon.

What the hell happened to me? … And where on earth am I?

She can't see anything. An impenetrable darkness. She blinks to see if there's any contrast between eyes open or eyes shut.

There isn't.

As she swallows, her throat is red raw. Similar to when she used to suffer from tonsillitis as a child. Like swallowing fragments of glass. Bracing herself for each swallow and the intense pain it brings.

Still fighting to remain conscious. Slipping in and out of a heavy stupor.

And her head.

Jesus! She has a throbbing headache like someone is hitting the

1

inside of her skull with a claw hammer. Is it a hangover? It feels like a bad one.

If it is, she hasn't had a hangover like this since she was a student nurse and drank half a bottle of Jameson's whiskey. Why can't she piece the last few hours together? And why is she lying in the darkness?

I'm definitely not in my bedroom.

Starting to move a little, she can feel the hard surface beneath her back. It certainly isn't a bed. With a tiny stroke of her forefinger, she touches whatever it is she is on top of. It has texture. A wood of some sort. A floor?

Am I lying on a wooden floor? Did I pass out?

Too soft to be a floorboard.

She tries to move again.

Nothing.

There is also a stinging pain coming from the back of her scalp.

As if someone's hit her hard on the back of the head.

What the …

She gives an exasperated sigh.

Her body seems unable to respond to the simple request that her brain is making to move her limbs.

With focussed concentration, she wills her legs to move.

Come on, you can do this.

Nothing.

Another audible gasp of frustration.

'Jesus!'

Then a wave of terrible, terrifying fear.

Am I paralysed?

She tries to move again.

Nothing.

Legs, feet, arms react as if made from heavy lead.

Oh my God, what's happened to me?

Her pulse starts to race, thudding rhythmically like a drumbeat. Getting faster. Louder.

Have I been in an accident? Have I fallen down some-where when I was drunk?

The only thing she can do is slowly wiggle her fingers.

Then she fixates on listening closely to the room she's in. She hears something. Or is it just some white noise? The slight ring of tinnitus that came with age. She's in her mid 60s.

But then a sound comes out of the thick darkness.

A rustling or swishing.

As if someone is entering the space where she is lying. Not the sound of footsteps. More the soft noise that clothing makes when you walk. The material of trousers as legs rub together. Maybe the gentle pad of a socked foot.

'Hello?' she croaks. 'Is someone there?' *Her words sound stran-gled. What she'd give for a swig of cold water.*

A penetrating silence.

Her pulse quickens again. Growing fear pulsating. A bass rhythm in the carotid artery in her neck.

'Yes,' *says a man's voice. It sounds strange. Electronic.*

Jesus! If she could have moved, she would have jumped out of her skin.

'Where am I? What's going on?' *she asks as her body floods with an overwhelming fear.* 'Who are you? I … I can't move.'

'I know,' *the man says as if she's being idiotic.* 'That's the point.'

Searching the darkness, she can roughly locate where the terrifying voice has come from but it's just too black to see anything.

'Why are you doing this to me?' *Her eyes fill with warm tears. It's all too much for her to bear.* 'Please …'

'I'd hoped it wouldn't come to this.'

It sounds as if the man is using some kind of machine to make his voice have an electronic tone to it. Like a dalek from Dr Who, or one of those American films where a kidnapper uses a device to disguise their voice over a phone line.

Silence.

She squints into the darkness. The man, whoever he is, seems to have gone.

Disappeared.

Or has he?

A horrible, overwhelming nothingness.

Moving her feet, she realises that she can now roll her ankles around. She feels an object against her skin. Then she remembers. It's her mobile phone. She shoved it into her sock as soon as she realised that she was in danger. Thank God her abductor hasn't found it.

As she checks, there's also movement in her wrists and elbows. It's as if she is slowly coming back to life.

Maybe she can reach down to get the phone in a second or two. Make an emergency phone call.

For a moment, she has hope that there might be a way out of this.

Then she hears movement again. The same gentle swishing of material.

Her heart sinks.

She freezes and holds her breath.

Suddenly, a single bulb hanging from the ceiling explodes into light.

After the darkness, her eyes sting from the bright whiteness. Squinting, she opens her right eye by a millimetre. The glare is intensifying her headache.

Blinking, she tries to adjust her eyes to see where she is and who is in front of her.

A dark figure slowly approaches where she's lying.

'What do you want from me?' she asks as fear sweeps through her. Had he turned on the light because he was now going to kill her?

As her retinas finally grow accustomed to the light, she focusses on the man standing in front of her.

He is dressed in black, and has a black Japanese-style mask that covers his face except for his eyes.

It's petrifying to look at it.

'What the hell do you want from me?' she whimpers as she takes in her surroundings. She's lying on top of a large wooden table in some kind of cellar. There are empty metallic shelving units on the far side. A step ladder. The ceiling is made up of white square polystyrene tiles, some of which are stained brown at the edges.

'Don't worry, you'll get used to the light in a minute,' the man says calmly. His tone is almost caring and gentle.

'Who the bloody hell are you?' she snarls.

He ignores her. 'You've been sedated. That's why you've got a headache, sore throat, dry mouth. And I had to hit you on the back of the head to stop you struggling. There's a nasty gash. Lots of blood. But it's stopped bleeding now. And it's good to see the movement has come back to your arms and legs.'

'Please, just answer me,' she says, sounding desperate. 'What am I doing here?'

'Once the sedative wears off, I'm going to need you to come with me,' he explains softly.

'Where?' she asks.

The man snorts an amused laugh. 'That's for me to know, and you to find out. A little magical mystery tour, as it were.'

She doesn't say anything for a few seconds.

Then she asks, 'Are you going to kill me?'

He shrugs. 'I haven't decided yet.'

Chapter 1

Annie Taylor sat up in bed. Reaching over to the bedside table, she took her reading glasses, popped them on the bridge of her nose and then grabbed her phone. She could hear her husband Stephen downstairs in the kitchen. As usual, he had come home very late and slept in the spare room. She didn't know why they called it the *spare* room. Stephen had been sleeping in there for the best part of three years. Their marriage was one of resigned tolerance. A loveless convenience. Stephen was having yet another affair. Annie didn't care. He was quite simply a prick.

Feeling a sharp twinge in her hand, Annie shifted her right arm so that she was comfortable. She'd had two minor wrist operations in recent years and had a very slow degeneration of the bones. Her doctor had told her that at the age of seventy-two, it was just a result of getting old. Seventy-two! Wow. How the hell did that happen? In her head, she was about nineteen. *Bewitched* by *Doris Day* was the number one single on the day she was born in April 1950. *Annie Get Your Gun* was the popular film at the time. To say that it was such a different time didn't really do justice to the extraordinary events and changes that she'd witnessed in her lifetime.

Looking at the screen of her iPhone, Annie glanced down to see if her younger sister, Megan, had replied to several messages that she had sent her in the past two days. Meg was eight years younger.

Annie could see from WhatsApp that her sister hadn't picked her messages up. No little blue ticks. And that was worrying. More than worrying actually. And the half dozen or so phone calls had all gone to voicemail. Why the hell wasn't she responding?

They messaged or called each other nearly every day, so it was completely out of character for Meg to go off radar like this. In fact, it had never happened before. Technically, Meg's last message had been 48 hours ago and since then, nothing.

Annie had also tried to contact Meg's son, her nephew Callum.

Taking a deep breath, Annie could feel the growing anxiety in her stomach. It felt tight and uncomfortable. She would get dressed and drive over to Megan's home. Disturbing images flashed in her mind. Maybe her sister had had a fall or a stroke and was lying there helpless. Even though Megan was only sixty-four years old, the stress of Callum's lifestyle as an alcoholic and drug addict seemed to have taken its toll on her. She had developed heart arrhythmia that doctors thought had been brought on by prolonged stress. What if she had had a heart attack?

Annie had sent Denise Thomas, the woman who lived in the next caravan, a text message to ask her to check on Megan and see if there was anything wrong. Denise hadn't replied yet.

As Annie pulled back the duvet and swung her legs over the side of the bed, her mind pulled up even darker thoughts. There had been several occasions when Megan had confronted Callum, and six months ago she had even tried to prevent him from leaving the static caravan that they lived in a few miles west of Dolgellau. It had resulted in an altercation. Callum had slapped his mother and pushed her to the floor when she stood in front of the door to prevent him leaving and driving because he was hammered. What if Callum had just snapped and attacked Megan?

Annie's pulse quickened. *Keep it together, Annie. Just keep it together.*

Moving quickly towards the en suite bathroom, she showered, dressed and left the bedroom in less than ten minutes. She knew something was wrong. That something had happened to her sister. It was starting to overwhelm her.

Going into the kitchen, she saw that Stephen was sitting on his usual stool at the breakfast bar reading *The Daily Telegraph* online.

'Going somewhere?' he asked in his public school accent.

'I can't get hold of Meg,' she said.

He didn't reply, but instead carried on reading.

For a moment, her eyes moved around her beautiful, high-spec kitchen. The marble worktop, bespoke cupboards, AGA, and vast American-style fridge freezer.

If only that man wasn't sitting there ruining everything, she thought to herself.

Grabbing the car keys, Annie headed out of the kitchen, down the carpeted hallway and out of the front door.

The low, early morning autumnal sun glared angrily off the frosty path and garden, making her squint. Shielding her eyes as she went, she got to her new black

Land Rover Discovery Sport and opened the driver's door.

She glanced at the outbuildings that were over to her right. Stephen had had a snooker room built, along with a room that had an indoor putting mat and computer golf driving simulator. She rarely went over there. Boys and their toys.

Taking a breath as she got into the car, Annie took her phone and rang Megan's number again.

Nothing.

Come on, come on. Why aren't you answering my bloody calls?

She started the car and drove across their huge, u-shaped gravel drive, the icy stones crunching loudly under her tyres.

There would be some perfectly logical explanation. Maybe she'd simply lost her phone somewhere. *Yes, that would explain it. Meg just lost her phone. Why am I getting so stressed?*

Annie's phone rang and she stamped on the brakes.

Grabbing it, she prayed that it was Meg.

Please God, let it be her.

It wasn't.

It was Denise Thomas.

Her heart sank.

She answered it.

'Hi Annie, I got your message,' Denise said. 'I've knocked a couple of times on Megan's door but there's no answer.'

Annie's chest tightened. 'Okay. When did you last see her?'

'It's been a couple of days now,' Denise admitted.

'Is her car there?' Annie asked, sounding fretful.

'No. And all the blinds and curtains have been pulled, even during the day.'

That rang alarm bells.

Oh God. This isn't good.

Annie felt her voice break with anxiety. 'Okay, thank you, Denise. I'm on my way over.'

Blowing out her cheeks, she took a breath to try and compose herself. Then she stamped down on the accelerator, wheels spinning on the gravel driveway as she sped away to find out what had happened to her sister.

Chapter 2

My eyes flickered open, and for a few seconds I'm still haunted by my dream. I could feel it consume me. It's invaded my whole body. I'm riddled with it. Tightness around my throat. Anxiety in my chest and stomach. Taut muscles. Pulse racing. Mouth dry.

James. Jim. Jimmy.

And then I'm jolted awake. The feeling of loss is excruciating. It always is.

I needed to pee. I *always* needed to pee. At a guess, I'd been up to pee four times during the night. Maybe five. It might be an age thing but it was frustrating. Happy seventieth bloody birthday. Technically, I was now seventy years and one week old.

I remembered the days when I could go all night. It was a distant bloody memory now. Pee like a sodding racehorse in the morning. A continuous, thunderous, glorious stream of urine for well over a minute. Those were the days, eh?

I stared up at the ceiling and started to get my breath back after my dream. Then I rolled onto my side. My eyes rested on Rachel, who was lying sleeping next to me, as she had done for forty-five years. A slice of vanilla light fell across her cheek. She was beautiful. Serene. The autumnal light of Snowdonia, North Wales. Where I lived and worked. Where I was born and grew up. Home. *Aelwyd*.

But Rachel was slowly fading away from me with every day that passed. The woman I have loved for forty-five years was gradually fading like an old polaroid photograph that had been left in the sunlight. And the pain of that fact was constantly with me. Everyone says it, but dementia really is a bloody cruel disease.

I studied her face. That beautiful face. I slowly traced it with my eyes. I had no idea how many more mornings I'd be able to do this. It's so wonderfully symmetrical. A little button nose, rosebud lips. I wondered if I could still see the young woman who I fell in love with all those years ago. And I could.

I sensed movement from the bottom of the bed. A familiar and welcome distraction from my sad thoughts.

Jack, my three-year-old German Shepherd stood and circled up towards me slowly as he did every morning. He sniffed and licked me as I scruffed and stroked his head. And then he leapt down onto the carpet and gave me an expectant look.

It was time for me to make a strong, black coffee and take him out.

I quickly brushed my teeth. No fillings in seventy years! Then I peered in the mirror and ran a brush through my generous head of silver-white hair and neatly trimmed beard. There were still days when I was surprised by the old man who peered back at me. In my head, I was still twenty-seven years old. There was still part of me that expected to see that younger, stronger version of myself in the mirror.

I was never comfortable looking back at myself. I wondered if everyone had that slightly uneasy, scratchy discomfort when staring at their reflection. As if in that moment, you get a glimpse of the person you really are.

Hello, Frank, I said to myself. *You stupid old bastard.*

I got dressed. Thick black cargo trousers, fleece, walking socks, and a baseball cap with a name and logo on the front – a snowcapped mountain, two daffodils, and the words FRANK MARSHAL – RANGER *Parc Cenedlaethol Eryri Snowdonia National Park.*

I leaned down and strapped the small, sharp knife that I kept in a leather sheath to my ankle. It was force of habit from my time in the police, and had come to my rescue on several occasions. There were far less sinister reasons for wearing it these days. Cutting rope, wire or undergrowth was about as exciting as it got.

Today I had some work to do. It's fifteen years since I became a Park Ranger, or *Ceidwad Parc* in Welsh, for the Snowdonia/Eryri National Park. I only worked part-time. Some basic troubleshooting, repairs, protecting the landscape and wildlife. I also managed some of the local volunteers, which had its own challenges and frustrations. But in my view, it was the best job in the world. It had to be. I got paid to work outside in the most beautiful scenery on the planet. And that was a gift.

Walking along the landing, my eyes locked onto a closed bedroom door, as they did every morning. Several large stickers were stuck on to the white, tired-looking, paintwork – a Wrexham FC sticker, an Acid House smiley face, and a blue logo for the band Oasis. Another sign read *James' Room – KEEP OUT!*

I couldn't bring myself to ever remove them. As usual, I reached out and touched the wooden frame around the door. I patted it, as if trying to make a connection.

I went downstairs, knee deep in my own self-loathing when my phone vibrated in my pocket.

It was a message from Dai Thompson, Eryri National Park's Head Ranger.

I read it.

Frank, we've got a report of poachers on the east bank of Afon Mawddach. About 3 miles north of you. Can you have a look? Ta, Dai

The Afon Mawddach was a nearby river that ran about 30 miles north to south at the centre of Eryri. It was bordered to the east by the Aran Fawddwy massif, and to the west and north by the Harlech Dome. It was a rich source of salmon, which is what the poachers were after. I'd known poachers to be caught with over £5,000 worth of salmon in the back of a pick-up or a boat. Thieving bastards. Ruining the stock for everyone.

Glancing at my watch, I saw that there was no time to lose. As soon as it was full daylight the poachers would be gone, as the light drove the salmon to the bottom of the water.

As my pulse quickened, I jogged outside and messaged Dai back as I went.

YEAH, *no problem. I'll let you know how I get on. Frank.*

THAT PART of the river was virtually inaccessible from the road. The poachers had probably come upstream on a boat. The only viable way for me to get there was by horse. It wouldn't be the first time that I'd chased or caught scumbag poachers. And I guessed it wouldn't be the last.

Going to my gun case, I unlocked it, grabbed my Winchester Select shotgun and a box of shells. I got the familiar smell of gun oil. For some reason, it smelled reas-suring. I loved the feel of it, the weight of it in my hands. And I had to admit it, I loved the power of holding a heavy Winchester. No one dared mess with me.

The sight or sound of my shotgun usually scared poachers enough to run. I had no time for them. There were moments when I wanted to shoot them rather than just scare them. They were the worst kind of bloody scav-engers. Selfish and immoral.

'Come on, boy,' I said to Jack as I raced towards the front door and went outside.

Striding down the uneven track towards the paddock, the autumnal leaves crunched under my thick-soled work-boots and sounded as if I was walking on crisps.

The jagged mountains of Snowdonia were still a dark plum colour at that time of the morning. They rolled into the distance and it was impossible to see in the light quite where they ended. And at this time of year, their tops were often painted with ribbons of snow and patches of mist. The sun had just started to frown hesitantly over their tops.

Jack and I continued as he trotted away before circling back as if to remind me to keep up. He's a German Shep-herd so it was instinctive.

As we went around the bend, I could see more fields and more dry stone walls. There were a handful of houses dotted around the landscape like smudges against the morning light. And past that, a dark, heather-clad moorland.

Arriving at the paddock, I went into our stable and untethered 'Duke', my chestnut-coloured Welsh cob. At seventeen hands, Duke was a big bugger of a horse with a slightly aloof, even arrogant, nature that I loved. He took after me. I'd had him since he was a yearling and trained him myself. I didn't trust anyone else to do it properly.

I pulled on the bridle, then took my heavy Thorowgood saddle and threw it over Duke and fastened it. That great smell of ageing leather.

Going out into the paddock, I strained as I put my foot up in the stirrup. I wasn't as supple as I used to be. Then with a groan, I swung my leg over and I was on.

I pushed the shotgun down into the long, dark leather holster.

Jack looked up at me expectantly.

I felt more at home sitting in a saddle like this than almost anywhere else. Maybe I'd been born in the wrong bloody century.

'Come on, boys,' I said as I gave Duke a nudge with the heels of my boots. 'We've got some bad guys to find.'

3

2 days 1 hour missing

Speeding through Dolgellau, Annie took the turning to a small caravan park where Meg and Callum lived. Annie had offered to lend her sister money after one of Meg's boyfriends ran off with her savings five years ago. But Meg was too proud to accept what she termed 'charity'.

The caravan park was cold and deserted at this time of the morning. There were about twenty static caravans in total. According to Meg, there were only about nine permanent residents, and the rest of the caravans were used by people as holiday homes.

Annie stopped the car outside her sister's caravan. It was painted white, although it was starting to fade and looked like it needed a new coat of paint.

Just as Denise had described, all the curtains and blinds were closed. Maybe she was still asleep?

Annie got out of her car, trying to reassure herself that all would be well. But there was a dark, uneasy feeling deep in the pit of her stomach.

Walking quickly up the wooden steps and along the decking, she got to the front door which Megan had recently painted a fashionable grey. It had a black metal handle.

Her breathing was getting shallow as she knocked on the door loudly. Her heart was now thumping against her chest.

Come on, come on. Open the door, Meg.

Nothing.

She knocked again. Louder and harder.

Nothing.

Taking her phone, she rang her sister's number again and listened carefully with her ear to the door.

Nothing.

Shit, this is not good.

Feeling the anxiety surge through her body, Annie crouched down, pushed the letterbox open and peered inside the caravan.

She could see the tiny hallway and then the kitchen beyond that.

What the …?

Something wasn't right.

The hallway rug was gone. The coat rack on the wall. Megan and Callum's coats were also gone. It looked as if her sister and nephew had moved out. But that didn't make any sense at all.

Jesus, the caravan has been stripped, Annie thought in a panic. *What the hell is going on?*

'Meg? Meg? It's Annie!' she shouted through the letterbox.

Then she held her breath, straining her ears to see if she could hear the faintest sound or movement from inside.

Nothing.

Try to keep calm, Annie. There has to be a logical explanation for all this.

'Callum? Callum?', she shouted. 'It's Auntie Annie. Can you come and open the door please?'

Nothing.

What the hell do I do? Call the police?

Having worked as a High Court Judge for over twenty years, Annie knew that the police would do little to begin with. Megan and Callum were two adults and there was no immediate danger to their lives.

Then she had a thought. She would ring the one person on the planet who she trusted more than anyone else.

Frank Marshal.

Chapter 4

Galloping at full speed across the Snowdonia moorland, I had the poacher on his quad bike in my sights. He was wearing a black baseball cap with a hoodie pulled over the top of it. I wondered if it was one of the usual suspects that I'd encountered over the years.

When I'd arrived, the poacher was knee deep in the river and hadn't managed to catch anything. As soon as he spotted me and Duke, he'd run like the chicken-shit coward he was over to his green, mud-splattered Suzuki quad bike and taken off.

The muscles in my thighs were burning, my knee joints sore, reminding me that I was no longer a young man. The icy morning air numbed my face and ears. There was no feeling quite like it.

The poacher was about fifty yards ahead of me as we hurtled across the uneven terrain. Mud flew up from the quad bike's rear tyres.

Over to my right, the land was surrounded by crumbling dry stone walls, covered in weeds and dotted with dark green moss. Ahead of me, the landscape just tumbled away, unfurling itself like a great blanket of varying colours. I felt deep pride in being born and bred in Eryri. The old land of my fathers. *Hen Wlad Fy Nhadau.*

Jack was running alongside us, his pink tongue lolling with the effort of keeping up.

Duke was labouring under the strain of galloping for this long. He was built for short, fast gallops but we'd already covered a couple of miles.

'Come on, boy,' I shouted, using the reins to encourage him.

It was no use. The poacher was starting to get away.

Bollocks.

There was nothing for it.

Grabbing the reins with my left hand, I pulled the shotgun out of its leather holster.

It was incredibly heavy.

Using all my strength, I lifted it up to my right shoulder. Then I put it into the nook until I could feel it nestle comfortably there.

I aimed it directly at the poacher ahead of me.

The quad bike was bouncing over the rough terrain. A moving target.

The poacher was sitting lifted slightly off his seat, using his legs to keep his balance as if he was a skilled steeplechase jockey.

You cocky little fucker.

I curled my finger around the cold steel of the trigger.

Closing my left eye, I took aim.

I should shoot you in the back, right here and right now.

Instead, I chose a spot about twenty-five feet above his head. It was enough to ensure that no stray pellets hit him. I was too old to go to prison.

Then I squeezed the trigger slowly.

BANG!

The air exploded with the sound of both barrels.

The recoil jolted hard into my shoulder with a thud.

Startled, the poacher glanced back in terror to see where the gunshot had come from.

Yeah, that's scared the shit of out of you, hasn't it?

I couldn't see his face, but his loss of concentration had the desired effect.

The quad bike hit a large mound and left the ground for a second.

As it landed, it bounced and swerved out of control, throwing the poacher off.

Bingo!

He landed and rolled several times until he came to a stop in the thick heather.

Good.

With no accelerator, the bike came to a slow and rather ignominious halt.

'Woah, there,' I said, pulling the reins tight. 'Woah.'

Duke slowed to a trot and eventually stopped. His flanks and neck were covered in glistening sweat.

I circled him back.

My hands felt sweaty inside my leather gloves.

Keeping hold of the shotgun, I dismounted. My back and shoulders ached.

The poacher wasn't moving.

Christ, I hope he's not dead.

Jack, who was panting loudly and blinking, came to my side.

'Good boy,' I said as I scruffed his head as we approached.

Taking no chances, I clicked open the gun, pulled the

empty red shells out before reloading with fresh ammunition from my pocket.

I had no idea if he was armed with a weapon. I wasn't about to take any chances. I'd been attacked by a poacher with a knife a few years ago and had a scar on my thigh as a souvenir.

Giving the poacher's legs a little kick, I watched to see if he'd been knocked unconscious. Or worse.

He gave a groan and rolled over.

I instantly knew his young, ruddy face.

Ethan Jenkins.

Bloody idiot!

His clothes and forehead were covered in mud. He coughed, squinted up at me, and then gave me his usual boyish smirk. Even though he was only in his late teens, Ethan was a serial offender. He came from a local family with a long tradition of poaching and theft.

'For fuck's sake, Ethan, I could have killed you,' I snapped at him. 'You utter knobhead.'

'Hello Mr Marshal,' he said with a wince. Then he gave a little laugh.

'It's not bloody funny, Ethan. I thought community service and a fine would have put you off doing this type of bloody thing.' I sighed angrily.

In reality, nothing seemed to deter the male members of his family from a life of petty crime.

Sitting up, he gave a shrug. 'My dad says you're a total prick.'

'Does he now?' I gave a wry smile.

'Yeah.'

'This is your dad, the convicted burglar, thief and poacher, I take it?' I asked dryly.

Ethan seemed confused by my sarcasm. 'Said you used to give him and his brothers hell when you were Five-O.'

Five-O? Jesus! Since when did the word 'copper' go out of fashion?

'That's because they were always nicking stuff,' I growled in frustration, 'and that was my job.'

'He said you were a bloody hypocrite,' he continued, 'and that's why your son topped himself.'

Silence.

A wave of fury swept through my whole body.

I could hardly breathe. My hands shook with rage.

How fucking dare you!

'You what?' I snarled with gritted teeth as I pulled the shotgun up to my shoulder and pointed it at Ethan's head. I wanted to kill him. Maybe I should. Do the world a fucking favour.

'Don't shoot me,' he whimpered as he put his hands up defensively. 'Please.'

I tried to calm myself. *Come on, Frank, he's not worth going to prison for is he?*

I lowered the shotgun and instead moved closer and pointed it directly at his right knee.

'Close your eyes,' I barked at him.

His eyes widened with fear. 'What?'

'Do it! Now!' I snapped loudly at him.

'What? Why? What are you going to do?' he babbled in terror.

'I'm going to shoot you in the kneecap,' I explained calmly.

The blood drained from his face. 'No, no. You can't do that,' he said, his voice trembling in utter panic.

'Why? It's what the punishment gangs in Belfast do to little scumbags like you so they don't steal or deal drugs again,' I said with a shrug, enjoying watching him squirm. 'Maybe it'll teach you a bloody lesson.'

'No, please.' He shook his head, took a nervous gulp as

he scurried backwards on the ground. 'I won't do it again. I … I promise.'

'Stop bloody moving!' I yelled at him.

He froze.

I pulled a dubious face. 'Sorry. I don't believe you won't do this again.' I took a step forward, glanced down at his knee and made as if I was about to shoot. 'This is going to really hurt. And you're going to need to get someone to take you to hospital.' Then I locked eyes with him. 'Oh, and you might have a permanent limp.'

He screamed with tears in his eyes, 'NO! PLEASE!'

I waited for a few seconds.

'Right, Ethan,' I snorted. 'If I catch you again, I really will shoot you.' I gestured to his quad bike. 'Now fuck off and make sure I never catch you again.'

He scrambled to his feet in panic. 'Sorry. Yeah, you won't,' he whimpered as he sprinted over to his quad bike and jumped on.

For a few seconds, I watched him go. Even though I might not show it, I did have some empathy for the Jenkins' family. Ethan's maternal grandmother, Linda Jenkins, had been murdered by the serial killer Keith Tatchell in the summer of 1998 in North Wales. It had obviously devastated the family at the time, and I often wondered what impact such an event might have long term. But they were still a family of scumbag thieves.

My phone buzzed in my pocket.

I took it out.

There was a message from an old friend, Annie Taylor. The signal was terrible out in this area so it must have gone straight to voicemail.

Taking off my leather gloves, I pushed the button to play it.

'*Frank,*' Annie said. She sounded flustered. '*I need your help with something.*'

Despite being born and bred in North Wales, she had no real accent. She sounded English. It was probably because she'd studied law at Cambridge.

'*It's my sister Meg. I think she's missing.*'

5

2 days 2 hours missing

As I turned onto *The Vale Caravan Park*, I saw Annie's black Land Rover Discovery parked up close to her sister's caravan. *Lost Highway* by *Hank Williams* was playing on my car stereo.

I took a moment to look out across the landscape. We were high up. Out to the east, the valley dropped away dramatically. Beyond that, clusters of frost-covered trees huddled together in the folds of the hills.

The park itself was scruffy. Grass was gouged by deep muddy troughs where mobile caravans had been towed into position. Two rusty oil drums and a broken trestle table stood outside a nearby caravan. An ugly clump of trees was over to the right, its branches dense and tangled. Exposed roots uncomfortably twisted into muddy pockets of water - the daylight seemed greyer and more forbidding. A colourless blanket that seemed to bleach any warmth or colour from the landscape. It was bleak, desolate and isolated.

The concrete shower block was old, with crumbling

brickwork that was dotted with black mould. I shuddered to think what it might be like inside.

On returning home, I'd called Annie back. She'd explained that there was no sign of her sister Megan at her caravan, and that she wasn't answering any calls or text messages. Annie was clearly agitated. It had been over two days since they'd had any contact.

Parking my muddy old blue Toyota Hilux pick-up truck beside Annie's 'gleaming *Disco*', I got out. Over by the caravan, Annie cupped her hands as she peered in through the windows on the raised wooden platform to the side.

'What's going on?' I called over as the wind picked up and cut into my face. It was so exposed up here.

Annie turned to me. The worry was clear on her face. She had high cheekbones, silver-blonde hair cut into a bob, and piercing blue eyes.

'I can't get any answer,' she shouted over the noise of the wind, shaking her head. 'All the curtains are pulled,' she explained with a frown, 'but I've looked through the letterbox and it looks like Meg's moved out.'

'You didn't know she was moving out?' I asked as I approached.

'She hasn't moved out. I know she hasn't. She can't have done. I only spoke to her on Thursday,' Annie stated in a concerned but confident tone. 'It doesn't make any sense. Where would she go?'

I didn't have an answer to that, but Annie's implication was clear.

'No answer from her phone?' I said.

'Nothing.' Annie put her hand to her temple and rubbed it nervously. 'I've sent her half a dozen messages.'

'On WhatsApp?' I enquired.

She gave a diminutive nod.

I squinted at her and pulled down the brim of my cap. 'Can you see if she picked them up?'

'No. She hasn't.' Annie gazed into space, her mind was racing away with a million different thoughts. 'As far as I can see, she hasn't picked them up. I don't understand why.'

I furrowed my brow. 'You talk to her all the time, don't you?'

'At least two or three times a week. Sometimes more. We message each other several times a day.' Annie nodded as a little strand of blonde-silver hair over her forehead blew and flickered in the strong cold wind. She was bewildered. 'I'm really worried, Frank.'

I gestured to the caravan with a sense of urgency. 'We need to get inside,' I said calmly. 'Have you got keys?'

Annie pulled an exasperated face. 'Callum lost a set when he was out drunk. For about the tenth time. Meg changed the locks. She hasn't given me the spare set yet.'

I tried to remember the layout of the caravan. I'd been to a small party there about three years ago. Megan's birthday, if I remembered correctly. Rachel came with me and we got drunk and slow danced to Lionel Richie.

'Isn't there a door round at the back?' I asked, as a couple of tiny raindrops fell and touched my cheek. I glanced up. The sky had started to darken to a steel grey overhead. It was about to throw it down.

'Yes, but you'd have to get over that.' She gestured to a gate that was halfway down the raised platform to the side of the caravan. It was made from stained wood. 'Meg had it put in for extra security,' she added.

Thirty years ago, when I was a CID detective, I would have been up and over it in a flash. My pride and ego kicked in. It was stupid, but I didn't want Annie to think less of me. And I could see how desperate she was.

'No problem,' I said as casually as I could. 'Not my first time climbing over a fence.'

'Sure?' Annie asked. 'Be careful.'

I guessed that what she was really thinking was *'But you weren't seventy years old the last time you did it.'*

I jumped and threw my leg up. The base of my back twinged and my hamstrings protested strongly, but my right leg landed on top. Then I pulled myself up, noticing how I was struggling more than a few years ago. I swung my leg over and dropped down the other side. I felt the drop jarr my knees and ankles – but I was over.

Bloody hell, I'm getting old!

'You okay?' Annie called from behind the gate.

'Fine,' I lied, as a pain shot through my left knee.

The white wooden slats at the side of the caravan beyond the gate were stained, and the paint was flaking off. There was a miniature garden with cheap-looking gravel which crunched under my boots as I made my way down the side of the caravan and round to the back.

On the grass beyond the caravan sat a long, dark wooden shed. I vaguely remembered being told that it was a storage shed for use by the permanent caravan owners.

Moving across the small, damp wooden patio, I reached the back door that had been painted black a long time ago. The paint was now peeling like sunburned skin.

There was a plastic door handle which I tried to turn. It gave a loose rattle but it was locked. *Bugger.*

'I don't suppose Megan leaves a key to the back door out?' I called back, mildly irritated that I hadn't thought about this possibility before. My aching back twinged to add to the annoyance.

'Try the flower pots by the back door. I'm sure I remember her leaving one under there a few times,' Annie replied.

Crouching down, I heard my knees crack like gunshots as I began to turn a series of flimsy brown plastic flower pots over.

Nothing.

I stood up and then reached on top of the wooden frame of the door to see if there was a key there.

Nothing.

There didn't seem anywhere else where a key might have been hidden. At least, nothing obvious.

'Excuse me, sir,' said a stern male voice. 'Can you tell me what you're doing?'

I turned and saw a young, male police officer in black uniform walking across the patio towards me. He must have come the same way as I'd done – over the fence.

Great, this is all I need.

'My friend is worried about her sister who lives here,' I explained, confident that this could all be resolved in a few seconds.

The police officer gestured to the adjacent caravan to the right. 'We had a call from a neighbour. She reported seeing someone snooping around and trying to break into this caravan.'

'I'm not trying to break in,' I snorted.

'Can you explain what you're doing here, please?'

My irritation and impatience grew.

Take it easy, Frank, I told myself.

'I just told you that,' I said forcefully. 'My friend, Annie Taylor, is standing outside the front. You must have seen her?'

'I did,' he admitted, 'but I was more concerned about the report of a burglar.'

I sighed in frustration. 'Do I look like a burglar?'

He didn't answer.

'Are you going to arrest me?' I joked in an annoyed tone.

'Not yet, sir.'

I gave him a forced smile. 'We're worried about her sister, Megan, who lives here. She isn't answering her phone or answering the door.'

The police officer raised an eyebrow. 'So, you climbed over the fence and tried to break in?'

'Jesus Christ! I didn't try to break in,' I snapped. 'I tried the door to see if it was locked, and searched around to see if there was a spare key. And as far as I remember, that's not a bloody criminal offence.'

'If you could calm down, please,' he said. 'Have you got any ID?'

'Are you joking?'

'No, I'm not.'

I shook my head, took out my wallet, and showed him my driving licence.

He then peered at me with a quizzical expression. 'Frank Marshal?' he asked, as if this was significant.

'Yes,' I replied as I took the driving licence back.

He raised an eyebrow. His whole demeanour had changed. 'DCI Frank Marshal?'

'Not anymore,' I said dryly, 'but once, yes.'

He gestured towards the front of the caravan. 'DCI Humphries is out the front, sir. We were in the area so we picked up the call.'

'Great. That's all I need,' I groaned. 'And please don't call me sir again.'

He gave me a slightly embarrassed look.

I followed him back down the side of the caravan and over the fence.

I immediately spotted a man in his early 50s, salt and

pepper hair, smart navy suit, talking to Annie by a police car.

The man saw me and gave me a withering look.

My heart sank. DCI Dewi Humphries.

Just when I thought my day couldn't get any worse.

Dewi and I went back years. And there was little love lost between us. We had worked at St Asaph nick together twenty-five years ago. He was a pompous prick who had just been promoted to Detective Sergeant. Dewi was riding high after being the arresting officer of the serial killer Keith Tatchell. There had been a series of murders in North Wales in the late 90s in which three middle-aged women were murdered and then dumped at remote locations over a space of eighteen months. They had all been romantically involved with the murderer, Keith Tatchell, a builder from Caernarfon. And Tatchell had strangled them all using wire. One of them had been killed with electrical lead, one with fencing wire, and the last of his victims, Linda Simmons, with piano wire. Their bodies had been left in remote locations. Even though the senior investigating officer had been DCI Ian Goddard, it had been Dewi who had finally tracked Tatchell down and made the arrest. It seemed to have gone to Dewi's head, and until I left the force he'd been increasingly arrogant and unpleasant.

I went over and gave him a sarcastic smile. 'Hello, Dewi.'

He returned my sarcasm. 'Good to see you, Frank.' He gave me a smirk. 'Some kind of misunderstanding, was there?'

'Not really.' I forced a smile over at the officer. 'Just doing your job, weren't you, son? No harm done,' I reassured him, trying not to be too patronising. I remembered being an enthusiastic bobby on the beat in my 20s.

He gave the officer an ironic grin. 'This man is <u>the</u> Frank Marshal. A legend in his own lunchtime. Queen's Police Medal back in the 80s, wasn't it?'

'Long time ago, Dewi,' I muttered under my breath. What I wanted to say was *Why don't you just fuck off?*

Then I gestured. 'This is my friend, Annie Taylor.'

Dewi nodded. 'Annie's been telling me that she believes her sister is missing.'

'But I know the protocol,' Annie stated. 'She's only been missing for two days. My sister isn't going to be a priority for you as a missing person. But I know her. And I know that something is wrong.'

Dewi raised an eyebrow curiously. 'Don't I recognise you from somewhere?'

'Yes,' Annie replied. 'Mold Crown Court, 2017. You were the senior investigating officer in the Stephen Henry murder trial.'

'That's right,' he said, puffing out his chest. 'I was, but I …' Clearly he still didn't know how he recognised her.

'I was the woman sitting behind the big table with the funny wig,' Annie said dryly.

Dewi's eyes widened as the penny dropped. 'You were the judge. Of course,' he said, almost as if talking to himself. 'Judge Taylor. Sorry, I just didn't recognise you.'

'Not many people do when I'm out of fancy dress.'

'You don't have access to your sister's house?' Dewi asked her.

Annie shook her head. 'She changed the locks.'

'And I tried the door at the back,' I explained.

Dewi purposefully ignored me and instead looked at Annie. 'Well, if a Crown Court judge is genuinely worried, then I'm worried. Are you okay for us to break in?'

He couldn't have sounded more smarmy if he'd tried. *Fawning little sycophant.*

'Please,' she said, unable to hide her distress.

'Right, let's get it open.'

I glanced over at Annie. She was understandably concerned. We had no idea what we were going to find on the other side of that door. With Megan not answering the door, phone calls and text messages, Annie might be fearing the worst.

Putting a reassuring hand on her shoulder, I gave her a sympathetic look. 'You okay?' I asked quietly. I knew that she wasn't, but it was a way of me letting her know that I was there to support her.

She gave me an uncertain nod. 'Yeah.'

The young officer came forward and gave the door a hefty kick.

It flew open with a bang.

There was tension in my stomach as we followed Dewi and the officer inside. A refillable lavender air freshener had been left running somewhere, presumably in an effort to offset the musty aroma of the caravan. Then I realised that the 'musty aroma' was the smell of weed.

Casting my eyes around, it was obvious that the place was completely empty. Moving slowly down the tiny hall-way, I glanced into what I remembered was the living room.

'Meg? Meg?' Annie called out frantically as she hurried through the interior of the caravan.

Silence.

No furniture, no pictures on the wall. The floors were now bare.

Annie was behind me with an anguished look on her face. 'This is just so strange,' she said quietly under her breath.

Dewi came out of the kitchen and shook his head.

'Nothing in the cupboards. Looks like your sister has moved out.'

Annie shook her head in disbelief. 'No, that's just not possible. My sister wouldn't have done that without telling me.'

There was an unnerving silence as we walked slowly towards the back of the caravan. Our shoes echoed around the empty shell.

Annie hastily checked inside the two bedrooms. They were also empty.

Then she marched into what appeared to be the main bedroom, went to the flimsy built-in wardrobe and pulled the doors open frantically. Nothing.

Pushing past me, she went into the bathroom and yanked open the mirrored cabinet on the wall.

Nothing.

She came back to where I was standing.

'Okay, this just doesn't make any sense,' she said desperately. Her breathing was shallow. 'Something is very wrong. I can feel it.'

We moved back to the living area of the caravan.

Dewi raised an eyebrow. 'Do you know if the property was rented?'

Annie nodded. 'Yes it was.'

'Any idea who the letting agent is?'

She took a moment. 'I might have their name at home.'

'There aren't many letting agents dealing with Dolgellau,' I stated. 'It wouldn't take long to track them down.'

Dewi blanked me again and looked at Annie. 'Does your sister have any financial worries?'

'She didn't have lots of money but she got by.'

'Does she have any medical conditions or significant mental health issues?'

SIMON MCCLEAVE

'No. Nothing like that.'

'What about arguments or disputes? Is there anyone who might want to harm her?'

'No.'

'And she lived alone?'

'No. My nephew lived here too.'

'And what's his name?'

'Callum. Callum Taylor.'

Dewi frowned. 'And you can't contact him either?'

'No. I've messaged and called but nothing.'

Dewi took a few seconds as he processed all this. 'Was your sister in a relationship?'

Annie shrugged. 'She was seeing someone. It was a relatively recent thing.'

'Do you know who?'

'No, sorry. She didn't tell me details. She was pretty private about that sort of thing.'

'Private?' Dewi snatched at the word and its significance. I knew exactly what he was thinking. 'Isn't it possible that your sister and nephew are with this man? Maybe they decided to move in together?'

'No,' Annie insisted. 'She would have told me.'

Dewi narrowed his eyes. 'But you've just told me that your sister was private about her relationship, or relationships, with men.'

'She was.' Annie gave a frustrated sigh.

I fixed Dewi with an icy stare. 'I think we've established that Megan wouldn't have moved out without telling Annie first. It's suspicious.'

'Is it though?' Dewi sounded very dubious. 'You know the statistics. There are nearly nine hundred people reported missing in this country every day. Back at the station, we've got at least thirty ongoing missing persons cases.'

Annie shook her head. 'What am I going to do?' she said as her voice dropped to a whisper and she ran her hands through her hair.

'Listen, I am taking your concerns seriously,' Dewi replied calmly, 'but you know how this works. There is nothing to suggest that your sister or your nephew are in any immediate danger. Megan doesn't have any medical or mental health conditions. You don't know of anyone who might want to harm her.' He gestured around the caravan. 'And there's nothing suspicious here. It just looks as if your sister and nephew packed up and left.'

Annie groaned. 'Except that I know for a fact they wouldn't do that.'

Dewi looked at her. 'I'll talk to our Missing Persons Unit. That's all I can do at the moment. Good to see you, Frank.'

And with that, he and the police officer headed for the front door and left.

Annie had tears in her eyes. 'What the hell am I going to do, Frank?'

'Dewi is a useless, self-serving prick. Don't worry, we'll find her ourselves if we have to,' I reassured her. 'I'm just going to have another nosy round.'

As I went into the kitchen, I could now sense how dark, quiet and still everything was. Just the low hum of the fridge and the smell of the surface cleaner. The wind outside picked up and I heard the fence creak.

Then all the noise seemed to drift away, replaced by a sad, suffocating silence.

What happened in here, Megan? And where the hell are you?

6

2 days 3 hours missing

Annie came back to where her car was parked. She had been over to the caravan to the right-hand side of Meg's. I had just knocked on the door of the caravan to the left-hand side, but there was no reply.

'Anything?' I asked as I walked over.

She shook her head and sighed. 'No answer.'

We both scanned the caravan park. It was deserted.

'We'll come back later and try again,' I reassured her.

'I don't know what to do with myself,' Annie admitted.

We stood out by her car in silence for a few seconds, both lost in thought about what had transpired in the last hour. The police had now left, with promises to contact the Missing Persons Unit but little more at this stage. Annie was desperate.

Above us, the autumnal sun shone in the clear blue sky. The air was icy and I could see my breath.

My phone rang.

I saw it was my daughter Caitlin. We spoke at least a couple of times a week. Now living in Watford with her feckless boyfriend TJ, Caitlin worked part time as a travel agent. And TJ and Caitlin had a son, Sam, who was ten years old. Rachel and I doted on Sam as he was our only grandchild. I wished he lived closer, but Caitlin visited as often as she could with him. TJ rarely came with her.

'It's Caitlin,' I explained to Annie as I gestured to my ringing phone.

Annie and Caitlin had met on several occasions and got on like a house on fire.

'Take it,' she insisted. 'Please.'

I shook my head. 'It's fine. She's just ringing for a chat and to see how her mum's doing ... and probably asking for money.'

Annie laughed. 'Oh dear.'

'They don't have much money.' I then gave a withering look. 'And TJ is looking for a new job. Again!'

'What does he do?'

'To be honest, I've no idea. I think he sells weed.' There was little love lost between myself and TJ. I was pretty sure that he sold drugs, but it wasn't something I could ever prove. And I feared that if I pushed too hard, Rachel and I wouldn't see Sam. And of course TJ had made his feelings about me being an ex-copper very clear. 'If I could get them both away from him, I would,' I admitted.

As the wind picked up, Annie folded her arms and shivered.

Then she gave me a meaningful look. 'What now?'

I took a moment to think. Then I got myself into detective mode. How would I approach this if it were a missing persons investigation?

'We need to talk to the letting agent for starters. See if Meg has moved out. If not, why has the caravan been cleared out?'

Annie nodded. 'And where's her car? None of this makes any sense to me.'

My phone buzzed with a text.

Glancing down, I saw it was from Caitlin.

DAD, *me and Sam are on our way up to yours. I'll explain when I get there but we're going to need to stay for a bit. Be with you about 10am xx*

I FROWNED. There was definitely something wrong.

I looked at my watch and saw that it was 9.30am.

'Do you need to go?' Annie asked.

I nodded. 'I've got to go and meet Caitlin and Sam at the house. I'm not sure why, but they're coming to stay with us which doesn't bode well. Once I've sorted them out, we'll make a plan.' I gave her a reassuring look. 'We'll find Meg and Callum, don't worry.'

'Thank you, Frank,' Annie said gratefully.

7

2 days 4 hours missing

Looking at my watch, I calculated that Caitlin and Sam would arrive in the next fifteen minutes. I had tried to call her back but her phone had just rung out. I knew that if she was driving, Caitlin wasn't reckless enough to answer it. And I didn't imagine that the old Citroen she drove had any fancy Bluetooth phone system inside it. It would be lovely to see her and Sam, although I couldn't help but worry at the impromptu nature of her visit. Usually her visits were organised around school holidays and planned weeks, if not months, in advance. Something was definitely wrong, but there was nothing I could do until she arrived.

I stirred the teabag in the boiling water, took it out, and then added a dash of milk. Rachel liked her tea strong. 'Nothing worse than insipid, milky tea,' she always used to say. Those little acerbic asides were now long gone.

Taking a few chocolate digestives, I put them on a patterned plate and then went out of the kitchen. I glanced down at the plate. I remembered that we'd had that set of plates since Rachel and I had got married. We'd picked them out in a department store in Liverpool with vouchers that we'd been given as a wedding present. That must have been 1978, I thought to myself with a quick calculation. They've lasted over forty years which I considered to be pretty good value for money.

I padded down the hallway and entered the living room where Rachel was sitting watching television. There was a programme on about people moving from UK cities out to the countryside. We used to laugh together at what the programme used to categorise as 'the countryside'.

For a moment, I just watched her staring at the screen. I had no idea if she was taking any of it in, or if she was lost somewhere in her own head. If I allowed myself to dwell on it too much, I'd get upset. Rachel had been so fiercely intelligent – 'sharp as a bodkin' was the description a colleague of hers once used. And independent.

I spotted the book that rested on the arm of her chair. Rachel was also a voracious reader. Two or three books a week once she'd retired. But in recent months I'd noticed that she'd either labour through a book at a snail's pace, or whizz through at breakneck speed, turning pages after a couple of seconds. Sometimes we used to read the same book and then talk about it in depth. The last time we tried that – a crime thriller set in London during the Second World War – Rachel couldn't remember the plot in any meaningful way. She ended up in tears at the frustration of not being able to remember the story.

Taking a small side table, I set the tea and biscuits down.

'You are a dear,' she said with a vacant smile.

'I am a dear, you're right,' I replied and smiled back at her.

It was a little exchange, a funny little saying, that went

back many years when we brought stuff to each other. It felt reassuring to hear her say it.

Rachel looked up at me. 'Did you know that Linda Collier had died?' she asked.

Linda Collier was an old friend of ours who lived over towards Corwen. Her husband, Roy, a retired English teacher, was a lovely man who now spent his time volunteering for the National Trust and the RSPB.

'Has she?' I asked dubiously. This wasn't the first time that she'd had delusions about someone that we knew dying.

'Yes,' she replied with a nonchalant nod of her head. Then she casually sipped her tea and went back to watching the television.

'Oh right,' I said, playing along. There's no point challenging her. 'Who told you that?'

She pointed over at the phone. 'Someone rang here earlier and told me.'

'Oh, well that is sad, isn't it?' I said. I knew that no one had called. It was just another one of her delusions, but it broke my heart.

I took a breath.

Rachel didn't reply. I could see that her attention had drifted away again.

'Let me know if you need anything,' I told her, the words sticking in my throat as I made my way out of the living room. I knew she wasn't listening.

I would give Roy a ring later, just to make sure.

I gave a little whistle. 'Come on, Jack,' I called. He came trotting out from his bed in the kitchen and looked up at me expectantly. I stroked his head. 'Let's go.'

We went outside and I tried to clear my head.

The sign beside our farmhouse read *Yr hen dy Fferm*.

Translated from Welsh it simply meant *The old farmhouse*. I liked the lovely modesty of it. The wooden sign was weather-beaten, rinsed pale over the years that it had stood guard over the house and land that Rachel and I have called home for over thirty years.

Built in 1824, it had one large bedroom and two further small ones, plus a basic bathroom on the first floor. Downstairs comprised of a large traditional farmhouse kitchen, living room with an open fireplace, and a small room beside the front door off the hallway that I used as a study.

There was a one-storey annexe over to the right that the previous owner built back in the 60s for his mother to live in. Self-contained with a bedroom, bathroom and decent-sized living space. Rachel and I considered renting it out but we never got around to it. I'm not sure we ever will.

Beyond the sign, we had a muddy track littered with potholes, bumps and stones. And as Jack bounded away and sniffed at the verges, I surveyed the surrounding land. We were high up, with stunning views west towards the highest peaks of Snowdon/Eryri. *Yr Wyddfa*. The Welsh word for 'grave'. Legend had it that Eryri was the burial site of the giant Rhita Gawr.

It was so hard to accept that this is what Rachel was like now. It was never going to change. And it was never going to get better, only worse. Maybe I was avoiding thinking about how it would all end. A care home, incontinence, total loss of memory, and finally death. I tried to put that out of my mind. I'd deal with it on a day-to-day basis for now.

I didn't realise how cold it had got. The wind whipped in from the mountains and across the fields. The morning autumnal sun was now lost behind banks of bruised clouds. The fierce gusts numbed my face – or at least those bits not covered by my greying beard. It felt clean and refreshing.

My mind refocussed on what had happened to Megan. I'd spent thirty-five years as a police officer, so I'd dealt with more than my fair share of missing people. However, most of them had very obvious reasons for going missing. Skipping bail before a trial. Committing a crime and vanishing. Or going into hiding rather than give evidence. There didn't seem to be anything like this yet for Megan. Of course, something might surface in the coming days that would explain her disappearance. Or the whole thing could be resolved with a perfectly logical explanation.

Annie's reaction at being unable to contact her sister concerned me. I'd known Annie long enough to know how pragmatic, worldly, and calm she was day-to-day. Nothing seemed to faze her. Clearly, as a High Court judge, Annie – or *the Honourable Mrs Justice Annabelle Taylor* - had seen humanity at its worst or at its most vulnerable. If she felt that something was suspicious about Megan's disappearance, then it was something I needed to take seriously.

The sound of crunching tyres pulled me out of my thoughts. Looking up, I saw a red Citroen trundling up the track. It was Caitlin. My face softened to a smile just at the thought of seeing her and Sam.

They both gave me an enthusiastic wave from the car as they pulled up and parked outside the farmhouse.

Before I could take more than a step, the back door of the car flew open and Sam came hurtling towards me at full pelt.

'Taid!' he shouted as he wrapped his arms around me.

'Hello mate.' I laughed at his exuberance. Then I ruffled his coal-black hair. 'You okay?'

'We got a McDonald's breakfast,' he announced excitedly.

'Did you now?' I said with a chortle.

Crouching down, Sam started to make a fuss of Jack as I wandered over to the car where Caitlin was standing.

As soon as I saw her expression, I could see that something was wrong.

'Hello Dad,' she said quietly, but it was clear that she was holding back tears.

'You found us all right?' I teased her.

Caitlin's sense of direction was terrible, and even though she'd lived up here for years, she had still managed to get lost on several occasions.

She laughed. 'Yeah, I used *what3words*, that three-word location website. This place is *lamp, mirror, shoe*.'

I vaguely remembered reading about *what3words* in the paper.

Then I noticed that she had some purple and black bruising around her left eye.

'Jesus, Caitlin,' I said very quietly as I gestured to her face. 'Are you okay?'

She didn't reply as she came towards me and hugged me tightly.

I took a deep breath as the rage swept through me.

'I've left him,' she whispered.

All I could think about was how much I wished I could get my hands on TJ and teach him a lesson. I wanted to kill him.

'Okay,' I said as I held her for a few seconds, my hands pressed comfortingly against her back, trying to hide my fury from her. 'You know you can both stay here for as long as you need.'

She took a step back as she wiped tears from her eyes. 'He's such a prick, Dad.'

'Yeah, well I'm not going to disagree with you there, love,' I said.

Now wasn't the time to flag up the number of times I'd suggested that she leave that feckless moron. If TJ came anywhere near the farmhouse, I would shoot him dead and then take him out into Eryri, dig a hole, and bury the scumbag.

Caitlin then nodded over at the farmhouse. 'How's Mum?'

'She's okay,' I said unconvincingly. 'I guess I see her all the time so it's hard for me to gauge. She'll be so pleased to see you and Sam though.' I pointed at the car. 'Let's get your stuff indoors, shall we?'

Caitlin gave me a meaningful look. 'Thanks, Dad.'

'How long do you want to stay for?' I asked. 'Not that it matters to us.'

She pulled a face. 'Permanently?'

'Great.' I smiled reassuringly. 'That's more than fine by me.' Then I gestured to the single-storey annexe that was on the far side of the farmhouse. 'If you're really serious, we can spruce up the annexe for you.'

'Really?'

'Of course,' I said. 'You've got everything in there. A bedroom, kitchen, bathroom and living room.'

She gave me a beaming smile, and I could see the little girl that she had once been. James' death had hit her particularly hard, and she'd admitted that for a few years she'd found it hard to return to our farmhouse where he'd taken his own life.

Before we could continue, my phone rang.

I looked at the caller ID. It was Annie.

'I've got to take this,' I said to Caitlin and then answered it. 'Annie?'

'Is everything okay with your daughter and grandson?' she asked.

'Sort of,' I replied. 'I'll explain, but they're fine.'

'Good … I've tracked down the letting agency that my sister used,' she explained. 'Harrisons in Dolgellau.'

'Okay,' I said as I glanced down at my watch. 'I'll see you there in an hour.'

8

2 days 5 hours missing

Andrew Harrison ran the Harrison Letting Agency in the centre of Dolgellau. Its offices were modest and old fash-ioned. Black and white photographs of Dolgellau from a bygone era were dotted along the wall.

I shifted in my seat to get comfortable and then took a sip from my questionable-looking coffee. The rim was stained on the opposite side so I politely set it down on the table and sat back.

Jesus, that's not coffee.

Annie had briefly explained to Harrison that she was worried about Megan's whereabouts and the fact that she had moved out of the caravan.

'I've got your sister's paperwork here somewhere,' he said as he fumbled through a folder. He was in his early fifties. His mousy-coloured hair was patchy, his face covered by a thick beard, but it was hard to say if he appeared older or younger than his actual years. His face was marked by deep lines, giving him the weary look of someone permanently harassed.

I sat forward on my chair. 'The first thing we need to

know, Mr Harrison, is when Megan gave notice on her rental agreement.'

He nodded as he shuffled the papers. I was astounded that in 2022, the information wasn't all kept on a computer.

'Yes, right, here we are,' he said triumphantly as if he'd been searching for a lost key. Then he frowned. 'That's right. The tenancy agreement for the caravan stipulated that your sister and nephew needed to give three months' notice.'

Annie raised an eyebrow. 'And did they?'

Harrison blinked. I noticed that his forehead was a little sweaty. Given the cool temperature in the office, I wondered if he was a heavy drinker. I'd seen it countless times before. The glistening sheen of sweat on the face of a heavy drinker or alcoholic the following day. It was a tell-tale sign.

'No.' He frowned again. Then he nodded as if a memory had suddenly come back to him. 'Yes, that's right. It was your nephew, Callum, who came to see me.'

Annie squinted in confusion. 'Callum?'

'He came in to say that he and your sister Megan wanted to move out,' he explained.

'Callum came in?' she asked in disbelief.

'Yes, that's right.'

Annie glanced over at me. She'd made it very clear on many occasions what type of man Callum was.

'And he came in on his own?' Her tone suggested that she was more than surprised.

Harrison nodded. 'Yes.' He clearly didn't understand the implication of Annie's surprise.

'When was this?' I asked.

He squinted down at the document. 'Monday of last week. The 15th.'

Annie's eyes widened. 'Really? But that's only eight days ago. We've been over to the caravan and everything has gone. They've moved out.' She sounded utterly baffled.

'That's right,' Harrison said. 'Callum explained he was happy to pay for the full month but they needed to move out now. Technically, he and your sister still have access to the caravan for the next couple of weeks.'

'Isn't that highly irregular?' Annie asked.

'It is,' Harrison agreed. 'Normally landlords want three months' notice so that we can find them new tenants to move in.'

I raised my eyebrow. 'Why was this different?'

'Mr Thomas, who owns the caravan your sister and nephew lived in ...' Harrison explained, '... has been debating whether or not to sell it. I rang him and he told me that he'd gladly accept your sister and nephew giving one month notice so that he could get the caravan on the market as quickly as possible.'

'That just doesn't make any sense,' Annie said under her breath. 'I had a text message from Meg on the 15th. I'd messaged her because it would have been our father's birthday. She sent me a message back but she didn't say anything about this.'

Harrison frowned at us. 'I take it you didn't know they were moving out?'

'No,' Annie sighed in exasperation. 'Surely it was my sister who signed the tenancy agreement? Legally you would have needed her consent to do all this.'

Harrison shook his head. 'No. Callum was a co-signatory on the agreement. Is something the matter?'

Annie nodded. 'I didn't know they were going to move. And I haven't had any contact from my sister or nephew in the past two days. I'm just very worried.'

'Oh dear,' Harrison said, pulling a face. 'I'm sorry to hear that.'

'Have you seen my sister at any point in the last eight days?'

'No, sorry.'

'What about a deposit?' I asked.

'Yes, there was a three-month deposit.' He looked at Annie. 'Your nephew said that he had a new bank account. He gave me the details and Mr Thomas paid the deposit back to Callum via us.'

'The money went back to Callum?' I asked to clarify.

'Yes, that's right. It only cleared this morning,' he confirmed. 'It was about £2,500 in total.'

Annie gave me a dark look. Neither of us liked the sound of that.

9

2 days 5 hours missing

Twenty minutes later, Annie and I sat in the *Popty'r Dref Bakery*. I stirred my black coffee as Annie dunked a fruit teabag into her cup of hot water. We sat in silence for a few seconds. Annie rubbed her forehead and let out a frustrated breath.

A blackboard behind one of the counters read *Large people are harder to kidnap. So eat cake.* The dark irony of the joke wasn't lost on me.

'Used to be called 'The Tea Rooms' didn't it?' I asked.

Annie nodded. 'My nain used to bring me and Megan here on a Saturday when we were little for squash and a bun.'

'Bara Brith?' I asked, referring to traditional Welsh fruit cake.

Annie shook her head. 'No, they were fingers with white icing on top. Nain called them 'school buns'. She used to tell me and Megan off for licking the icing before eating the bun.'

'I remember,' I said with a half-smile as I sipped my

scalding hot coffee. It was strong, and a million miles from the muck I'd been served by Andrew Harrison. 'Just.'

Annie gave a sad smile at the memory.

I reached across the table and put my hand on the back of hers for a moment. 'We're going to find her. I promise you.'

She gave me the same nod that she'd given me a couple of times already today. It was a nod that was devoid of all certainty. A nod full of fear and apprehension.

'You can't promise me that, Frank,' she said quietly.

There was silence for a few seconds. Annie was deep in thought as her eyes roamed around the room and her brow was furrowed.

She looked at me as if she had suddenly drawn a conclusion from these thoughts.

'I think Callum has done something to her,' she whispered.

I frowned, looking for her to be less vague. 'How do you mean?'

'Callum hasn't ever taken responsibility for anything in his life,' she explained. 'Meg wouldn't have sent him to talk to the letting agent. Never. And he has never had any money. Meg has subsidised him every step of the way. So why did he give Harrison Letting Agency his new bank details? Meg would have paid the deposit on that caravan.'

I took in the seriousness of what Annie was suggesting. 'Do you think Callum is capable of harming your sister to get the deposit back?'

'I don't know. Maybe,' she replied with a shrug. 'He's an addict. You know how far an addict will go to get drugs or booze. We both do. £2,500 is a lot of money.'

'I do. More than most ... We have to find Callum,' I said, thinking out loud.

Annie shrugged. 'The only thing I've got is his mobile phone number.'

'We don't have any way of tracking his signal. And the police aren't going to do that unless they think Meg is in danger.'

'Which we can't prove in any meaningful way.'

'No, we can't.' I said.

Annie moved a strand of hair off her face and tucked it behind her ear. The light from outside reflected on the left-hand side of her face.

Then I said, 'There must be something. Where would Callum go if he wanted to get away or if he was in trouble?'

'He has turned up at his father's house in Barmouth a couple of times when Meg kicked him out. Maybe he's gone there?'

'Are he and his father close?'

'Not really.' Annie shook her head. 'He left Meg when Callum was two. But they've been in touch a bit more in recent years.'

'Has to be worth a try,' I suggested. 'Have you got an address?'

'Yeah, I know where Bryn lives,' she said as we got up from the table.

10

2 days 6 hours missing

We arrived in Barmouth, a seaside town that lay on the estuary of Afon Mawddach and Cardigan Bay. Technically it was just outside Snowdonia National Park, although Cadair Idris, standing nearly 3000ft, loomed over the town.

I spotted the Mermaid Fish Bar on the front as we drove past.

'Best fish and chip shop in Wales,' I said.

'The Mermaid?'

I nodded.

'It's been there since I was a child,' she said.

'My father insisted that we go there for tea on his birthday every year,' I said, thinking back. 'My mum would drive and he'd have a couple of pints at that pub on the front. Then fish and chips from the Mermaid.'

'Sounds nice.'

I glanced over at her. 'I genuinely think it was the only time that my dad was ever happy. He sometimes managed a smile if Wrexham won.'

Annie pulled a face. 'That's sad. You said he was a farmer?'

I nodded. This wasn't the time to describe the kind of man my father was. 'Yeah. Very old fashioned. Cattle. Bred horses. He was as hard as nails and miserable as sin. And partial to showing us the back of his hand on a regular basis.'

'The good old days,' Annie joked darkly as she then opened the piece of paper and reminded me, 'The Grange, 7 Mynach Road.'

'I looked at Google Maps before we left. I know where it is roughly.'

'What if Callum isn't there?' Annie asked as the worried expression returned to her face.

'We keep looking,' I said in a determined tone. 'What's this Bryn like?'

Annie let out a sigh. 'I haven't seen him since Callum was born. He was just a selfish prick. Fancied himself as a bit of a hippy. He was in a band, long hair, smoked a lot of hashish. He got Meg pregnant and promised that they would build a life together. Then he just fucked off.'

'Yeah, he sounds like a prick,' I agreed. 'And he didn't keep in touch with Callum?'

'Very sporadically. The odd birthday or Christmas when he could be bothered. I think Callum has seen a lot more of him in the last few years. I've no idea why.'

We turned into Mynach Road and I saw the sign that read *The Grange*.

The house was larger than I thought it would be but it was in a state of disrepair. The grey stone walls were covered in moss, and the wooden window frames were rotten and needed to be replaced. On the driveway was an old, battered wooden rowboat and a small blue caravan that had to be over fifty years old. There was a relatively new-looking Leeway Falcon 125cc scooter. Next to the front door was a rusty bicycle and old pots of paint and a stepladder.

I parked the pick-up about thirty yards down the road so as not to draw attention to our arrival. We got out and made our way back up the road to the drive.

A crow flew overhead. It wheeled around and landed on a dirty grey wheelie bin. Two more joined it. The first crow then jumped down onto a weed-strewn flowerbed, its scrawny feet scratching angrily at the earth, searching for worms or bugs. I shuddered for a second. There was something horribly ominous about crows. There always had been.

I looked at Annie. 'We should have a look around before we knock,' I said under my breath, 'in case Bryn covers for him.'

She nodded in agreement.

Treading as carefully as we could on the gravel drive, we made our way up to the house itself. Straining my ears, I couldn't hear anything but the sound of someone cutting a hedge somewhere nearby. My hearing had deteriorated in recent years, so I now had tiny digital hearing aids in both ears. Rachel used to tease me when I first got them. She'd mouth words but not say anything so I would have to check that they were working. Then she'd have fits of laughter when I realised what she'd done. That's what I loved about our relationship. The teasing, the jokes, the little sayings or snippets from films that no one else understood. And then the easy ability to slip into a more serious conversation. I'm aware that I now think of that as all being in the past. We just don't have that connection anymore.

The squawk of the nearby crows broke my train of thought.

Annie walked over gingerly to a ground floor window, cupped her hands to shield her view from the sunlight, and peered inside.

'Anything?' I asked, as I went further down the side of the house.

'No one in there,' she replied.

Suddenly, there was a thunderous barking and scratching from behind the wooden fence and gate that clearly led to the back garden.

I pulled a face at Annie. 'Christ, he sounds big.'

'And very friendly,' she joked.

'Front door?' I suggested.

She nodded in agreement. 'Sensible idea I think.'

As we turned to head back, the garden gate burst open.

A man in his 60s, greying beard and hair tied into a ponytail, came out holding an enormous American X Bully dog straining at a thick red rope leash.

'What the fuck do you want?' he shouted angrily as he advanced.

The muscles in my stomach tensed as, instinctively, I stepped in front of Annie to protect her. If the man let go of the lead, it was likely that the dog was going to attack us.

'Take it easy ...' I said, holding up my hands to pacify the man and persuade him to keep his dog on the leash. I didn't have a gun to reach for.

'Bryn, you idiot!' Annie shouted at him. 'For God's sake, put that bloody thing away!'

He frowned at her for a few seconds.

'It's me. Annie,' she explained loudly.

'Annie? Jesus,' he said, now realising who she was. 'What the fuck are you doing down here? Why didn't you just knock on the front door, you daft cow?'

'We did,' she lied.

Bryn shrugged. 'Didn't hear it. But my hearing is shot to fucking pieces these days. All that touring back in the day.'

'This is Frank,' Annie explained over the noise of the dog's barking and snarling. 'He's a friend of mine. Can we come in for a few minutes?'

'Erm, yeah, yeah, course,' he said, now calmer. 'I'll keep Rocky out in the garden. Don't worry, he's all mouth, no trousers. Wouldn't harm a fly.'

As I looked at the long globules of saliva that dripped from Rocky's fangs, it wasn't a theory that I wanted to put to the test.

'Okay,' Annie said. 'I'll see you in a second.'

Bryn disappeared with Rocky back through the garden gate, which he then closed behind him and locked.

'Rocky?' I said in a withering tone.

She shrugged. 'Told you he was a prick.'

Annie and I went around to the front door, and a few seconds later Bryn opened it and ushered us inside. The hallway was cluttered and messy. There was the distinct smell of weed in the air, along with air freshener of some kind.

'Sorry about the mess,' he muttered as we stepped over a box containing old music cassettes and VHS tapes. 'Come through.'

He led us into a living room. The walls had patterned, oriental wall hangings. Sofas were covered in patterned throws. A low table had a Buddha's head, a wooden carved statue of the Indian god Shiva, and a red lava lamp. There was a bong on the table along with a pile of scruffy books about mysticism. It was like walking into a time warp from 1969.

And this peace-loving hippy owns a dog like Rocky? I thought to myself dryly.

'Sit down, sit down,' Bryn said in a friendly tone. Then he looked over at Annie and shook his head. 'It's been a while, hasn't it?'

'Nearly thirty years, Bryn,' she replied guardedly. 'Two years after Callum was born.'

Bryn shrugged defensively. 'Oh come on, Annie.' He laughed nervously as he began to roll up a cigarette. 'That's all water under the bridge isn't it?'

'We're looking for Meg,' she said, ignoring his comment. 'Or Callum. Have you seen either of them recently?'

Bryn narrowed his eyes. 'No. What's the urgency?'

'It looks like Megan and Callum moved out of their caravan,' I said. 'We don't know where they've gone.'

Bryn shrugged. 'I haven't seen them,' he said defensively.

Annie sat forward on her chair. 'Something's wrong, Bryn. I talk or message my sister nearly every day. She would have told me if she was moving.'

'Did Callum say anything to you about it?' I asked Bryn.

He raised an eyebrow. 'You a copper?'

I looked at him for a moment. 'Used to be.'

'Thought so,' he said with a smirk. If he was trying to irritate me, then it wasn't working. I'd come up against far more sophisticated 'wind-up merchants' than him.

'Have you seen or heard from Callum recently?' Annie asked, now sounding desperate.

'I just told you. No.' Bryn shook his head adamantly. But as he went to lick the cigarette paper, he scratched the side of his nose. It was 'a tell'. He was lying.

'Bryn, this is serious,' Annie said forcefully. 'Callum went to the letting agency to tell them he and Meg were moving out. He took the deposit.'

Bryn scowled. 'That's not what he told me.'

'You just told me that you hadn't heard from him!' Annie growled.

There was an awkward silence as Bryn squirmed and then lit his cigarette. 'I didn't know what you meant,' he mumbled.

Annie shook her head. 'Don't be ridiculous.'

'Can you tell us what Callum *did* tell you?' I asked, trying to focus back on getting information.

'He said that Meg had vanished about a week ago,' he explained awkwardly. 'He said that she must have run off with her 'fancy man'.'

Out of the corner of my eye, I saw movement outside. A figure was taking the scooter off its stand.

It was a man in his 30s who I assumed was Callum. And he was clearly about to do a runner.

Standing up quickly, I glanced at Annie. 'Callum's out there. Come on.'

Turning on my heels, I heard the scooter's engine burst into life. Annie and I jogged down the hallway, threw open the front door and jumped down the stone steps.

As the scooter crunched on the gravel, Callum stared at us. He wasn't wearing a helmet.

'Callum! Just stop. Stay there!' Annie yelled at him as she held up her hand.

Striding across the driveway, I positioned myself between Callum and the drive's entrance to the road. It might have been foolhardy but it felt instinctive.

Callum pulled the throttle, revved the engine and sped towards me.

Oh bollocks.

I dived out of the way and crashed to the ground. A sharp pain went through my shoulder and neck.

'Are you okay?' Annie cried as she got to me.

'Hurt pride, that's all,' I groaned as I got to my feet. 'Come on. Let's see if we can catch him up.'

Annie nodded, looking concerned.

Jogging along the road with my shoulder still throbbing, I unlocked the Toyota pick-up and we jumped in.

I started the ignition, spun the steering wheel, and screeched into a fast U-turn as Annie gripped the ceiling strap.

Stamping down on the accelerator, the pick-up lurched forward, throwing us both back in our seats.

'Sorry,' I said as we picked up speed. 'I'm a bit out of practice when it comes to high-speed pursuits.'

'Don't worry. Just catch him up. Callum's the only person who can tell us what's happened to Meg.'

Turning left onto the A496, we hammered along with the estuary and Aberamffra Harbour to our right.

Glancing down at the dashboard, I could see we were now travelling at 65mph.

The trees were flashing past in a blur. I just prayed that no one pulled out from one of the side turnings or entrances to the fields along the way.

Peering up the road, I could see a shape up ahead.

Callum.

'There he is,' I said, gesturing as the shape became clearer.

70mph.

It was clear that Callum held the answer to whatever had happened to Megan. Had he harmed her in an argument? Or had he seen an opportunity to get the deposit back to feed his various addictions?

Pushing the accelerator another inch, I gunned the engine.

The speedometer hit 85mph.

Callum was getting closer.

We were now less than 50 yards behind the scooter.

I glanced over at Annie whose face was gripped with grim determination.

'This is getting dangerous,' I warned her.

'I know,' she said under her breath.

'I can back off or slow down?'

'Don't slow down.' She shook her head adamantly. 'If Callum gets away, he'll disappear. And so will the one person who knows what's happened to Meg. I can't let that happen.'

Annie had read my mind.

'Okay,' I said as I gripped the steering wheel with both hands. My eyes were now locked on to Callum and the scooter.

We careered around a long bend and could hear the tyres of the Toyota starting to squeal.

A huge articulated lorry came thundering past in the opposite direction.

Callum wobbled a little.

We cut right for about thirty seconds and then left.

'Where the hell is he going?' Annie said, sounding exasperated.

I shrugged. 'The next place we get to is Ffestiniog.'

Then Callum took a hard right.

As we hurtled along the country lane, there was something about the area that I recognised.

'I know where he's going,' Annie said. 'Look.'

Up ahead, there was a large steel gate between two wooden bollards. A red traffic sign showed there was no access for cars or motorcycles.

Llanelltyd Bridge.

'Shit,' I groaned. 'Sneaky fucker.'

The 18th century stone bridge at Llanelltyd was closed to traffic these days and was merely a footbridge.

Smart move.

Callum was using it because we couldn't follow him in the truck.

He slowed quickly, manoeuvred the scooter around the gate, and then sped away down the deserted track.

'We can't let him get away!' Annie insisted.

As we got to the gate, I could see that there might be just enough verge to the side of it to squeeze the Toyota through and continue our pursuit.

There wasn't.

I hit the wooden bollard with a thud and knocked it, and the steel gate, to the ground with a thunderous metallic crash.

But we were through. I could try to explain later.

Pushing down the accelerator, we lurched down the lane, hitting potholes and bumps which threw us around the inside of the pick-up.

'Bloody hell!' Annie yelled, holding on for dear life.

As we turned the bend, I could see Callum heading towards the old, stone bridge. He clearly thought that he'd lost us at the gate.

He was now about seventy yards ahead of us.

With a quick turn back, Callum spotted us behind him.

Oh shit, I thought.

The high-pitched whine of the scooter's engine pierced the air as Callum hammered away like a maniac towards the old stone bridge, trying to escape.

The bridge was narrow and full of pedestrians.

I slammed on the brakes and stopped.

Throwing open the pick-up door, I got out.

There were shouts from a middle-aged man that I was 'a moron'.

I spotted Callum weaving his scooter over the bridge and jogged off after him.

A mother with a pushchair walked obliviously into his path.

She spotted Callum and froze.

Callum swerved violently to avoid her.

He lost control.

The scooter ploughed into the side of the bridge.

Callum was tossed high off the scooter and into the water below.

'Oh my God!' Annie cried as she jogged beside me.

Despite my aching knees and shoulder, I had already gone into full police officer mode.

I needed to get to Callum as quickly as possible so that he didn't drown.

There was a scream and shouting from people on the bridge.

Some of them rushed to the edge to look down and see where Callum had been thrown.

'Out of the way!' I yelled.

I sprinted to where the scooter had crashed into the stone wall.

Peering down, I saw Callum's body lying face down in about five feet of water. Even though it was a good twenty feet down, I had no choice.

Sitting on the edge of the bridge, I threw my legs over the side.

'Frank!' Annie shouted nervously.

'It's fine. I've got to get him out of there.'

With a quick push, I dropped down into the water, keeping my legs bent as much as I could. As I hit the river bed, a searing white hot pain pierced through my right ankle. But I couldn't stop.

Wading rapidly through the water, I reached over and grabbed the back of Callum's jacket. I pulled him up out of the water with all my strength.

Turning him around, I managed to loop both my arms under his armpits from behind. He was unconscious. I didn't even know if he was still breathing.

I needed to get him to the riverbank.

I could hear the shouts from people on the bridge calling for an ambulance. Others ran down to the far side of the bridge to get to the riverbank.

My arms were burning with the stress of holding Callum. I waded backwards through the water.

Thank God he's a skinny bugger, I thought to myself.

I interlocked my fingers to try and pull him higher. His cold wet hair from the back of his head was pressed against the right-hand side of my face. For a second, I could even smell the shampoo he used.

With a quick glance back, I could see that I was now about fifteen yards from the riverbank.

However, my arms were starting to go numb with exertion.

Don't drop him, I said to myself.

Hearing some splashing, I saw that a young man in his twenties had jumped into the river and was now wading out to help me.

'Thank you,' I sighed through gritted teeth.

'Here you go, mate,' he said, as he helped me take Callum's weight.

We both pulled him back through the water.

Getting to the riverbank, a few others helped to put him on his back on the grassy bank.

Annie crouched down next to me. 'Jesus, Frank,' she gasped.

I quickly checked to see if he was breathing.

He wasn't.

I checked his pulse. He still had one but it was weak.

Pinching his nose, I opened his mouth and checked to

see that his airways were clear. I held his mouth open by the jaw and began mouth to mouth resuscitation. I must have performed it over a dozen times as a police officer.

A second later, Callum groaned and coughed up some water but didn't regain consciousness.

But he was now breathing. I could see his chest moving up and down.

In the distance, the noise of sirens. The paramedics were on their way.

Callum was alive. Just.

The woman who had been pushing the pushchair looked down at me with widened eyes. 'You saved that bloke's life. If you hadn't jumped in and done that, he'd be dead.'

I didn't reply.

Annie met my eyes and nodded. 'She's right.'

11

2 days 9 hours missing

Annie and I sat in a long row of red seats outside the Acute Medical Unit (AMC) at Glan Clwyd Hospital. The air smelled of dreary, flavourless hospital food and disinfectant. The corridor was empty and seemed to echo as if we were in a church. The caramel-coloured laminate floor was dirty and needed a good mop.

It had been over two hours since we'd followed the ambulance up from Llanelltyd Bridge. However, a doctor had told us about twenty minutes ago that Callum was out of danger and his injuries weren't as serious as they'd first anticipated.

Looking down, I massaged cramp from my right hand and then stretched out my fingers. My ankle was still throbbing from where I'd jumped off the bridge but I was pretty sure it was no more than a minor strain.

Annie caught me. 'You're not meant to do stuff like that at your age,' she said under her breath. She had a half-smile as if she was in fact very grateful that I had. She had such a lovely smile. It just lit up her face.

'What stuff?' I asked, playing along a little.

'Jumping off bridges, pulling people out of rivers ...'

'He's your nephew.'

'I know, but ...'

Looking directly at her, I gave an expression of mock indignation. 'And anyway, what do you mean "at my age"? Bloody cheek.'

She laughed. It was a good laugh. Full and throaty. 'You're seventy, Frank.'

I tapped my forefinger against my temple. 'Yes, but up here I'm twenty-seven. And I tend to forget my age when things get a bit hairy.'

She smiled. 'Gosh. I'm actually nineteen in my head. A little bit younger than you. And then I walk past a mirror and say "Bloody hell, who's that old woman looking back at me?"'

I nodded in recognition. 'Hey, 70s are the new 30s.'

She gave me a suspicious look. 'Who told you that?'

'No one.' I shrugged. 'I just made it up.'

'You're a daft bugger, Frank Marshal,' she said as she leaned in to give me a playful little shove.

'It's been said before. On many occasions.'

My phone buzzed. It was Caitlin checking in and telling me that Rachel was fine and that they'd had tea together.

'Just Caitlin checking in,' I explained, gesturing to my phone.

'How do you feel about her and Sam staying?' she asked. I'd filled her in very briefly earlier.

'I'm made up.'

'Really? It's quite a big change, especially with how poorly Rachel is,' she said gently.

'To be honest, it's a huge weight off my mind. I've lost sleep over Caitlin and Sam being down there with that dickhead waste of space. We've got the annexe, and I know Rachel will love having them around more.'

Annie gave me a knowing look. 'And so will you.'

'Of course.' I smiled. 'I'd like to get Sam riding again. Maybe get him a pony.'

'You want to spoil him, which is exactly what you're meant to do,' Annie said, but then she looked sad and shook her head. 'For the briefest of seconds there, I forgot that Meg was missing.'

I gave her an understanding look. 'I know that I keep saying it, but we will find out what's happened to her.'

She gave me a quizzical look as if she'd noticed something.

'What?' I asked.

Silence as she took a few seconds. I couldn't work out what was wrong or what I'd said that seemed to have upset her.

'Up until now you've told me that we're going to <u>find</u> Meg,' she explained, 'but you've just said we're going to find out what's happened to her. It feels like you're less sure that something terrible hasn't happened to her.'

'No, that's not what I meant. Sorry…' I said, floundering and wondering how to backtrack. Deep down in my gut I'd started to worry that something terrible <u>had</u> happened to her, but it wasn't something I could share. 'I've gone into detective mode. I'm not going to make any assumptions until we have more concrete evidence or leads.'

'Mrs Taylor?' said a young woman's voice interrupting us.

A doctor was approaching. She wore a white coat and was holding a folder.

'Yes?' Annie replied.

'Your nephew has regained consciousness.'

'How is he?' she asked.

'He's had a nasty bang to the head but he's going to be okay. CT scan shows there's no damage to his brain. We just need to keep him under observation for the next couple of days.'

'Good,' she said with a sigh. 'Can we go and see him?'

'Yes, but not too long. He's still a bit groggy.'

'Thank you,' I said as the doctor turned and left us.

Annie put her hands on her thighs and then stood up with a sense of purpose.

'Right, let's go and find out what he knows,' she said as she gestured for me to follow her.

For a few seconds, we walked down the corridor before arriving at a small single room that we'd been told Callum was in when we first arrived.

Annie knocked on the door and then opened it.

Callum was lying propped up in bed. He had ECG electrodes attached to his chest, and the right-hand side of his head was heavily bandaged.

'Callum?' Annie said gently as she went over and took a grey plastic chair and sat down.

He frowned as he looked at Annie and then at me.

Annie reached across and took his hand which had nasty grazes from where he had hit the bridge.

'How are you feeling?' she asked.

He shrugged but didn't answer.

Then she leaned closer. 'Callum, where's your mum?' she asked quietly.

Callum squinted with a quizzical expression. Then he shook his head very slightly.

'Where is she, Callum? Where's Meg? I don't understand why you both moved out from the caravan without telling me.' Annie started to sound both concerned and frantic. 'What the hell happened, Callum?'

Callum narrowed his eyes and then glanced suspiciously at her.

'Who are you?' he asked in a very croaky voice.

'What?' Annie asked, looking thoroughly perplexed. 'I'm your Aunt Annie. I've known you all your life. What on earth are you talking about, Callum?'

Callum shook his head. He was genuinely upset. 'I've never seen you before.'

12

2 days 11 hours missing

Once we'd left the hospital, I'd driven Annie home. We had been driving in a pensive silence for about ten minutes. I guessed that we were both running over the events of the day and trying to piece together all that we'd learned. The doctor had assured us that temporary memory loss after an accident wasn't that uncommon. However, she'd also explained that it might last for a day or two which was frustrating.

Winding down the window, I took a deep breath. The night air was cold and fresh. The moon had sloped unnoticed behind a swollen grey cloud so that the road ahead was now enveloped in darkness.

'Penny for them,' Annie said quietly.

'I just wish we had something concrete to go on,' I admitted.

She sighed. 'I've started to think that maybe I'm overreacting. Maybe there is going to be a perfectly logical explanation for all this.'

'I've known you for a long time.' I shook my head. 'You're not someone who is prone to overreact, catastrophise or be melodramatic. If your instinct tells you that something is wrong, then I think you're almost certainly right.'

'What do you think?' she asked.

'I agree with you. None of it adds up.'

'Thank you, Frank.' She sounded relieved that she wasn't just imagining it all.

I turned right, headed slowly up the gravel driveway and then stopped.

Annie leaned in and gave me a kiss on the cheek. She lingered a little and I could smell her perfume.

'I don't know what I would have done without you today,' she admitted as she took off her seatbelt.

'No problem.'

'I could do with a drink.'

I sighed. 'So could I.'

She glanced over. 'Why don't you come in? Stephen's away overnight. A mixture of business and golf apparently,' she said. 'That's if he's there at all.'

I HESITATED BEFORE ANSWERING, and smiled as our eyes met. 'I'd better get back actually. See how Caitlin and Sam are settling in.'

Annie tutted. 'Oh God, that sounded weird, didn't it? Saying that Stephen's away.'

I gave a chortle. 'No, not at all. I knew what you meant. To say that Stephen's not my cup of tea would be an understatement.'

She leaned over and gave me another kiss on the cheek. 'Oh God, I've already kissed you,' she said, getting flustered.

I laughed. 'It's fine.'

She waved her hands. 'Don't worry, I'm getting out of the bloody car.'

Closing the door, she went around to the other side of the car as I wound down the window.

I looked directly at her. Even though she was still clearly anxious, her blue eyes seemed to twinkle at me.

'It's going to be all right,' I said in a reassuring tone.

'Frank, you're a perfect gentleman and a very dear friend.'

'Let's talk first thing in the morning,' I suggested, 'and if you think of anything or just need to talk, call me. Whatever time it is.'

'Thanks again.' She turned, fished her keys from her bag, and headed for the front door.

13

3 days 1 hour missing

It was early morning as I held the dark green throw at one end and Caitlin held it at the other. We slowly placed it down over the old burgundy sofa that rested against the living room wall and stood back.

'That's better already, isn't it?' I said to her.

'Yeah,' she agreed, and then pointed to the blank walls. 'I'll get some pictures up on the walls. This place will feel like home before you know it.'

'Did you guys sleep okay?' I asked.

'Yes. Great.'

I gave her a warm smile.

'What's wrong with the wi-fi here?' said a voice.

Sam was sitting over in the corner holding his phone with a perplexed look on his face.

'This place is like a lead bunker when it comes to getting wi-fi or a phone signal,' I joked, but I could see that he didn't really understand what I was talking about.

Caitlin looked at me thoughtfully. 'Maybe we could get separate wi-fi in here rather than piggy-backing yours from the main house?'

'Sounds good,' I said encouragingly as I went over to an old, dusty uplighter floor lamp. 'This doesn't work anymore so I'll put it in the shed.'

'Taid, we haven't even got a TV,' Sam said, pulling a face.

'Sam!' Caitlin said in a reprimanding tone.

'It's fine,' I reassured her. 'I don't suppose there's much point telling him that when I was his age, we had a tiny black and white tv set in the kitchen with three channels.'

Caitlin shook her head. 'Probably not,' she said dryly.

I laughed as I headed out with the lamp. 'One thing at a time, mate. I've got a credit card so don't worry. We can get a huge TV for in here. As long as we can watch the footie together.'

'Cool,' Sam said with a beaming smile.

'Don't spoil him,' Caitlin called as I left the room.

'I'm his Taid. That's my job.'

The back door was open, so I went outside and over to a large garden shed which had become a dumping ground for things that essentially needed to be thrown out.

Then something occurred to me. There was the residents' storage shed at the back of the caravans where Megan and Callum had lived. No one had checked it when we and the police were at the property. I knew it was a dark thought, but if Callum had done anything to Megan, putting her body in the shed and locking it up would be the easiest way of buying him some time. Especially if his plan was to use the deposit money to disappear and start a new life somewhere else.

'You okay, Dad?' Caitlin asked, breaking my train of thought as she came beside me.

'Erm yeah. Sort of.'

'You look like you've seen a ghost,' she said as she put some very dusty old cushions into the shed.

'I've just got to pop out for a bit,' I explained. 'Can you keep an eye on your mum?'

'Of course.'

I took out my phone as I headed around the side of the annexe and towards the Toyota pick-up.

I rang Annie.

'Frank?' she said, answering her phone.

'I'm coming to pick you up now,' I said with a sense of urgency.

'Why?'

'I'll explain when I get to you. See you in a bit.'

I ended the call, put my fingers to my mouth and gave a loud whistle.

'Jack!' I shouted.

He came bounding out of the farmhouse.

I clicked my fingers and he jumped up the bumper and into the back of the pick-up truck as he'd done hundreds of times before.

I was starting to feel a little uneasy about what we'd find at the Vale Caravan Park.

14

3 days 2 hours missing

Standing outside Megan's caravan with Annie, I grabbed the iron crowbar from the back of the truck.

The air was filled with the musty smell of damp autumnal leaves. As the wind soared, the leaves in the trees and hedges rattled with a strange skittering noise.

As we walked down the side of the caravan that led to the storage shed, I could feel Jack by my feet.

Annie was wearing a woollen hat and scarf. The apprehension was deep in her eyes.

'Do you want to stay here while I have a look first?' I asked her. I'd told her my fears about the shed on the way over. I wondered if I should have made the journey on my own in case we did find something.

'No,' she said, shaking her head with quiet resolve. 'I'm fine.'

Making our way down the side of the caravan, we then came to the storage shed. It was made from wood that had been stained a dark green.

Jack immediately made for the door and began to sniff.

Then he backed away, barked and scratched at the wood, and barked again.

I shared a dark look with Annie. It wasn't a good sign.

I approached and then levered the crowbar into the middle of the padlock. With a quick jerk I pulled, and the padlock and metal panel behind it came clean off the wood.

I pulled the door to the shed open slowly as Jack scampered inside and disappeared into the darkness.

I was hit instantly by an overwhelming putrid smell.

Annie put her hand over her nose and mouth as we moved inside.

'Jesus,' she gasped as she pulled a face. We both knew what the smell was.

It was the unmistakable stink of death – of rotting flesh.

This isn't good.

The inside of the shed was bigger than it appeared from the outside, and shadowy. There were shelving units stacked against the walls, along with a ladder, a small pile of chairs, and objects covered with dark green tarpaulins.

I used my torch to see where I was going and stepped over some old pots of paint. I just prayed that the stench wasn't anything to do with Megan.

Jack was barking and whining about five yards in front of us.

Moving my torch slowly over the area where Jack was, I saw a large shape under a dark green tarpaulin. Looking down I saw a small tyre and realised that there was some sort of trolley underneath.

Annie appeared next to me. The colour had drained from her face.

'You okay?' I asked quietly. She was breathing through her mouth given the terrible odour.

She didn't answer but instead just stared at the tarpaulin. I knew she was wondering if her sister's body was underneath it.

Jack's whines and nervous barking intensified.

'It's all right, boy,' I reassured him. Then I gestured to the tarpaulin. 'Annie, can you give me a hand to move this so we can have a look underneath?'

She hesitated for a moment before reaching over to take it.

We pulled back the tarpaulin to reveal a small flat trolley with four rubber wheels. It was covered with an old, dirty yellow blanket. The smell had intensified significantly now that the tarpaulin had been moved.

I took my torch, moved its beam and saw the tell-tale sign of blowflies buzzing in the air. They seemed to be circling the trolley and whatever it was underneath the blanket.

The light disturbed the flies who began to swirl noisily, adding to the eerie scene.

Jack's barking got louder.

Reaching over, I held my breath as I pulled the yellow blanket back.

I saw a shape inside the trolley and my pulse quickened as I took an unsteady breath.

Jack backed away with a high-pitched whine.

I squinted.

The shape was small – too small to be a person.

Then I saw fur. Black and grey fur.

'It's a badger,' Annie whispered with a sigh of complete and utter relief.

'Yeah,' I mumbled.

We backed away and then out of the shed.

'I'll call the letting agents and let them know,' Annie said very quietly.

15

3 days 3 hours missing

Annie and I had started to search through the caravan once again. It had to be worth checking in case we'd missed something. It wasn't as if the place had been searched by scene of crime officers or a forensic team. It had been given the once-over by a few uniformed officers.

While Annie searched the kitchen and living area, I entered the bedroom to the rear of the caravan. As I entered, I dropped my torch. It landed with a noisy bang on the wooden flooring. Crouching down to pick it up, I spotted something out of the corner of my eye.

A small luminous pink piece of paper stuck to the wall just behind the bed. It was barely visible but it looked like a post-it note.

I crawled over, reached out and took it. It was a square post-it that had part of a cobweb stuck on its sticky edge.

'What's that?' Annie asked as she came over, and I used the bed to push myself to my feet.

Scribbled at the centre of the note was *TAP 134 3A*.

I showed it to Annie. 'This mean anything to you?'

She shrugged. 'No.'

'TAP? Is that someone's initials or something?' I asked, thinking out loud.

'Maybe.'

Putting the note carefully into my phone wallet, we went out into the narrow hallway. I had no idea if the note had any relevance to what had happened to Megan. Probably not.

As we went down the hallway, I glanced up. There was a hatch up above us on the ceiling. It clearly led up to some kind of loft space. I wasn't even aware that caravans had such things as loft spaces.

My mind was drawn back to a terrible case that I'd worked as a detective up in Llandudno. A young twelve-year-old girl, Lilly Tranter, had been reported missing from her home in 1998. She had been to town to meet friends and go to McDonalds. Dozens of officers were assigned to the case. CCTV footage was scoured. Lilly's mother Sally and her boyfriend Geoff Mann pleaded for her safe return at a televised press conference. We visited their home on several occasions to take statements. Three days after she'd been reported missing, Lilly's body was found hidden in black bin liners in the attic at the family home. Mann was eventually convicted of strangling her. The prosecution revealed that he had secretly taken photos of Lilly over the previous 12 months and had clearly become obsessed with her. When he was convicted of her murder, the head of North Wales Police had made a public apology that Lilly's body hadn't been found sooner.

Walking into the bedroom, I grabbed a small chair and pulled it so that it was underneath the hatch.

'What are you doing?' Annie asked.

I pointed at the ceiling. 'We need to have a look up there.'

Then I stepped up onto the chair and tried to balance.

Even though I was 6ft 2', and the ceilings were very low, I still needed a few more inches to move the hatch and look inside.

'Be careful,' Annie warned me yet again.

'I'll be fine,' I reassured her, and then pointed. 'I've left my torch on the floor there. Can you pass it up to me, please?'

She nodded as she reached down, picked up the flashlight and handed it to me.

Pushing the hatch up, I slid it over and stood on my tiptoes so that I could stick my head up inside and look.

Clicking on the torch, I slowly moved the beam around the loft.

It was small and smelled musty.

A huge cobweb glowed in the beam of my torch. It was dotted with the corpses of about a dozen flies.

Some of the lagging close to me had been torn or scratched at by something. A mouse or rat at a guess.

As my torch beam scanned the whole loft area, it seemed as if it was completely empty.

No boxes, no bags, nothing that would suggest that anything untoward had been stashed inside.

I looked down at Annie and shook my head. 'Nothing. It's empty.'

I could see the relief on her face again as she gave an almost imperceptible nod. 'Good, that's good,' she said under her breath.

I stepped down from the chair and then put it back in the bedroom.

I went into the bathroom while Annie continued her search.

I opened the medicine cabinet and I peered inside. It was empty.

As I closed the mirrored door, I spotted something in

the reflection of the house next door. Someone was peering out of a window over at me from the adjacent caravan.

A man wearing glasses.

I quickly closed the cabinet door, turned to the window and gazed across at the neighbour's caravan.

The man had vanished.

I wondered if I'd imagined it.

Crouching down, I used my flashlight to look behind the waste pipe that led down from the sink.

Nothing.

Then I opened the cistern lid and looked inside the tank.

Nothing.

I glanced over at the bath. It had an old wooden panel down the side that had been painted white but was now a little stained.

Of course, the panel, I said to myself as I reached into my trouser pocket and retrieved my Swiss army knife.

Pulling out the small screwdriver, I knelt on the floor beside the bath. Jack came over to look at what I was doing. He nuzzled into me and licked my neck.

'Not now, mate,' I said as I patted his head and gestured for him to lie down on the floor.

I twisted the screws anti-clockwise and removed the panel.

Sitting inside was a black holdall.

I zipped the top open and peered inside.

The thick smell of weed hit me immediately.

Jesus, that's strong.

There were five sealed cellophane bags of marijuana – 'weed' – inside. I wasn't an expert, but it looked like a couple of pounds. At a rough calculation, I thought it probably had a street value of at least £10,000.

On the other side of the bag were around forty small plastic bags with white powder inside. I took one out to look at it. I'd worked as a police officer long enough to know that it was cocaine. Ten grams in each bag by the look of it. Probably £20,000 on the street.

'Annie,' I called, 'you need to come and look at this.'

Within seconds, she had come back down the caravan.

'What is it?' she asked, sounding alarmed.

I opened the bags to show her. 'I found these hidden behind the bath panel.'

'For God's sake,' she sighed. 'Callum.'

'Did you know he was dealing drugs?'

She shook her head. 'No. I had no idea.'

'Why did he leave the drugs here?' I wondered.

'He has access to the caravan for another two weeks,' Annie suggested. 'Maybe he thought this was a safe place to store them until he sold them?' Then she gave me a dark look. 'Do you think this has anything to do with what's happened to Meg?'

Getting up from the floor, I shrugged. 'It's possible, isn't it?'

Annie furrowed her brow. 'I guess we have to call DCI Humphries?'

I nodded in agreement but then thought for a moment.

'Where did Callum get £30,000 to buy these drugs?' I asked her.

She shrugged. 'I've no idea. There's no way he could get his hands on that kind of money.'

'And the deposit didn't clear until yesterday, so he didn't use that,' I concluded. I pulled a face. 'I've got a horrible feeling that Callum might have stolen these drugs from someone.'

'Really?'

'He didn't have the money to buy them,' I said. 'And I

can't see any dealer with half a brain trusting him to take the drugs on tick and then hand over the money when they're sold.'

Annie gave me a dark look. 'Do you think that's why Meg has gone missing?'

'I don't know,' I replied. 'Possibly.'

I reached into the bath panel and pulled out the black holdall. Then I took one of the bags of marijuana and put it back where I had found it under the bath. I took two wraps of cocaine and placed them on top of the marijuana.

'Frank, what are you doing?' Annie asked slowly.

I stood up with the holdall. 'I'm leaving these here so we can call the police, but we're taking the rest of the drugs with us.'

'Because you want to be Snowdonia's answer to Pablo Escobar?' she quipped darkly.

'No.' I gave a wry smile. 'If Meg is missing because Callum has stolen drugs from some nutcase dealer, we might need the drugs to barter with.'

'Jesus, Frank.'

I sighed. 'I know.'

Then I spotted something in my peripheral vision.

The man with glasses was looking out of the window from the next door caravan again. I definitely hadn't imagined it.

As I turned to look out, he moved out of sight.

What the hell is he playing at?

'We're being watched,' I said.

'Really? That's a bit creepy.'

I frowned at Annie. 'Do you know anything about the neighbours?' I asked as I gestured out of the window towards the caravan.

'No. I think Meg said there was some bloke who lived

there. An ex-pilot or something like that. She said that he kept himself to himself. Bit of an eccentric. Why?'

'I think it might be worth us going to have a quick word with him before we make that call to the police,' I suggested.

16

3 days 4 hours missing

I gave a gentle knock on the door of the caravan next to Megan's. It was newly painted in a fashionable olive green.

'My thinking is that if someone in this caravan is looking over there, maybe they saw something in the past few days?' I suggested.

Annie nodded. 'Yeah, you read my mind.'

A few seconds later, a man in his late 50s came to the door. He had a chiselled face, swept-back sandy hair and designer glasses. He wore a navy American college sweatshirt.

He gave us a quizzical look. I noticed that it looked like he'd had 'work' done to his face – Botox, fillers. There was something decidedly unnatural about his appearance.

'Hi,' Annie said in a calm voice. 'My sister Megan was living in the caravan next door.'

'Megan, yes,' he said guardedly. 'Is something wrong?'

The man deliberately moved his body in front of the gap between the door and the frame. He wasn't going to invite us in.

From his appearance and manner, I immediately had him down as a cock.

I rubbed my hands together to demonstrate how chilly it was. 'Mind if we come in for a second?' I asked in a friendly voice. It was an old police tactic. There was a big difference to what people would say or how they would act inside their own home, in comparison to having someone standing on the doorstep. In my years as a detective, the first thing was to get inside.

'Erm, I suppose so,' he said uncertainly as he reluctantly opened the door wide and gestured for us to come in.

'I'm Annie,' she explained, 'and this is my friend Frank.'

'Right. I'm Simon,' he said, but his tone was less than friendly.

The small hallway was fashionably decorated. A couple of framed black and white photographs of classic aeroplanes from the past. I clocked an envelope on the hall table. It was addressed to *Simon Bentley*. Now I knew his surname.

I stopped to look at the photos on the wall for a second.

'Bit of a passion of mine,' he explained, pointing to the photos. 'I was a pilot. Just passenger jets, but I've always loved planes.'

Why did he tell us all that? I wondered.

I nodded anyway. The house smelled of recently cooked food – garlic and possibly cheese.

Annie looked at him. 'The thing is, Simon, my sister seems to have gone missing.'

I watched for his reaction. He took a few seconds to process what she said, which was odd.

'Really?' He narrowed his eyes. Then he pointed to a

half-open door. 'Why don't you come and sit down for a minute?'

'Thanks,' I said as I allowed Annie to go into the living room first.

As with the hallway, the room was fashionably decorated and furnished. I spotted a record player on the far side with a couple of vinyl record covers – *Kind of Blue* by *Miles Davis* and *A Love Supreme* by *John Coltrane*. Classic jazz albums. I had them both at home, which meant that Simon dabbled in jazz rather than being a jazz bore.

Annie and I sat down on the comfortable coffee-coloured sofa.

'If I can explain,' Annie said sitting forward, lacing her fingers together and looking directly at Simon. 'I have regular contact with Megan. We speak three or four times a week. We text each other a couple of times a day. But two days ago, she stopped replying to my texts and phone calls.'

'Maybe she's not well,' Simon suggested immediately as he fidgeted on the dark leather armchair he was sitting on. 'Or she's gone on holiday.'

His eagerness to offer two instant explanations without listening to what we had to say seemed strange.

'No. She would have told me either of those things,' Annie explained assertively. 'Frank and I came round early yesterday morning to see if she or Callum, my nephew, were in. But we discovered that they moved out about two days ago.'

'What?' Simon's eyes widened. 'I didn't know they'd moved out.' The tone of his voice just wasn't convincing.

I glanced over at him. There was something 'off'. I couldn't put my finger on it, but my instinct was that he was uncomfortable as he shifted on the chair and scratched at his nose.

'You didn't know that they'd moved out?' I asked.

'No.' He blinked and then shook his head in surprise. 'I don't know how I didn't notice.'

He's definitely lying about something.

I raised an eyebrow. 'Do you mind if I ask how long you've lived here?'

'No. I moved in here about three years ago,' he explained as he sat forward, his body hunched and defensive. 'A failed second marriage.' Then he looked as if he'd caught himself giving too much detail and frowned. 'Are you a police officer?'

'Used to be,' I admitted.

He nodded at my disclosure, but it seemed to make him even more guarded.

'If you could think back to the last two days, was there anything strange or out of the ordinary that you noticed going on next door? Or did you see anyone coming or going apart from Megan or Callum?' Annie enquired.

He pulled an apologetic face. 'Sorry, no. Nothing that I remember.'

He was hiding something. It wasn't the actual words he'd said. It was his mannerisms, body language and facial expressions. He was jittery, but doing his best to hide it. I'd seen it a thousand times before.

'Did you know Megan and Callum very well?' I asked.

He shook his head instantly as if it was important for him to signal that he didn't. 'No. Not really.' Then he rubbed his nose. 'Just to say hello to. Nothing more than that.'

Annie moved a strand of hair and tucked it behind her ear. 'This might sound strange, but did you ever see my sister with a man? We're trying to find out if she was in a relationship of some kind.'

He sighed. 'I'm really sorry,' he said with a shrug. 'Like

I say, I didn't know her very well at all. Have you spoken to Denise on the other side?'

'I spoke to her yesterday. She'd been round to knock on my sister's door but there was no reply.'

'Right. I know that Denise and Megan were very friendly. I'd seen them chatting on a few occasions,' Simon stated as he stood up to signal that he wanted us to leave.

'Thank you,' Annie said as we got up from the sofa.

'I hope you find her,' he said as he ushered us towards the door and down the hallway. 'I'm sure there's a perfectly logical explanation.'

I frowned at Annie as we stepped out of the front door. He hastily closed it behind us.

Simon seemed very keen for us to leave.

17

3 days 5 hours missing

'I didn't even know that Meg wanted to move out,' Denise said, looking confused.

We'd been sitting in Denise's kitchen for about five minutes. It was small, and virtually identical in layout to Megan's caravan next door. There was the distinct smell of musky aftershave as if a man had been there just before we had arrived.

Denise had already told us how fond of Megan she was, but she'd had some concerns about Callum and his behaviour over the years.

She was in her late 50s, dyed blonde hair in a bob, small features and piercing green eyes.

'The thing is,' Annie said, pulling a face, 'I know for almost certain that my sister had no plans to move out. It's my birthday next week and we'd made plans to go out for the day. I said I'd pick her up and we'd drive up to the coast.'

Denise was baffled. 'That is strange,' she agreed.

'I'm very close to Megan,' Annie explained. 'We told

each other everything. If she was planning on leaving her caravan, she would have told me.'

Denise furrowed her brow. 'And I know that she would have told me too. Even if she was leaving, she would have come round to tell me and say goodbye. She wouldn't have left without a word.'

I shifted forward on my chair. 'And that's why we're concerned. It all seems completely out of character for her to just vanish without telling anyone.'

'God, do you think she was kidnapped or something?' Denise asked, looking frightened.

Annie blinked at Denise's suggestion.

Kidnapped. Neither of us had actually used that word yet, and her question seemed to hang in the air for a second or two. But with the discovery of the drugs, it was a possibility that we needed to look at.

'We just don't know,' Annie admitted, 'but she's not answering her phone to me.'

'Oh God, that's terrible,' Denise said under her breath. 'Have you reported it to the police?'

'Yes, but there's not a lot they can do until we can prove that she was in some kind of danger.'

'But she's missing,' Denise said, shaking her head.

'Is there anything in the past couple of weeks that seemed out of the ordinary?' Annie asked. 'Or did you see anyone at Meg's caravan who you didn't recognise?'

Denise didn't say anything for a moment as she trawled her memory. 'I did see her being picked up one night,' she said, gesturing outside. 'About three weeks ago.'

'Did you see who picked her up?' Annie asked.

'No.' She shook her head. 'It was quite a fancy car though because I remember wondering if it was a man. You know, picking her up. And it looked like he had money.'

'Can you remember anything else. Was it a 4x4?' Annie said.

Denise put her hand to her mouth in confusion.

'A big car. Like a Range Rover,' I said to clarify.

'Oh no. It was smaller than that, but long. 'You know, like a Jaguar or a BMW. It was a dark car. Black maybe.' Then she pulled a face. 'Sorry I can't remember any more than that.'

'That's fine,' Annie reassured her. 'Did you see who was driving it?'

'No, sorry. I just assumed because of the car that it was a man though.'

'And you haven't seen it since?'

'No. But I did hear a car pulling up outside a few times recently. I just didn't bother to go and look out. Tell a lie. I did look out about two weeks ago because it was late. Gone midnight. I saw that someone had dropped Meg home, and she was opening her front door.' Denise shook her head. 'God, I sound like a right old nosy busybody, don't I?'

Yeah, you do, I thought to myself.

'It's fine,' Annie said supportively. 'Anything you can tell us really helps.'

I looked over at her intently. 'And Meg never mentioned that she was seeing anyone, or that she'd met someone?'

'No. I was really pleased for her when I thought she had. It can't have been easy with all the stuff that Callum had put her through over the years.'

Annie gave her an understanding nod. 'No. It's been very difficult for her.'

'Did you ever hear or see Meg and Callum rowing?' I asked.

'Yes. Quite a lot. Especially if Callum had been drinking. He had quite a temper on him.'

'Did you ever hear them fighting?' Annie said.

'I'm not sure. I did see Meg with a bruise on her face a couple of months ago. I wondered if it had been Callum.'

'What about the last week or so?' I prompted her.

She scratched her nose and squinted as she thought. 'Yes. A few days ago there was a right old ding dong over there. It was the night that *Vera* was on the telly 'cos I had to turn the volume up to hear it over the shouting.'

'I think that's a Sunday night, isn't it?' I suggested.

'Sunday. Yes, that sounds about right,' she agreed. 'And then …' She tailed off.

'Go on,' Annie encouraged her.

She shrugged. 'It was just a bit weird.'

'Anything, however small, might help us find out what's happened to Megan,' I said firmly. It had amazed me over the years as a detective how the tiniest of details could open up an investigation.

'It was about 1am,' she said. 'I heard this weird sound coming from next door. It woke me up. I went to the window in my bedroom and looked outside. And I saw Callum … well, I assume it was Callum. He was sweeping the decking at the back of the caravan. There was a bucket, so I thought he might have been cleaning. I just thought that he'd been sick out there and was cleaning up after himself. I'd seen him being sick before when he was pissed up.'

Annie raised her eyebrow. 'And you're sure that it was Callum?'

'Actually no,' she conceded. 'Whoever it was, they were wearing a woolly hat and a hoodie pulled over the top. I couldn't see who it was.'

'But you thought it was a man?' I said.

'Oh yes. It was definitely a man. Then I saw him kneel down and start to scrub the wooden decking.'

That does sound weird.

I gave Annie a quizzical look. What the hell was that about?

18

3 days 5 hours missing

Ten minutes later, Annie and I were back at the rear of Meg's caravan. The air was bitterly cold and stung the tops of my ears. We both peered down at the wooden decking, which was covered in an array of gold, red and lemon-coloured autumnal leaves.

A deathly silence only broken by the wind that swept around the deserted caravan park. Then the loud malignant squawks of two gulls that swooped high above us.

Crouching down, I used my hand to sweep leaves off the wood.

We gazed at the dark, stained slatted wood of the decking, searching for something that might give us a clue as to why Callum had been cleaning up a few days earlier.

I rubbed my finger along the wood, then sniffed it.

'It's definitely been bleached,' I said, glancing up at Annie.

'What the hell was Callum doing washing down and scrubbing the decking with bleach at one in the morning? That doesn't sound normal.'

I gave Annie a dark look. 'It sounds suspicious. And that's if it was Callum.'

Annie's face fell.

I moved a few more leaves to inspect the far side of the decking.

Something metallic glinted in the sunlight.

What's that?

Whatever it was, it was located underneath the decking.

'What is it?' Annie asked as she came over.

'I'm not sure yet.' I grabbed my torch from my pocket. Holding it close to the small gap between the boards on the decking, I could see something silver on the original wood underneath. I couldn't make out what it was. I had no idea if it was important either.

Annie crouched down next to me. 'Anything?'

'I can't really see it. Could be a piece of metal or jewellery. Have you got a pencil or a biro?'

She reached into her coat pocket. 'Here you go.'

Holding the biro at one end, I pushed the nib carefully through the gap in the decking, seeing if I could loop up the object.

The first few times, nothing happened. I gave a frustrated sigh.

Then I managed to get the biro nib under it and then very slowly I pulled it up and out of the gap in the decking.

Annie immediately reached down and picked it up.

'What is it?' I asked as I crouched down beside her. Then I could see that she was holding up a silver earring.

She was overwhelmed. 'It's one of the earrings that I bought Meg last Christmas.'

We could both see that the curved bar that went through the ear was severely bent out of shape and had blood on it.

Silence.

Annie now had tears in her eyes. 'She loved those earrings. She wouldn't have just left it down there if she'd dropped it.'

As I looked down again, I noticed something else.

Although the tops of the decking had been scrubbed clean, I saw that there were tiny splashes of black on the sides of some of the slats. It was as if a dark liquid had dripped through them. It wasn't a huge leap to think that it might have been blood. It would explain Callum's clean-up job in the early hours.

I felt my stomach tighten. I wasn't going to raise my suspicions with Annie yet. Not until I was certain.

She held up the earring. 'What the hell happened here, Frank?'

'I'm not sure yet. I need to get these boards up to see if there's anything else down there.'

Annie shrugged. 'Frankly, I don't care what you do if it helps us find Meg.'

I nodded as I reached for the screwdriver that was nestled in my toolbelt.

Wedging it in between the boards, I pushed down. 'Bugger.' I could see that it wasn't going to give. I needed to get something much bigger.

Then I remembered seeing a spade in the storage shed earlier.

'Hang on a second,' I said. 'I just need to go and get something to shift these.'

I walked down the side of the caravan and over to the storage shed. Unlocking the padlock, I went inside. The putrid smell of the badger's corpse wasn't any better second time round.

I spotted a large steel spade with a green handle, grabbed it, and headed back.

'Hopefully this will do the trick,' I said under my breath as I wedged the metal blade of the spade in between the wooden planks and then pushed down on the shaft.

It didn't work, although I could hear the wood creak under the strain.

I tried it again.

This time I stamped down on the shaft, using my bodyweight.

There was a loud crack of wood as the decking plank came free.

Reaching down, I pulled the plank up and put it down to one side. I then pulled up another, twisting it free.

Underneath the decking was the original wood which, like the rest of the caravan, had been painted white.

Where I had removed the decking, there were dark splashes on the white paintwork.

Blood?

I reached down and rubbed my finger hard against one of the splashes.

Looking at the tip of my forefinger, I saw my skin was now stained dark red.

Definitely blood. And a substantial amount.

Annie saw it too.

She dissolved into tears.

'I'm so sorry, Annie,' I whispered as I put a comforting arm around her.

19

3 days 5 hours missing

I gazed across the scene laid out in front of me. The area outside Megan's caravan was now ablaze with strobing blue lights. A major incident crime scene. The air filled with the crackle of police radios. Three marked patrol cars had pulled across the entrance to the caravan park to stop all traffic. Uniformed officers in high vis luminous yellow jackets had cordoned off the area with blue evidence tape, and several neighbours were huddled together outside their caravans trying to find out what had happened. Near to where Annie and I were standing was the white scene of crime forensics van. Its back doors were open, and a scene of crime officer – SOCO – in full nitrile forensic suit, hat and mask, was carefully putting evidence away inside. I could see that they had taken samples of wood from the decking and the wooden base of the caravan.

Dewi appeared from the side gate and looked over at Annie and I.

'Annie,' he said in a sombre tone as he approached. 'The forensic team want you and Frank to explain exactly what you did and where you went in the caravan and round the back tonight. They're going to need to photo-graph your shoes to eliminate any prints they find. And we're going to need fingerprints and DNA off both of you too.'

I narrowed my eyes at Dewi. I definitely got the feeling he was about to say something disparaging. I assumed he wasn't best pleased that I'd found evidence that he and his officers had missed.

'Yes, of course,' Annie said very quietly. She had been in a state of shock since we found the earring and then the blood.

Dewi then fixed me with an icy stare. 'If I'm honest, Frank, I don't know what the bloody hell you were doing here,' he said in a withering tone. 'I know being retired must be tedious for you after being a big shot …'

'Hold on a second,' Annie snapped, interrupting Dewi. 'If Frank hadn't had the foresight to go and talk to the neighbours here, and then take a proper look at that deck-ing, you'd still be treating my sister's disappearance as an unimportant missing persons case. He was doing your job for you.'

There was an awkward silence. Dewi bristled.

I stopped myself from smiling at Annie giving him a dressing down. However tempting, it would have been inflammatory.

'As I said,' he continued, trying his upmost to be polite as he pointed to the caravan. 'If you can go and show the forensic team your movements, I'd be very grateful.'

A female detective wearing a full white forensic suit approached – 30s, brunette, attractive.

'Boss, canine unit is on its way,' she explained. 'POLSA search of the caravan park is underway. No CCTV or security cameras anywhere up here though.'

'Shame,' Dewi said. 'ANPR on the approach roads?'

The detective pulled a face. 'Won't get those until the morning, boss. And there aren't many around here I'm afraid.'

'No, I don't suppose there are.' Dewi glanced at Annie. 'This is DS Kelly Thomas. She'll be the deputy SIO on this investigation. I'll leave you in her capable hands.'

Dewi walked away and back towards the caravan.

'Hi Annie,' Kelly said. 'I'm really sorry, but I'm going to have to ask you a few questions that no doubt you've been asked already.'

'That's fine,' Annie replied in a virtual whisper. 'I'll do anything to get my sister back.'

'Do you have anything of Megan's that we could use to get her DNA? Hairbrush, toothbrush?'

'Yes. I have the spare toothbrush she uses when she stays over.'

'Good. I'll send an officer over to get that as soon as you're back home. And I'd like you to do a press conference first thing in the morning.'

'Really?' Annie asked with a frown.

'Having looked at what you found today,' Kelly said, 'we are now working on the assumption that your sister has been taken by force and is being held against her will somewhere. We need the search for her to be as visible as possible. As you probably know, time is crucial in an investigation like this. If we can engage the media and the general public, then the greater the chances of finding Megan quickly.'

20

3 days 9 hours missing

As the light faded over Eryri, I sat astride Duke in the paddock with Sam sitting on the saddle in front of me. It had been an hour since I'd dropped Annie back home. There was little else we could do for the rest of the day. We would start again in the morning after the press conference. After the stress of the day, it was good to be out in the cold mountain air and try to clear my head.

'You see you've got to bounce with the horse,' I explained to Sam as we trotted in a wide circle around the paddock. 'Or it gets very sore.'

'Like this?' he asked, trying to demonstrate.

'Yeah, nearly got it,' I said encouragingly as I took his hands. 'Here, take the reins with me.'

He reached uncertainly and then took the reins in his hands.

'There you go. You've got it … It'll be different when you have your own pony or horse. Then you can use the stirrups to ride properly.'

He turned to me and frowned. 'But I haven't got a pony or a horse, Taid.'

I raised an eyebrow. 'Would you like one?'

'Erm, yeah!!' he exclaimed as though this was a silly question.

'Then I think I can sort that out for you,' I said with a smile. 'Start you off with a pony to get you going.'

'Mum!' Sam shouted to Caitlin who was watching us from behind the wooden fence of the paddock. 'Taid is going to get me a pony!'

Caitlin laughed. 'Is he now?'

I shrugged. 'He's got to learn to ride … You had a pony.'

'Yeah.' Caitlin then gave me a meaningful glance. 'Well, I shared one with James.'

There was a little moment of understanding between us. I knew how much she missed her younger brother but we hadn't spoken about it for over a year.

Caitlin glanced at Sam. 'It's hard work having a pony, Sam. Mucking out, grooming, cleaning the tackle.'

He grinned. 'I don't mind.'

'Right, mate,' I said as I pulled on Duke's reins and brought him to a stop. 'Lesson's over for the day.'

Throwing my leg back, I jumped down and then lifted Sam down.

'There you go,' I said as I plonked him down on the ground.

'Thank you, Taid.'

'You're welcome.' I put a comforting hand on his shoulder. 'I'm glad that you and your mum are here.'

I watched as he ran over to Caitlin.

For a moment, I was overwhelmed by emotion. He looked so small, so vulnerable. I couldn't bear to think of all the chaos and aggression that he'd already had to witness in his life so far. I consoled myself with the fact that now he and Caitlin were under my roof, I could protect them. All I wanted was for them both to have happy and peaceful lives. I'd do anything to make sure that happened from now on.

And then I remembered when James had been Sam's age. He loved riding and being around horses. Rachel and I were convinced that being outside, riding, and looking after the horses would help alleviate his worsening mental health.

Taking a breath to stop myself from getting over-whelmed by grief, I led Duke over to where Caitlin and Sam were standing.

I handed Sam the reins. 'There you go. Take Duke up to the stables for me, will you? I'll be up there in a minute. I'll show you how to take off his bridle.'

Sam beamed with pride at being given such respon-sibility.

Caitlin and I walked slowly behind as he led Duke away from the paddock.

'You're spoiling him,' she said.

'That's my job, isn't it?' I let out an audible sigh. 'What a day.'

'Everything okay? You seemed a bit stressed earlier?' Caitlin asked.

I spent the next few minutes filling her in on all that had happened that day, and the police investigation into Megan's disappearance.

'Oh God, that's terrible,' Caitlin exclaimed, blinking as she took in what I'd told her. 'Poor Annie. Isn't her nephew a bit of a wrong 'un?'

'Callum. Yes, you could say that.'

'Where's he at the moment?'

'In a coma. He had an accident.'

'Christ.' Caitlin's eyes widened. 'Do you think he's involved in what's happened to Megan?'

'Possibly,' I replied. 'Probably. But he can't tell us anything at the moment.'

Sam had now disappeared into the stable with Duke.

Caitlin pointed towards the annexe. 'Do you want to come in for a beer or anything, Dad?'

I pointed over towards the farmhouse. 'Once I've sorted out Duke, I'd better go and check on your mother. Did she go to bed okay?'

'Yeah, she seemed fine this evening. She did ask where you were about ten times so I kept having to remind her where you'd gone.'

I gave Caitlin a grateful smile.

Sam appeared from the stable wearing a black riding hat. 'Look what I found,' he said with a cheery grin and pointed to his head.

'Take that off right now!' I thundered as I clicked my fingers angrily at him. It had been James' riding hat and no one had worn it since he'd died.

Sam's eyes widened. He was startled.

'Dad, for God's sake!' Caitlin protested.

Bollocks. I hadn't meant to react like that.

'Sorry,' I said quickly as Sam pulled off the hat. 'Sorry, Sam. It's fine. We'll get you your own hat, okay?'

He nodded, but he still looked upset at my outburst.

I went over to him, putting my hand on his head. 'I'm sorry I snapped, mate.'

He lowered his head and wandered back into the stables.

I looked at Caitlin apologetically.

'Sorry. Bloody hell,' I sighed as I rubbed the stubble on my chin. 'It still gets to me.'

'I don't think it ever goes away,' Caitlin said gently.

'No … Anything from TJ?' I asked, keen to change the subject.

'A string of abusive texts,' she said, narrowing her eyes. 'And threats.'

I felt my stomach tense with anger.

'Make sure you double lock all the doors tonight,' I said with a serious expression.

'It's all right, Dad,' she said reassuringly. 'He won't come up here.'

'Yeah, well just to be on the safe side, eh?'

'You worry too much, Dad.'

'You're both precious to me.'

Sam came out of the stable. He had clearly put James' riding hat back where he'd found it.

I put my hand on his shoulder. 'Right mate, let me show you how to take Duke's bridle off.'

21

3 days 16 hours missing

Annie sat in the living room gazing at the television. It was agony not knowing what had happened to Meg. It came in waves of excruciating fear and anxiety. Uniformed police officers had arrived an hour ago to take Meg's toothbrush to collect her DNA. It had felt utterly surreal.

Where was she? What Annie would give just to know that she was safe. She didn't care if her sister had run off somewhere without telling her. It didn't matter. All that mattered was that Meg was okay. Annie ached for that knowledge. She'd do anything for her sister.

Please God, let her be safe and alive, she thought, as the emotions got too much for her and her eyes filled with tears.

She wiped the tears away and reached for her phone. Maybe someone had tried to get in touch and she hadn't heard it.

A *Facebook Memory* popped up on her timeline. A lovely photo from around twenty years ago. It showed Callum, aged about eight or nine. He was dressed just in his shorts and doing a jokey 'muscle man' pose. She remembered the beautiful summer afternoon when the photograph had been taken in hers and Stephen's garden. Callum had been over to stay for the weekend, as he did on a regular basis in the summer holidays, especially if Megan was working shifts at the hospital. Stephen and Annie couldn't have children. She suffered from polycystic ovary syndrome (PCOS). She and Stephen had talked about adopting for a while, but Stephen had grown increasingly against the idea. Maybe that's why she had begun to resent him.

Annie knew that she had spoiled Callum over the years. She didn't have a child of her own so it was natural. Even at that age, it was clear that he had a reckless streak. Stephen used to joke that Callum had 'ants in his pants'. Annie was convinced that he had ADHD. Not only could he not sit down or concentrate, he also had an impulsive nature that got him into trouble. He would act first and think later. Annie had told Meg to get him tested for ADHD but she said that he would grow out of it.

As a teenager, he continued to come and stay, especially as Megan had a series of relationships with some very questionable men. At that time, Callum saw very little of his father, Bryn. But the signs of addiction had already started. Annie had had to pick up Callum several times from parties where he had drunk too much and passed out in his own vomit. Then she caught him smoking weed in their house when he was only fourteen. Meg maintained that that's what teenage boys did, but Annie knew there was a problem. And she also knew that if he did have undiagnosed ADHD, there was a higher likelihood of him becoming an addict.

The front door bell rang. Annie glanced at her phone. It was 10.45pm.

Who the hell is that? It's late.

Then she had a dark thought.

The police.

Her stomach lurched.

Getting up from the sofa, she padded down the hallway towards the front door. Her breathing was fast and shallow. Her mind racing.

She opened the door and saw that DS Kelly Thomas was standing on the doorstep. It had started to rain.

For a split second, Annie held her breath.

'Have you found her?' she asked.

'I'm sorry. No,' Kelly said gently as she shook her head, 'but I do need to ask you a couple of questions. Can I come in?'

'Of course. Sorry,' Annie sighed. She couldn't decide if she was disappointed that the police hadn't found her sister, or relieved that Kelly hadn't come to give her terrible news. Both probably.

Kelly came inside. Her black raincoat and hair were wet from the rain.

Annie closed the front door and gave her a quizzical look.

'Have you spoken to the guy Simon in the caravan next door to Meg's?' Annie asked.

'We've taken statements from everyone who lives on the site.'

'I think you should take a proper look at him,' Annie insisted. 'He was a real oddball. And he was definitely hiding something when Frank and I spoke to him.'

'Okay. I'll make a note of that and go and speak to him myself.'

'Thank you. Sorry, you said you wanted to ask a couple of questions.'

'Our digital forensics team have managed to locate a historic signal from Megan's mobile phone,' Kelly explained. 'It means we can track where it's been.'

'That's good, isn't it?' Annie's spirits lifted with some renewed hope.

'Yes. Her phone was active on Sunday night in the Dolgellau area. And then at 1.30am, it travelled across country to Barmouth where it stopped for an hour. Then at 2.30am, the phone travelled north. Then it stops in an area inland from Benar Beach.'

'Okay,' Annie said optimistically. *This is a significant lead, isn't it?* 'Well, where is it now?'

If they could locate the phone, then they might find Meg.

Kelly pulled a face. 'That's the problem. The phone stopped registering at 6am on Monday morning, which is when we assume the battery ran out.'

Annie's heart sank. 'But you know where the phone was before the battery ran out?'

'Not really. The phone signal only registered on the Llanbedr mast at 3.30am. I need to know if you can think of any reason why your sister would drive out to Barmouth in the early hours of Monday morning or then drive north to the area around Tal-y-bont.'

'She wouldn't,' Annie said with certainty.

'Friends, relatives?'

'Sorry, no. She doesn't know anyone there that's of any significance.' Annie shook her head. 'Can't you triangulate the final signal from her phone to pinpoint where it is?' Annie had spent enough time in criminal trials to understand some digital forensics.

'There's only one mast down there. It's in the middle of nowhere,' Kelly replied. 'We do have a defined search area, but unfortunately it's about three and a half miles. It takes in Cors y Gedol neolithic site.'

That's strange. Annie didn't like the sound of that. She knew the Cors y Gedol site. It was a Bronze Age burial ground and ceremonial tomb. She felt a shiver down her spine.

'Cors y Gedol?' Annie said quietly.

Kelly knew what Annie was getting at. 'I've got officers and a canine unit over there right now.'

Silence.

'Maybe Meg had a car accident, she's been injured and she's just lying there,' Annie suggested.

Kelly nodded unconvincingly. 'That is possible, but I think that the blood we found at the caravan might suggest that she's been taken against her will.'

Annie narrowed her eyes angrily. 'You don't even know that the blood is hers. What if she's lying in her car in a ditch somewhere?'

'We're looking at every possibility.' Kelly gave her an empathetic nod.

'I'm going to print off some leaflets with Megan's photo and details on it,' Annie said, thinking aloud.

'That's a good idea,' Kelly agreed. 'And when the weather clears, we'll be sending up a helicopter with a thermal imaging camera. If your sister is in that area, we'll find her.'

'Do you think my nephew is involved?'

'I've just come from the hospital, but as you know, Callum has memory loss from his accident. He wasn't able to shed any light on where your sister might be or what happened on Sunday night.'

Annie closed her eyes. It was all getting too much for her.

'I know that this is incredibly difficult for you,' Kelly said gently. 'At the moment, we're not giving up hope that your sister is still alive. And that we'll find her.'

22

3 days 20 hours missing

I'd been drifting in and out of sleep for a while. Annie had sent me a text just before midnight to update me on the news of Megan's mobile phone and that her signal had been traced to an area around Tal-y-bont. We had agreed that after the press conference we would head over there to help in any search of the area. And we'd used social media to see if we could drum up any volunteers to help. It was incredibly frustrating that we had no idea to what extent Callum was involved. After finding the drugs, the blood, and talking to the neighbour Denise, my instinct was that Callum was almost certainly responsible for whatever had happened to Megan. It was too coincidental for him not to be. And the old police adage was *'there's no such thing as a strange coincidence'*.

As I turned over in bed, I felt Rachel's hand stretch out and take mine. Opening my eyes, I saw that she was asleep. I wrapped my fingers around her hand. She felt cold, so I used my other hand to pull the duvet up around where her neck met her ear. Then I reached over to make sure that she was tucked in properly. I used the warmth of my hand to thaw out Rachel's hand and closed my eyes again.

My thoughts turned to Caitlin, fast asleep over in the annexe. I remembered the day that she'd been born. 29th September 1984. It was a particularly chilly autumnal day in London. I remembered pacing around the café on the ground floor of St Thomas' Hospital in central London. The song *Careless Whisper* by *George Michael* seemed to be playing in the café on a continual loop. Rachel had been in labour for over twenty hours, and in those days fathers weren't allowed to be present at the births of their children. It just didn't happen. Rachel had told me on several occasions to go home, and that the maternity ward would call me when the baby arrived. But I didn't want to leave. Instead, I'd taken myself off towards the Embankment where there was a little garden overlooking the Thames.

There was a beautiful stainless steel modern sculpture and fountain in the garden. The plaque said that it was by the Russian Constructivist sculptor Naum Gabo and had been there since 1975. I'd never heard of the sculptor. The sound of the water and the way that the light reflected off the steel made the garden seem very peaceful.

I'd found myself reflecting on the impending birth of a child and all that went with it. I had just turned thirty so in terms of friends, colleagues and relatives, it had been suggested that it was time for me and Rachel to start a family. I'd recently moved to the anti-terrorist unit of Scotland Yard. In fact, Canon Row nick was only a five-minute walk across Westminster Bridge from where I'd sat that day.

As far as I could see, Britain was in a terrible state and I wondered what kind of world Rachel and I were bringing a child into. Unemployment had hit record levels not seen since the Great Depression of the 1930s. The miners' strike had seen pitched battles between police and striking miners in places such as Orgreave. I was completely over-whelmed in that moment by the thought of our innocent, vulnerable child.

Having smoked a couple of B&H cigarettes, I had then wandered back to the hospital, headed up to the maternity ward to find out that I was now the father of a beautiful baby daughter who had weighed in at a very healthy seven pounds and five ounces.

I wasn't sure how long I'd drifted off to sleep for. It felt like a couple of minutes. The first indication that there was something wrong was Jack stirring at the edge of the bed. As I blinked open my eyes, I saw him jump off the bed, trot over to the large bay window, jump up and look out. Then he growled.

Something was up.

As my senses kicked in, I could hear a noise.

A low droning sound.

At first, I thought it was a tractor.

But as my hearing adjusted, I recognised it as the deep rumble of a car engine.

I immediately sat up in bed.

Then I heard angry shouting and banging outside. It was a man's voice.

It was coming from the annexe.

I quickly swung my legs out of the bed and down onto the carpet.

Hurrying to the window, I moved the heavy curtains out of the way and peered over to my left where the annexe was located.

I could see an Astra, headlights on full beam, engine running with the driver's door open.

Over at the front door, I could see TJ in a baseball cap.

What the fuck?

He pounded his fist angrily against the door and shouted.

Then I saw something glint in his other hand.

A knife.

Shit!

With a mixture of anxiety and anger, I pulled a dressing gown on and ran across the room, down the landing, and then the stairs. Jack was at my side.

He gave another growl as he sensed my panic.

Taking my phone, I dialled 999 and put the phone on speaker.

Heading over to the gun cabinet, I quickly unlocked it, grabbed the double-barrelled shotgun and a packet of shells.

'What service please?' asked the emergency call handler.

'Police,' I said immediately.

A moment later, a man's voice came on the phone. 'Hello. Police, what's your emergency?'

'I have a man with a knife at my property making threats. Address is *Yr hen dy Fferm*. It's a farmhouse in Llanelltyd, Snowdonia. Take the turning off the A470 towards Cymer Abbey. My name is Frank Marshal. I have to go now.'

I ended the call, hoping there would be a patrol car on its way very soon.

I then grabbed a thick lead and clipped it to Jack's collar as I threw open the front door.

Wrapping the lead around my left forearm, I opened the shotgun, put two cases in and clicked it shut.

I ran outside and headed towards the annexe.

Jack started to bark loudly.

'Don't open the door, Caitlin!' I bellowed. 'Don't open the door!'

TJ groaned sarcastically, his attention drawn by my shouting. 'Oh, here we go. For fuck's sake. Mr Billy big bollocks himself.' His eyes were glazed either from drugs or drink, or both.

I tied Jack to a fence pole. He was snapping and snarling so I was hoping that the sight of him and my shotgun was going to convince TJ to stand down.

Nestling the gun into the nook of my shoulder, I aimed it directly at him.

'Drop the knife and step away from that front door right now!' I snapped loudly.

'Why? What are you going to do? Shoot me?' TJ scoffed.

'Dad?' Caitlin called out from inside.

'Whatever you do, don't open the door. He's got a knife,' I thundered loudly.

'What?' she exclaimed.

'I'm not leaving until I see Sam,' TJ sneered.

I took a step forward and fixed him with an icy stare. If he tried to enter the annexe then I was more than prepared to shoot him.

'Step away from the front door and drop the knife TJ,' I said calmly, 'or I will shoot you.'

He laughed and shook his head arrogantly. 'No you won't, old man.'

I spun, aimed the gun at his car, pulled the trigger and the air split as the shotgun fired.

CRACK!

The headlight on TJ's Astra exploded in a shower of glass.

'Jesus! What the …' he exclaimed as I turned back to him, gun still raised.

Jack's barking was getting louder.

'Don't make me do it,' I said through gritted teeth as I

moved forward with the gun aimed at his chest. 'My daughter and grandson are in there. You've travelled all the way from London to confront them. You're either high, drunk, or both. And you're carrying a knife. If I shoot you while trying to enter the premises, I'll be able to show reasonable force was necessary … and you'll be dead.'

He took a few seconds to process what I'd said. Then he shook his head.

'I don't care,' he shrugged, looking at me. He had a wild, desperate look in his eyes. 'Just shoot me, because I really don't care anymore.'

I was now about ten yards away from him. His breathing was shallow and quick. He was broken.

Then he looked away for a moment. It was a tell-tale sign that someone was going to attack. I'd seen it hundreds of times before. There was a human instinct to try and lull the other person into lowering their guard.

Then TJ's arms and shoulders tensed.

Here we go, I thought, as I prepared myself for his attack.

He screamed as he ran towards me with the knife. 'Fuck you!'

Taking a step backwards, I managed to avoid his wild slashing.

The knife struck the barrel of the shotgun with a metallic clang.

TJ was now crouched, gripping the knife and glaring at me.

'I'm going to fucking kill you,' he sneered.

My heart was now thudding in my chest and adrenaline was coursing through my veins.

'Don't be stupid, TJ,' I said, trying to pacify him. 'You're the one who's going to get yourself killed.'

'Good,' he snarled.

'Dad?' Caitlin called. She was now looking out of the open living room window.

'Just stay there,' I called back.

TJ attacked again, slashing the knife backwards and forwards.

Moving towards him, I kicked out and hit his knee, hoping that this would put him down on the ground.

He stumbled.

With a quick whip, I smashed the butt of the shotgun against his jaw and he crumpled down to the ground.

In the distance I could hear a police siren.

Going over to where TJ was lying groaning on the ground, I could see that he was completely dazed. He wasn't going to be getting back up any time soon. I resisted the urge to give him an almighty kick just for good measure. I didn't want the police to accuse me of using excessive force.

I picked the knife up from where it had fallen and placed it on top of the fence post. I rested the gun against the post too and then marched over to my pick-up.

I needed to get all this done before the police arrived.

Inside the cab was a toolbox.

I opened it and grabbed a black plastic tie.

Then I circled around to the back, pulled back the tarpaulin and took the bag that Annie and I had stashed the drugs from the house in.

Reaching inside, I took a handful of cocaine wraps.

I then moved quickly over to TJ's Astra. I turned off the engine.

With a quick glance around, I placed the cocaine wraps on the floor behind the driver's seat. I had no reservations at setting TJ up. He'd come armed, and threatened my daughter and grandson.

Fuck him. I hope they lock him up for a very long time.

The police siren was getting louder.

I went over to where TJ was still reeling on the ground. His face was screwed up as he tried to open his eyes. The blow from the gun had knocked him for six.

I decided to give him a kick for good measure anyway.

'Hey, what are you doing?' he groaned.

'Shut up,' I growled.

Grabbing his shoulder, I turned him onto his front. Then I pulled his arms back, wrapped the plastic tie around his wrists and secured it until the plastic dug into his skin.

'Ah, that hurts,' he said.

'Good.'

The front door to the annexe was now open and Caitlin was standing looking out. She was wearing a big, fluffy, grey dressing gown which seemed incongruous after all that had just happened.

Sam was in his pyjamas behind her and peering out.

She sighed and shook her head. 'Jesus, Dad.'

'It's all right,' I reassured her as I walked over and gave her a hug. She was shaking. Then I put my hand on Sam's shoulder. 'It's all right mate. Your dad's just had too much to drink, that's all.'

He nodded but was clearly bewildered.

I could hear the sound of tyres and a car engine.

'I'm glad you didn't shoot him,' Caitlin said under her breath.

'Me too,' I replied as I stepped back and looked at her with a wry smile. 'It would have made a hell of a mess on your porch.'

She pulled a face and gave me a playful punch. 'Bloody hell. It's not the time for jokes.'

Before we could continue, the whole area was lit up by the blue lights of a patrol car which had *Heddlu Police* printed in black lettering on the bonnet. The rest of the car was white with fluorescent green and blue colouring.

As the two police officers got out of the car, I walked over to greet them.

The older officer – 40s, dark beard – looked at me hesitantly. 'Frank Marshal?'

'Yes.' I gestured to TJ who was starting to regain full consciousness. 'That's my daughter's partner. She's left him to come and live here with my grandson. He arrived from London about half an hour ago. I think he's drunk or taken drugs. He had a knife and was trying to get into that annexe where my daughter and grandson are staying.'

The younger officer went over to TJ's car. 'Is this his car, sir?'

'Yes,' I replied, hoping that he would give it the once-over.

'What's his name?' the older officer asked, taking out a notebook.

'Thomas Gilmore. Tom,' I explained. 'Everyone calls him TJ, which is short for Tom Junior.'

'Looks like you've done a thorough job of restraining him.'

'Yeah, I used to be on the job,' I replied.

He gave me a knowing look. 'I know. You're Frank Marshal. Most of us know about you.'

I suppose I was flattered by this but it wasn't important to me.

'Did he come at you with the knife?'

'Yes. He was trying to kill me,' I said with a serious expression. 'If I hadn't hit him with the butt of that shotgun, I think he would have succeeded.'

'Sounds like a charge of attempted murder for starters,' he said as he scribbled in his notebook.

'Sarge!' the younger officer called over.

'Everything all right?' he asked.

The younger officer held up the plastic bag with the cocaine wraps inside. 'I found this inside the car.'

TJ was now conscious and looking over from where he was lying on the ground.

'That's not mine,' he shouted. 'I've never seen that before in my life.'

'What is it?' I asked.

'Looks like wraps of drugs. Could be cocaine by the looks of it,' the younger officer said. 'There's five here, so it's not personal use.'

The older officer looked directly at me. 'Sounds like Thomas Gilmore is going to be spending a long time at His Majesty's pleasure.'

Relief swept through me at his comment. 'I really hope so,' I said.

23

4 days 1 hour missing

'Do you think Callum could be faking his memory loss?' I asked as Annie and I walked along the ground floor of St Asaph Police Station where the early morning press conference was going to take place. Annie had made a phone call to the hospital an hour earlier and there had been no change.

I looked over at Annie. My question had annoyed her.

'No, I don't think he could be faking it,' she snapped at me as we saw Dewi, Kelly and other officers outside the North Wales Police media room. 'Do *you* think he was faking it then?'

'I'm not sure.' I shrugged. 'My instinct when he couldn't remember you was that he was telling the truth. He seemed upset ...'

'But?'

'But over the years I've encountered people who have been incredibly convincing at faking amnesia. Especially when they have committed a crime. I just wanted to flag it up, that's all.'

'Right. Well I might be being naïve, but I think he's telling the truth.'

'Fair enough.' I wasn't going to pursue that theory for a while.

Dewi approached.

'Any news on the search?' Annie asked anxiously.

'I'm afraid not,' he admitted as he thrust his hands into his pockets, 'but we will let you know as soon as we find anything. I'd like you to sit between myself and DS Thomas when we get in there.' Then he gave a wave to a woman in her 40s with an abundance of curly red hair. 'Kerry?' he said.

She came over.

'Annie, this is Kerry Mahoney, Chief Corporate Communications Officer for North Wales Police. She'll run the press conference and explain the running order to you,' Dewi said. 'I'll leave you in her capable hands.'

'If you'd like to come with me,' Kerry said gently as she guided Annie into the media room.

'I hear there was a ruckus up at your place last night,' Dewi said under his breath.

'That's right,' I replied cautiously. Dewi said everything with a tone that suggested he had a hidden agenda.

'We've got your daughter's partner in a custody cell over in Dolgellau. He blew over a hundred and ninety when uniform got him back to the nick.'

'I'm surprised he could drive at all,' I said.

'So am I,' Dewi agreed. 'He's being taken up to Mold Magistrates this morning. But with the drink driving, the knife, the assault, a possible attempted murder charge and possession of cocaine with intent to supply, CPS tell me there's no way he's getting bail.'

Why is he telling me all this? I wondered.

'He'll be over at HMP Rhoswen then,' I said.

'That would be my guess,' Dewi said in a tone that bordered on friendly. 'I just wanted to let you and your daughter know that he's not going to be bothering you any time soon.'

'Thank you,' I said suspiciously. I had no idea why Dewi was being helpful or even civil. It made me feel uneasy.

After a few seconds, I showed my visitor's badge, went inside and sat at the back of the media room. My phone buzzed.

BBC Wales @ BBC Wales Breaking News

Missing woman in North Wales. Sources claim that forensic officers have discovered a significant amount of blood at the Vale Caravan Park where Megan Richards lived.

Megan's disappearance was now a lead news story. It had to help in a case like this. Having her image all over the media might jog someone's memory.

Annie looked incredibly uncomfortable sitting up on the raised platform next to the police officers. There were microphones and digital recorders on the table in front of them, along with a jug of water and glasses.

Dewi pulled his chair in and then peered out at the room. 'Good afternoon. I'm Detective Chief Inspector Dewi Humphries and I am the senior investigating officer for the investigation into the disappearance of Megan Richards. Beside me is Megan's sister, Annie, Detective Sergeant Kelly Thomas, and Kerry Mahoney, our chief corporate communications officer. This press conference is to update you on the case and appeal to the public for any information regarding Megan's disappearance from the Vale Caravan Park on the outskirts of Dolgellau. We believe this took place between 10pm on Sunday night and 1.30am on Monday morning. Megan's family are understandably very worried. We are looking for any information that can help us bring her back home safely. The caravan park and the surrounding area where she went missing is very quiet, so if you saw anything out of the ordinary, however insignificant you think it might be, please contact us so we can come and talk to you. Megan's sister, Annie, would now like to say a few words.'

The media room started to light up as cameras began to click noisily. Annie prepared to speak, but the colour had drained from her face. She moved the microphone towards her.

'Our family just wants to know that Megan is safe and for us to get her home. She's been missing now for over four days.' Annie cleared her throat. 'It's completely out of character for her not to be in contact for that amount of time. Someone out there must have seen Megan and know where she is. We just want them to come forward and contact the police. Thank you.'

The intensity of the photography rose.

'We do have time for a few questions,' Kerry said.

A sea of arms rose amongst the journalists.

'Can you confirm that a significant amount of blood was found at the caravan park yesterday?' a reporter asked Dewi from the front row.

'All I am prepared to say is that a thorough forensic examination is taking place at the Vale Caravan Park,' he said with a stony face. 'If there is anything significant, then we will let you know.'

'If blood was found, are you now treating Megan's disappearance as a possible murder?' asked another reporter.

For fuck's sake! I thought angrily. *Bloody reporters.*

'I can only reiterate what I've already told you. As far as we are concerned, Megan is missing and we are doing everything in our power to find her and bring her home safely.' Dewi was irritated.

A television reporter shouted from the back of the room. 'From the forensic investigation so far, do you think that Megan is still alive?'

'Right, thank you, everyone,' Kerry said, closing the press conference down. 'We're out of time, I'm afraid. No more questions.'

I locked eyes with Annie across the room. The questions about Megan's possible murder had understandably upset her.

24

4 days 3 hours missing

The torrential rain had stopped as I stared intently into the darkness of the forest. The search of Coed y Brenin had been going for over two hours now, but so far it had been futile. There were over a hundred volunteers. Locals who had seen the story on the news, as well as Megan's old work colleagues.

When Annie and I had arrived at the forest car park, there were already a legion of photographers and other members of the national press. Vans with satellite dishes, journalists talking to cameras, and a whole battalion of telephoto zoom lenses all trained on the search. Megan's disappearance was suddenly big news.

We continued to move slowly through the trees. There was the odd bark of one of the dogs from the canine unit but otherwise it was quiet. Once in a while there was the brush of a breeze through the leaves.

Annie slipped and lost her footing on the muddy bank that led up to the forest's edge. 'Bugger.'

'You okay?' I asked, as I reached out a helping hand.

She nodded but was lost in her thoughts.

The forest was dark and shadowy. Above us was a thick canopy created by the tightly knit rows of Welsh oak, pines and birch. The trunks reached nearly a hundred feet above our heads. There was a dark stillness as we walked. The air around us smelled of dampness and the decay of fallen leaves. But the rain had also made it fresh and light.

The stillness was broken by a thundering sound above us. I squinted, and through the trees above saw a black and yellow EC145 police helicopter. Even at that height, the branches of the trees rattled and swayed at the downward force of its propellors.

In my pocket I had one of the leaflets that Annie had printed off earlier and distributed when we arrived. There was a recent photo of Megan in the middle.

Help us find Megan Richards

We are appealing for the public's help in finding missing woman Megan Richards, aged sixty-four. Megan went missing on Monday evening from the Vale Caravan Park in the Dolgellau area.

ANNIE GAVE a frustrated sigh and stopping walking. 'This is ridiculous. I'm worried that we're wasting precious time here rather than actually doing something more useful.'

'What did you have in mind?' I asked. I agreed that walking slowly through this forest looking for tiny clues might not be the best use of our time.

'If Callum moved into Bryn's house, then all his stuff is there. Might be worth going to have a look through it all.'

I nodded in agreement but my focus was then taken as I saw Kelly heading our way.

'Have you found anything?' Annie asked immediately.

'Not here, I'm afraid,' Kelly said, but there seemed to be something troubling her.

'Everything okay?' I asked.

'I just had a call from our forensics lab,' she replied. They've tested the DNA from the blood we found at the back of Megan's caravan. It's a match. It's her blood. Forensics did find someone else's DNA too but that's not on the national database.'

25

4 days 6 hours missing

The journey over to Barmouth had been very quiet. Annie admitted that it wasn't a huge surprise that the forensic results had confirmed the blood at the back of the caravan was Megan's. However, it was still hard to hear. It confirmed that something terrible had happened late on Saturday night or early Sunday morning.

'Do we assume that the other person's DNA they found was Callum's?' Annie asked pensively.

'You told me that he had been arrested on several occasions, and that he'd had a suspended sentence for assault.'

Annie nodded. 'So his DNA would be on the national database.'

'Yes,' I agreed, 'but it doesn't help us narrow down whose DNA it could be.'

I saw that we were getting close to Bryn's house. This was the last place that Callum had been living before the accident. It was also where Annie and I assumed he'd stored all his possessions when he moved out of the caravan. We needed to look through his stuff. What I really wanted was a clue to any dealers that Callum had been

SIMON MCCLEAVE

involved with. It was a long shot but as Annie pointed out, we couldn't just sit around and do nothing.

The BBC News was burbling on the car radio:

North Wales Police are carrying out an extensive search of a section of Snowdonia Park in their ongoing search for Megan Richards who went missing in the early hours of Monday morning. An incident room has been set up at Dolgellau Police Station. Megan's sister, Annie Taylor, made a moving appeal earlier today in the hope of jogging someone's memory ....

Annie reached over and turned it off. 'Sorry. I know it's good that Megan's disappearance is everywhere now, but I just don't want to hear about it.'

I shrugged. 'No problem.'

Sleet had started to land and then melt on the windscreen. It clearly wasn't quite cold enough for snow yet. The sky above was a uniform cloak of battleship grey and made me feel slightly claustrophobic.

Annie raised an eyebrow. 'And you still think the drugs are the key to what happened to Meg?'

'I think it's too much of a coincidence for there to be that amount of drugs in the caravan, Meg to go missing, and the two not to be connected.'

Annie nodded in agreement. 'Maybe Callum had stolen those drugs from someone and they took Meg until he returned them,' she suggested.

It was a plausible explanation.

Bryn's dilapidated house came into view and I parked close to the driveway.

'Here we go,' I said as I turned off the ignition.

We didn't need to hide our arrival this time.

Getting out of the car, small flakes of sleet splattered softly against my face. One fell onto my eyelashes and I had to blink it away.

Annie's phone rang. 'DS Thomas,' she said, gesturing to the screen as she answered. 'Hi Kelly.'

Annie frowned. 'No, we haven't. Why are you asking me that? … Right. Okay, thank you,' she said, and then ended the call.

'Everything okay?' I asked, wondering what Kelly had asked Annie on the call.

'Someone has been up to Meg's caravan this morning after the police left and turned it upside down. Kelly said it might have been kids, but I don't believe that for a second.'

'Neither do I.' I narrowed my eyes. 'Someone is looking for their missing drugs.'

'That sounds more likely,' Annie agreed. She then pointed to the battered-looking blue transit van. 'Looks like Bryn's in.'

The pathway up to the front door was now dotted with sleet which looked like a scattering of confetti outside a church.

Annie knocked on the door and we took a step back.

A few seconds later, the door opened slowly and Bryn peered out. He was wearing a woollen hat, scarf, and padded coat.

Annie gestured. 'Okay if we come in for a second?'

'Not really,' he said. 'I'm going to the hospital right now.'

'You know Callum's got amnesia?' Annie asked. 'He didn't even recognise me.'

'What?' Bryn's eyes widened. 'Maybe he'll recognise me,' he suggested.

Annie gave a snort. 'Yes, of course he will.'

Bryn bristled but didn't respond. Then he gestured for us to come into the hallway.

I looked him in the eyes. 'They think it's temporary.'

'Think?' He pulled a concerned face. 'You mean it might not be temporary?'

'They won't know for a day or two.' Annie shrugged and then gestured upstairs. 'We need to look through Callum's stuff.'

'Why?' Bryn seemed suspicious.

Annie gave him a frustrated look. 'Because Callum can't tell us where Meg is or what's happened to her. And he might not be able to for a while. There could be something up there that will give us a clue as to what's going on.'

Bryn took a moment to process what Annie had said. Then he nodded. 'Okay. Just close the door on the way out.'

'Thanks Bryn,' she said with a forced smile. She wasn't doing anything to hide her animosity.

I watched him walk out of the front door and close it behind him.

I headed for the stairs. 'Right, let's have a look, shall we?'

The red carpet on the steps was worn and threadbare. There were old dusty books and a few magazines in piles on the first few stairs which we stepped over. The house smelled musty and damp, and Bryn had clearly been smoking weed that morning.

As we got to the landing at the top of the stairs, I saw that it was littered with cardboard boxes stuffed with clothes and general junk.

'This place is a dump,' Annie muttered under her breath.

'Yeah. It doesn't look like Bryn is a fan of throwing stuff away,' I agreed.

Walking along the landing, I spotted a bathroom that still had its original 80s avocado suite which was now stained and faded. Then there was a large bedroom with a double bed. In any other circumstances, I would have assumed that Bryn had been burgled. The floor was covered in clothes, shoes, towels, plastic bags and shoe boxes.

I also noticed a discarded black bra, knickers, a blouse and a gold can of cheap hairspray.

On the wall of the landing there were a few photos that had been put into cheap frames. Some featured Bryn playing a guitar in what appeared to be pubs or clubs.

'Complete fantasist,' Annie said witheringly. 'When he and Meg were together briefly, he acted like he was Eric Bloody Clapton. He'd say he was going on tour when he was playing a few pubs over in Cheshire or Liverpool.'

'And Bryn disappeared from their lives until very recently,' I said as I peered at more photos.

'Yes, but he and Callum did speak,' Annie replied, but then clearly thought of something. 'That's what Meg told me.'

Out of the corner of my eye I spotted two faded photos of Bryn, Meg and a baby. 'And this is Callum?' I asked as I pointed to them.

Annie frowned. 'Oh, I don't think I've ever seen those photos before. I'm surprised that Bryn's got them up on his wall.'

I looked at Annie and then back at the photograph. 'You said that Meg was seeing someone but you didn't know who.'

Annie gave me a sceptical look. 'You think Meg and Bryn got back together?'

I shrugged. 'Is it possible?'

'No. No way,' she replied adamantly. 'She couldn't stand him. And she was annoyed that Callum had got back in contact with him in the last few years. Bryn never gave her a penny when Callum was growing up. There's no way she'd let him back into her life.'

'Okay,' I said, but I wasn't fully convinced. 'There are some women's things in his bedroom.'

'No. There's just no way that would have happened,' Annie insisted. 'She would have told me.'

We moved along the landing and found a small room with a single bed. I assumed this was where Callum had been staying.

Rather surprisingly, the bedroom and Callum's possessions were relatively neat and tidy in comparison to the rest of the house.

As we went in, I spotted an ash tray filled to the brim with the remnants of spliffs. On the bedside table were a few empty cans of strong cider and a bottle of cheap Russian vodka.

'Right, let's see if there's anything useful in here,' Annie said as she started to search through Callum's possessions. 'To be honest, I've no idea what we're looking for.'

'If we're going on the theory that he had stolen those drugs from someone,' I said, thinking out loud, 'then anything that can narrow down who that might be.'

Annie gave me a dry look. 'It would be useful if Callum had written down that person's name and address with a heading '*drug dealer*'.'

I nodded sardonically. 'If only.'

Walking across the room, I went to the rickety pine wardrobe. As I opened it, it swayed and rocked where the joints were loose and unstable, and the glue had virtually disappeared.

Inside there were a few shirts hanging up and three pairs of trainers lined up at the bottom. I moved to the back to see if there was anything between the wall and the back of the wardrobe. On several occasions over the years I'd found stolen goods, drugs, and even weapons stashed in the gap between furniture and the walls behind.

There was nothing.

With a groan, I crouched down. My hands rubbed on the threadbare carpet that had definitely seen better days, and dust rose up into the air.

There was nothing hidden under the wardrobe either.

Out of the corner of my eye, I saw Annie pick something up from the bedside table and peer at it. It was a scrap of paper.

'What's that?' I enquired.

'Gobbledygook,' she said.

With some effort, I made a low groan as I got back to my feet. I felt a little dizzy for a second, but I was getting used to that these days. I glanced over at Annie. 'How do you mean?'

'Comb, fast, lame,' she said, and then turned the piece of paper to show me.

The three words were written in blue biro – *Comb / Fast / Lame*.

She furrowed her brow. 'Mean anything to you?'

For a second, I was baffled. 'Nope, nothing.'

Then I thought of something that Caitlin had said: *what3words*.

Grabbing my phone, I went on to Google.

'What is it?' she asked.

'Bit of a long shot but …'

I went onto the *what3words* location website. As far as I remembered, every house or property in the UK could be found by typing in a unique set of three words.

Typing them in, I saw an address come up.

'what3words,' I explained to Annie as I pointed to my phone. 'That location website with random words.'

'Yeah, I've heard of it. Never used it. What did you find?'

'A big house in Marford over in Wrexham,' I stated, giving her a meaningful look. 'Bit of a long shot, but my guess is that Callum has definitely been there.'

26

4 days 9 hours missing

Annie and I had been sitting outside a large detached house in Marford for about twenty minutes. It had been recently painted in a fashionable cream colour. On the enormous drive was a black Range Rover Sport and a white Porsche Cayenne 4x4. Annie was using her phone to see if she could find out the name of the owner of the house using various contacts in the judiciary and local government.

Narrowing my eyes, I looked at the high-tech gates, the video entry phone and the CCTV cameras that were dotted around the front of the house.

'What are you thinking?' Annie asked, as she continued to tap on her phone.

'I'm thinking that whoever lives in there has got more security than anyone else in this area.'

'But it doesn't mean that this is the right place,' she pointed out. 'Or that it's the home of a drug dealer.'

'No, that's true.' I didn't like to point out that this was all we had to go on right now.

'Nicholas Finn,' she said, pointing to her phone. 'Friend of mine at the Land Registry says this house belongs to a Nicholas Finn. He paid £1.7 million for it four years ago with cash.'

'Cash? Anything else?' I asked as I took my phone out. 'I'm going to ring Dewi Humphries.'

'What?' Annie raised an eyebrow quizzically. 'Is that wise? He's not going to tell you anything is he? He doesn't even like you.'

I shrugged. 'I'm aware of that.'

I called Dewi's number and he answered after five rings.

'Frank. I'm afraid I haven't got anything for you or Annie at the moment,' he said brusquely.

'Okay,' I replied. 'I just need to ask you something very quickly.'

'You want a favour from me?' he asked with a tinge of sarcasm.

'Does the name Nicholas Finn mean anything to you?'

A few seconds of silence.

I exchanged a meaningful look with Annie. Maybe we were on to something.

'Nicky Finn?' Dewi asked slowly.

'Yes. I take it you know him then?'

'Why are you asking me about Nicky Finn?' he asked suspiciously.

'Probably nothing,' I said.

'I've made no bones about what I think of you, Frank,' he said in a concerned tone, 'but you and Annie are not to go anywhere near Nicky Finn.'

'Okay. No problem,' I said calmly as Annie looked over at me.

'Where are you, Frank?' he asked.

'Sorry, Dewi. I can't hear you properly.'

'Frank?'

I ended the call and saw Annie staring at me.

'Yeah, I'm pretty sure we're in the right place,' I said to her.

27

4 days 10 hours missing

'We're here to see Mr Finn,' I said into the entry phone.

'No offence,' said a man's deep voice in a thick Wrexham accent, 'but if this is some religious thing, we're not interested, pal.'

'No, it's not that,' I replied. 'I've got something that belongs to Mr Finn. Some merchandise that I think he's been looking for. We'd like to come in and talk about how we can return it to him.'

Silence.

Another voice came on to the phone. 'Who the fuck is this?'

'My name is Frank Marshal,' I said calmly. 'Mr Finn?'

'What do you want?' he snapped.

'I think you were up at the Vale Caravan Park looking for something a few hours ago,' I explained. 'I'd like to return it to you in exchange for some information.'

'You taking the piss?' He sounded angry.

'No. I'm definitely not taking the piss. But if you're not interested, that's absolutely fine. Sorry to have bothered you.'

I turned around and took a step back towards the pick-up truck.

There was a high pitched buzz and the security gates made a metallic clunk and started to open slowly.

'Drive in and someone will come out and meet you,' Finn said.

We got back into the truck.

'Maybe you should wait out here,' I suggested to Annie. 'I don't know quite what we're walking into.'

'No chance.'

I took a breath, started the engine, drove slowly through the gates and parked next to the Range Rover.

As we got out of the truck, the front door opened and a huge man in his 40s, shaved head, black tracksuit and gold jewellery came towards us.

Well he definitely looks like a gang member, I thought dryly to myself.

The man looked at us. 'I'm gonna need to frisk you both before you come in,' he said in a Scouse accent.

Annie and I both nodded and held out our arms as he patted us down.

'Right,' he said, satisfied that neither Annie or I were carrying weapons or a wire. 'Follow me.'

We went through the front door and into a huge hall-way. It was tastefully, if a little garishly, decorated with tall plants, long mirrors, dark wooden furniture. A huge black and white photograph of a man dominated one wall. I assumed this was Nicky Finn. He didn't look quite how I'd expected. In the image, he had glasses, a bony face and a thin nose. Not only did he look unremarkable, he didn't look remotely threatening.

Annie and I followed the man into a large living room that had floor-to-ceiling glass doors at one end.

Finn sat on a long black sofa. He was wearing a navy

sweater with a white shirt underneath, jeans, and brown brogues. He looked like one of those middle-class dads you'd find sitting outside a coffee shop in Chester rather than a gangster.

'Come and sit down,' he said. His thick Wrexham accent betrayed his working class roots.

Annie and I sat down on a smaller sofa opposite him. There was a low coffee table between us with a couple of large photography books to one side.

Finn narrowed his eyes and pushed his designer glasses up the bridge of his nose. 'Frank Marshal? Do I know you?'

I shook my head, trying to remain calm. I had no idea how this was going to play out.

'And who are you, love?' he asked as he sat forward and stared at Annie.

'Annie Taylor,' she replied quietly as she fiddled nervously with a ring on her finger. 'We'd like to talk to you about my sister, Megan Richards.'

Finn shrugged. 'Yeah, well I think I'd like to talk to you about something that Frank here claims that he's got in his possession first, love.'

'Okay,' Annie conceded.

Finn fixed me with an icy stare. Behind the designer glasses and clothes, he wasn't someone to be messed with.

'Frank, I've got to hand it to you. A man of your age turning up here, claiming that you've got my gear. That takes balls,' he said. Then he continued to look directly at me.

'We're desperate,' I admitted with a shrug. 'Megan Richards, the woman who lived in the caravan you searched at the Vale Caravan Park, has gone missing. She's Annie's sister.'

'And you think I had something to do with that?' Finn asked calmly.

Annie looked over at him. 'Did you?'

'No, I didn't, love. I guess that makes Callum Richards your nephew, does it?'

'Yes, Callum is my nephew.'

Finn sat back deep in thought and took off his glasses. He cleaned them and then popped them back on again.

He raised an eyebrow. 'Where's Callum now then?'

'I'd rather not tell you that,' Annie admitted.

'Well, I hope for his sake he's a long, long way away,' he said ominously.

'He is,' Annie lied. 'He won't be around here ever again. But I do need to know what's happened to my sister.'

'I don't know anything about your sister.' Finn laughed. 'You think I've kidnapped her or something?'

'Yes.'

'That's not something I do. Not civilians anyway.'

Annie sat forward. 'Look at this from my point of view, Mr Finn.'

'Nicky, please,' he said.

'My nephew took something that didn't belong to him,' Annie said calmly, 'and you came to the caravan to look for it but you didn't find it. And now my sister has vanished.'

'I wish I could help you,' Finn said as he scratched his face. 'When we arrived at the caravan this morning, it was empty. That's all I know.' He narrowed his eyes. 'And if you think about it, if I had taken your sister as some form of collateral, I'd be mentioning it now so that I could guarantee that I get my gear back, wouldn't I?'

Annie nodded in frustration. 'Yes, that had crossed my mind.'

'Good. I'm glad we're clear on that then.' Finn turned

back to me. 'So, where's my gear, Frank? Outside in that truck of yours?'

I shook my head. That was a lie.

He snorted. 'You want money, Frank?'

'No. I came here because I want to help Annie to find her sister. That's all I'm interested in.'

'So, how do you propose I get my gear back, Frank?'

I took a few seconds to think. Then I shifted forward and looked directly at him. 'Okay. Let's say hypothetically that all your gear was in the black holdall in the back of my truck.'

Finn raised an eyebrow. 'I'd say that I'd be very pleased about that.'

'Hypothetically,' I reminded him.

He smiled. He was enjoying this little game. 'Hypothetically, of course.'

'Then you could get someone to go outside, retrieve it and confirm that for you, couldn't you?'

'Yes, I suppose I could.' Then he turned the large ring on his left hand. 'Hypothetically, what's stopping me taking you and this lovely lady and putting you in a hole in the ground?'

I gave him a wry smile but my heart was thumping. 'Ah, well I did think of that. I have a GPS tracker on my pick-up truck, and North Wales Police are aware that Annie and I are actively searching for Megan. If we suddenly go missing, they are going to pinpoint my truck to this address.'

Silence.

Finn furrowed his brow. I couldn't tell if he was about to explode in a fit of rage or not.

I held my breath.

Then he gave a roar of laughter and clapped his

hands. 'Fuck me, Frank, you've got some big kahunas on you, fella. Ever play poker?'

'Not my game,' I said.

He chortled. 'You should. You'd clean up, pal.'

I gave a half-smile back. 'So, given all that, my proposal is that I give you back what belongs to you, and Annie and I go on our merry way. How does that sound?'

Finn gave me a grin. 'Sounds like we have a deal, Frank. I don't have any reason to harm you or this lovely lady. But Callum? Well, Callum needs to watch his back for the rest of his life.' He glanced at Annie. 'But you knew that already.'

'Good,' I said as I got up.

Finn stood up too. 'You were a copper, weren't you?'

'That obvious is it?'

'Yeah.' He turned to Annie. 'I hope you find your sister.'

28

4 days 11 hours missing

Twenty minutes later, Annie and I were heading out of Wrexham as the light of the day started to fade. We travelled through Corwen on the A5 in silence. The visit to Finn had been a major blow to finding out what had happened to Megan. If her disappearance wasn't linked to the drugs that Callum had stolen, then who was involved? We were essentially back to square one. Except now it was over four days since Meg vanished – if not more.

'I thought that we were on to something,' Annie admitted quietly.

I sighed. 'So did I.'

'I'm sitting here wondering where to go next,' she said, her voice breaking with emotion.

'I know.' I nodded and gave her an empathetic look. 'But we're going to find her. I promise you.'

'It's got to be this man that she was seeing,' Annie said, as she dabbed the tears away from her face. 'He's got to be involved, hasn't he?'

'I think that's a distinct possibility,' I replied. As a detective I'd learned that the two most powerful motives for murder were love and money. We'd ruled out the stolen drugs as a motive, so Megan's relationship needed to be looked at more closely. But I was also aware that time was running out. It wasn't something I was going to share with Annie.

'What about the neighbour, Simon?' Annie asked.

'We haven't really got anything to go on other than he was a bit creepy,' I pointed out.

As we came out of Corwen, the houses, shops and buildings disappeared and were replaced by rolling fields on either side.

My phone rang and it registered on my internal Bluetooth speaker.

It was Dewi.

'Dewi,' I said cautiously.

'Is Annie with you?' he asked. He sounded more serious than usual.

'Nicky Finn isn't involved in Megan's disappearance,' he informed me. 'Don't ask me how I know, but I just know. You're going to have to trust me on it. But it would be a waste of precious time to go down that route.'

Silence.

Dewi didn't say anything for a few seconds.

'Dewi?'

'Yeah, I'm still here,' he said quietly. 'I just need to know if Annie is with you.'

The muscles in my stomach tensed. There was something incredibly ominous about Dewi's tone and it was making me feel very uneasy.

'Yes, she's sitting next to me,' I said, looking over at her. 'And you're on loud speaker so she can hear you.'

'There's no easy way of saying this, Annie,' Dewi said, 'but the body of a woman has been found on a small beach on a headland just outside Barmouth.'

29

4 days 11 hours missing

By the time Annie and I had arrived at Craig Fach car park to the east of Barmouth, a major incident had been declared. We had both been lost in thought on the journey. I had little doubt that the body would be Megan, even though I prayed that it wasn't. The anxiety was tight in my stomach.

The car park was busy with uniformed police cars, CID officers and a SOCO forensic van.

Annie shook her head sadly as she gazed out at the flashing blue lights and the SOCOs, who were now dressed in white nitrile forensic suits, masks, hats and white rubber boots. The back of the forensic van was wide open and a SOCO was clearly storing away evidence in a clear plastic bag.

'Oh God,' Annie whispered, as she took a deep breath to compose herself.

The scene in front of us sent a chill down my spine as I parked the truck. I just didn't know what to say. Obviously, I'd witnessed scenes like this dozens of times before. But this was so personal. I had known Megan. And Annie was my dear friend.

For a few seconds, we just sat in silence in the truck staring out. Neither of us wanted to get out. Once we went over to the beach, it would be clear if the woman they'd found was actually Megan. But while we sat here in the truck, there was still hope.

Annie visibly took a deep breath. 'I need to go and see if it's her.'

'I don't think that's a good idea,' I warned her. 'They probably won't let you anywhere near the crime scene.'

'I don't care, Frank,' she snapped. 'I need to know. You can stay here if you want.'

'No. I'm coming with you.'

Getting out of the truck, I stared up to the grey sky. I prayed that the person they'd found dead on the beach would not be Megan.

Making our way past two old boats that lay to one side of the car park, we headed over to a pathway that went up through the undergrowth. As we got to the top, the beach opened up in front of us.

The seaside town of Barmouth was about half a mile down the coast to our right. The estuary for Afon Mawd-dach was straight ahead, with the dark jagged line of mountains of Snowdonia behind that.

We stepped over the rusty railway track and then downhill through sandy dunes that were full of tall wild grasses. I heard the deep thundering sound of the black and yellow police EC145 helicopter as it swooped over-head and then hovered over the beach.

As my eyes focussed, I could see the white shape of a forensic tent about a hundred and fifty yards away on the wet sand to our left. There were various police officers, SOCOs and CID detectives moving around nearby.

I felt Annie reach for my hand as we tried to keep our

SIMON MCCLEAVE

footing on the soft sand. Her hand was freezing cold. I gave it a gentle, reassuring squeeze.

'Do you think someone drowned or something?' she said unconvincingly.

Given the number of officers and SOCOs, I knew that there was no way that whoever was lying dead under that tent had drowned. For this type of operation it must have been very clear from the outset that the person had been murdered.

'Maybe,' I said quietly.

We got on the wet sand flat and Annie let go of my hand. I looked down as I saw my boots making tiny splashes in the shallow rivulets of water that criss-crossed the beach.

A long blue and white police evidence tape stretched across the beach as we approached. A young male officer – sandy hair – was standing looking at us as we approached. He was there to make sure that members of the general public didn't encroach onto the crime scene, and that all visitors were logged in and out.

'I'm afraid I'm going to have to ask you to leave the beach please, sir,' he said sternly.

'We're here to see DCI Humphries,' Annie explained. 'He called us about twenty minutes ago. Or DS Thomas.'

The officer clicked his biro and inspected the scene log that he was holding in his other hand. 'Could I have your names please?' he asked.

'Frank Marshal and Annie Taylor,' I replied.

'Okay. If you can give me a minute, I'm just going to check if either of the officers is expecting you,' he said as he reached for his Tetra radio.

'We've just told you that DCI Humphries called us,' Annie said angrily.

'It won't take more than a minute, ma'am,' the officer

said politely as he moved away and used his radio to confirm who we were.

'Jesus Christ,' Annie sighed frustratedly under her breath. She was jittery, and her eyes roamed around as she became lost in her own dark thoughts.

'Okay,' the officer said, coming back to us. 'If you start to make your way over, then DS Thomas will come and meet you.'

'Thank you, constable,' I said with a friendly nod, realising that my use of 'constable' was an old force of habit.

The officer lifted the police tape. We ducked under it and started to make our way over towards the grisly sight of a forensics tent which was lit by huge halogen arc lights. The dim rumble of a diesel-powered generator filled the air, competing with the noise of the helicopter that circled around. White figures of the SOCOs in their forensic suits moved to and fro as the lines of blue police tape fluttered in the breeze.

Looking down, I started to tread carefully over the wet rocks which were covered in Chorda filum seaweed, known as bootlace weed or dead man's rope. I glanced over at Annie to make sure that she was okay and kept her balance.

Then I spotted a figure coming out of the forensic tent dressed in a white nitrile forensic suit and white rubber boots.

It was Kelly.

She started to head towards us.

Behind her I could see that SOCOs had laid down a series of aluminium stepping plates to preserve the sand around the crime scene for footprints and forensic evidence.

'I don't think you should be here, Annie,' Kelly said as she marched towards us.

'I need to know if it's her,' Annie said desperately as she searched Kelly's face for clues. 'Is it?'

Kelly took a moment and then said, 'I think so, but I can't be certain.'

Annie blinked nervously. 'You think she was murdered?'

Kelly nodded but didn't say anything.

Annie frowned. 'I gave you a photo of her. I don't understand why you can't tell me if it's Meg in there.'

Kelly hesitated. There was something that she wasn't telling us.

'I want to see her,' Annie said, sounding angry.

'I need you to go home, Annie,' Kelly said gently. 'We'll call you when you can see her and make an identification.'

'No. I want to see her now,' Annie insisted.

'I'm not sure that's a very good idea,' Kelly said, sounding a note of caution.

'Why?'

I looked at Annie and felt protective. 'Why don't I go with Kelly and take a look for you?' I suggested calmly.

'No, Frank,' Annie said, sounding annoyed. 'Meg was my sister. If it is her in there, I want to go and see her.'

Kelly frowned. 'I'd have to advise you against doing that. I don't think it's something you should see, Annie.'

'Nonsense! This is ridiculous,' Annie growled as she bristled.

Silence.

'Listen, I worked as a High Court Judge,' Annie said, sounding a little calmer. 'I've seen hundreds of terrible things in my time. If it's Meg, I want to know right now and I want to see her. And you can't stop me.'

Kelly looked at me and I shrugged.

'Very well.' Kelly sighed as she signalled for a SOCO

to bring us over forensic suits, masks and boots before we went any closer to the crime scene.

I pulled on the forensic suit. It was probably fifteen years since I'd worn one and I was surprised at how light-weight it was compared to the last time.

I watched Annie as she struggled angrily with the suit and mask. It was obvious that she was using anger to mask the overwhelming fear that she was feeling.

'Right, let's do this shall we?' she said.

Kelly and I exchanged a concerned look as we made our way towards the tent.

A SOCO took a photograph inside and the flash illuminated the material of the tent for a millisecond.

As we moved to the entrance, another SOCO moved out of our way.

My eyes slowly moved up the soaked clothing of the woman's body. Her legs were splayed at an unnatural angle.

I took two more steps into the tent before I saw the face.

However, even before I'd even registered the woman's features, I heard a terrible moan from next to me.

'Oh Meg,' Annie cried, her voice faltering, as her hands went to her face in horror. 'Meg … no … no … no …'

Annie moved forward and crouched down two yards from Meg's body.

My breath caught in my throat.

Megan's skin had a grey-blue tinge, and her hair was matted, dishevelled and sprinkled with sand.

Her eyes were open and there was a look of sheer horror on her face – the moment at which she had died.

Around her neck were deep lacerations that had been

caused by steel wire that was still wrapped around her throat.

I shuddered at my next thought.

Keith Tatchell? Megan had been killed in an identical way to the victims of the serial killer Keith Tatchell in the late 90s. But that didn't make any sense. Keith Tatchell was still in prison.

Annie took a step closer and crouched down. 'Megan, what happened to you? Look at you …'

Kelly crouched down next to Annie and touched her gently on the arm. 'Annie, I know how difficult this is for you but I'm going to have to ask you not to touch her at the moment. You can be with her once we've got her back to the hospital.'

Annie nodded, but her face was contorted with pain. 'Who did this to you?' she wept.

Chapter 30

It was about two hours later by the time Annie and I got back to where I'd parked my pick-up truck. We had stood and watched the forensic team for a while. Kelly had arranged for a family liaison officer to be based at Annie's home to support her and keep her up to date with the investigation into her sister's murder. However, I was pretty sure that Annie wouldn't be satisfied sitting at home waiting for updates from the police. She just wasn't that type of person, despite the terrible trauma of what had happened to Megan and what she'd witnessed on the beach. She had called her husband Stephen to tell him the awful news.

I still couldn't get the similarity to Tatchell's killings out of my head. I hadn't mentioned it to Annie. It didn't seem appropriate on the beach. I wondered if it had crossed her mind, or those of the CID officers yet? I assumed it would at some point. If not, I was happy to flag it up.

We got into the truck and for a few seconds we just sat in devastated silence.

'I'm so sorry,' I said under my breath.

Annie just nodded her acknowledgement as she wiped a tear from her face and sniffed.

Over to our right, more cars were arriving with CID officers and a couple of high-ranking uniformed officers from North Wales Police. An innocent woman had been found brutally murdered on a beach close to the seaside town of Barmouth. It was extremely unusual. There would be a media frenzy that needed to be managed. I wanted to make sure that Annie was protected from that.

I blew out my cheeks and glanced over at Annie. She was lost and broken.

I reached out and touched her arm. I knew there was nothing I could do to make her feel any better at this moment in time.

She didn't say anything for a while. Then a wave of shock and grief came flooding over her and tears rolled down her face silently. She took a tissue and wiped them away.

'I just want to be with her,' she said under her breath. Then she looked directly at me. 'Do you know what I mean?'

'Of course,' I replied with a reassuring nod.

'I hate the thought that Meg has been taken away and now she's going to be lying in a mortuary,' Annie wept, trying to get her breath back. 'I just want to be sitting next to her. Looking after her.'

'They will take good care of her,' I tried to reassure her, 'but I understand that you want to be with her. You'll be able to see her very soon.'

'And then I think about how scared she must have been in the final moments of her life.' She wiped her watery eyes with a tissue. Tears hung on her delicate eyelashes. 'I can't bear to think of her like that, Frank. She must have been terrified.'

I didn't know what to say. All I could do was sit with Annie and try and help her bear the incredible pain that she was experiencing.

She clutched at her chest as if the pain of grief was too much. 'Jesus. This just doesn't feel real, does it?'

'No,' I agreed. 'It really doesn't.'

She wiped her face again. 'I'm sorry to have put all this on you.'

'Don't be silly. I'm here for you. Whatever you need,' I said, trying to comfort her.

'You're one of the good ones, aren't you, Frank?' she said with a half-smile.

'I don't know about that.' I wasn't comfortable getting compliments. I never had been.

'Shall we go?' Annie asked. 'I'd like to get out of here now.'

I turned on the ignition. It seemed that sitting there in the truck was making things worse.

'Do you want me to drop you home?' I asked.

She shook her head. 'I need to tell Callum first.'

I frowned. 'He might not understand,' I suggested.

Annie shrugged. 'I have to tell him. And maybe that will jolt him out of his amnesia or something.'

'Okay,' I said, but I wasn't convinced. We pulled away from the small beachside road. 'We'll head to the hospital now.'

Chapter 31

We had been driving for about fifteen minutes in virtual silence when Annie spoke.

'I looked at what that person had done to Megan,' she said very quietly, 'and then I remembered ...' She trailed off.

I guessed that she was talking about the Tatchell murders but I couldn't be sure.

She glanced over at me. 'You do remember the case don't you?'

I nodded with a dark expression. 'Keith Tatchell.'

'You'd thought of that already,' she said. 'Of course you had.'

'But Tatchell is still in prison.'

'I know.' Annie took a deep breath. 'Is it the same, or just similar?' she asked very quietly.

'I didn't work on the investigation but I was still CID when it happened. And as far as I can remember, it's exactly the same.'

'But that doesn't make any sense, does it?' Annie said, as if she was thinking aloud. 'It obviously can't be him.'

'No,' I agreed.

I drove over the brow of a hill, and the rugged land-scape of Snowdonia lay out in front of us. Thick heath-land, scarred by rocks. Sheep dotted indiscriminately, moving slowly.

'I can't get what I saw just now out of my head, Frank,' Annie said, sounding very frightened.

I gave her a look to show that I understood and to try and reassure her.

'I'm scared that it's always going to be there,' she whispered. 'Her face like that. And I'm never going to get rid of it.'

Silence.

'Maybe we could go and see her in the hospital. After we've seen Callum?' I suggested. 'You could spend some time with her there.'

I was desperate to find something to give her any kind of comfort.

'Yes,' she nodded immediately. 'I'd like that. And I think it would help.'

I remembered a contact that I still had in the pathology department.

'I'll make a phone call.'

THE LIFT to the second floor of Glan Clwyd Hospital was slow and claustrophobic. Annie and I had been squeezed to the back of it by a family clearly celebrating the birth of a baby. Not only was the father there, but his three children, an uncle and the grandparents. As we made our way up the floors slowly, they chattered excitedly and noisily about the fact that 'he' – the baby – was a *whopper* at eight pounds eleven ounces and was therefore destined to play rugby for Wales. It was lovely to see their joy. That was the strange thing about hospitals. Relatives experiencing such extremes of emotion. Births or successful treatments of illnesses. Terminal diagnoses or even death. No one knew what those they shared the lifts, corridors and the cafés with were going through.

The lift clunked loudly to a halt and we followed the family out. They turned right towards the maternity wards. We turned left towards the ICU and the critical care wards.

As we strolled along the wide corridor, I opened the door for a young man in his 20s who was in a wheelchair attached to a drip. He was skin and bone, with a gaunt ghostly face. He looked up to give me a nod of thanks as he wheeled his way through. I could hear his wheezing as he went.

I studied his face for a split second. The substantial hollows in his cheeks where the translucent skin seemed to have been pulled too tight. He might have been young, but his eyes were old beyond their years. Weary from all that pain and worry. It was an unnerving sight. As if the man was caught somewhere in between. Neither old or young. Neither alive, nor dead. Just lost somewhere in between all that.

The air was thick with the usual smell of hospital food and cleansing fluids. The aroma of the mass-cooked food took me straight back to school for a moment. Queuing with wooden trays. Woolly mashed potato served in round dollops from an ice cream scooper. Eggs that had been fried into dry, flat discs. But when I gave it some thought, I realised that rationing from the Second World War had only finished two years before I went to school. Sometimes a thought like that struck me hard. How on earth was I seventy years old?

Bloody hell, I'm positively prehistoric.

Arriving on the ward, we walked down the corridor to Callum's room and went inside. He was still attached to an ECG and his eyes were closed. We pulled over two grey plastic seats and sat down beside the bed. A nurse had told us on our way in that he was on pain relief medication for the injury to his head, and that was making him sleepy and woozy. And he was still confused and having problems with his memory, which was making him agitated and upset. It wasn't good news.

Annie and I sat in silence for a while. Apart from the beep of the ECG machine, the room was still and quiet. We needed time to sit and process what we'd seen at the beach.

'Callum might not understand what's happened to Meg, might he?' Annie conceded in a low voice without taking her eyes off his bed.

'No, he might not,' I agreed. If there had been no progress since we'd last seen him, then Callum wouldn't have a clue as to who we were or understand what Annie was about to tell him. But it was clearly important to her.

'It just feels like I need to tell him,' she said gently. 'Does that make sense?'

'Yes, of course. It might even jog his memory,' I suggested, trying to reassure her that our journey wasn't futile.

Callum stirred a little and blinked open his eyes. Our conversation must have disturbed him.

He frowned as if he was trying to piece together something in his mind.

Annie leaned forward and put her hand on his.

He reacted by pulling it away. Clearly he still didn't recognise her.

'Callum,' she said, her voice now dropped to a whisper.

'Yes,' he mumbled as he wiped at his mouth and face.

'I need to tell you something about your mum, Megan,' Annie said. 'Do you know who that is?'

'Megan?' He blinked and then furrowed his brow. 'My mum's called Megan isn't she?'

'Yes.' Annie shot me a look and then glanced back at him. 'Do you know who I am?'

He shook his head but didn't reply.

'I'm Annie. I'm your Aunt. Megan is my sister,' Annie explained slowly as if talking to a child. '*Was* my sister,' she corrected herself. 'Do you remember me?'

Callum seemed frustrated as he blinked nervously. 'No. Sorry.'

'You don't need to apologise. You've been in an accident. Do you know that?'

'I remember there was a bridge. And I was under the water and someone pulled me out. Is that right?'

'That was my friend Frank.' Annie gestured to me. 'He pulled you out of the river.'

Callum peered at me. 'Thank you.'

'It's fine,' I reassured him.

The door began to open very slowly.

I turned to see who was coming in.

Even though there hadn't been a knock, I assumed it was just a doctor or nurse.

However, there was something about the speed at which the door was opening that immediately concerned me.

It was deliberately slow, as if the person on the other side was trying their best not to make a noise or be noticed.

I don't like the look of that.

Without hesitating, I got out of my seat and headed towards the door which was still inching open.

A man's head appeared and peered into the room.

He was in his 30s, shaved head, tattoo on his thick muscular neck.

'Can I help?' I asked. His arrival and his appearance had made me feel instantly uneasy.

'Sorry mate,' he said, sounding confused. He had a Scouse accent. 'Wrong room. My bad.'

And with that he was gone.

Annie was worried. So was I.

'I'll be back in a minute,' I told her.

'Frank …' she called after me, but I was already on my way out of the door.

Even though I couldn't be sure, the man who had just looked into the room seemed very suspicious. My instinct was that it wasn't coincidental or a mistake at all.

Glancing right, I saw him strolling down the corridor towards the exit of the AMC. If he had been searching for a patient but had got the wrong room, why was he now leaving? That didn't make any sense.

I sped up but he must have sensed this. He glanced back at me, walked faster, and turned out of sight.

I broke into a jog. I got to the main hospital corridor. The man was now waiting for the lift.

He saw me, and this time he turned in my direction and faced me head on.

I stopped in my tracks as my pulse quickened. He was over 6ft and very stocky.

The lift arrived with a beep.

The metallic doors clunked open and he stepped inside out of sight.

I jogged a little down the corridor again. I wasn't sure what I wanted to achieve but I needed to see his face again.

As I arrived at the lift, I saw that he was inside and alone.

He gave me an amused grin and then winked at me.

'You coming in or not, grandad?' he asked, gesturing to the empty lift.

Twenty years ago I wouldn't have hesitated.

The doors started to close.

My eyes were drawn to a shape under his Stone Island jacket.

It was a shape I'd seen many times before.

He had a handgun tucked into the waistband of his jeans.

The lift doors shut and he was gone.

Lucky I didn't get carried away.

'What was that about?' asked a voice.

It was Annie hurrying towards me.

I gave her a dark look.

'One of Nicky Finn's gang?' she asked.

'I think so, and that means that Callum is going to need protection while he's in here.'

Chapter 32

As Annie and I walked towards the mortuary that was located in the basement of Glan Clwyd Hospital, the drop in temperature was marked. I had pulled a few favours at the local coroner's office, explained who Annie was, and arranged for us to go and see Megan's body before the post-mortem started. I wasn't sure that Annie should see Megan again before the undertakers had done their work but she was insistent.

'Can we get Callum protection while he's here?' she asked.

'I think you should talk to Dewi. Explain about the mystery visitor and that you're concerned for Callum's safety. It'll be better coming from you.'

'Of course.'

'I've spoken to a contact I have in the prison service. I've put in a request to visit Keith Tatchell in HMP Wakefield.'

Annie's eyes widened. 'Really?'

'I think it has to be worth a conversation,' I said. 'I'm

also going to contact DCI Ian Goddard. He's retired now, but he was the original SIO on the Tatchell murders.'

'What am I supposed to be doing while you're doing all that?' she asked.

'What do you want to do?'

'I want to find out who did this to my sister,' she replied. 'I want to come with you.'

'I was hoping you were going to say that.'

We reached the black double doors that led into the mortuary.

'Are you going to be okay doing this?' I asked, as my voice dropped to a whisper.

'I don't know, but I want to see her so I have to just do it.'

As we made our way inside, the cold air was thick with the smell of disinfectants and other chemicals. It had been about fifteen years since I'd been inside the mortuary at Glan Clwyd. It was much like the dozen or so others that I'd visited over the years I'd been a police officer. The technology had changed significantly but the layout was virtually identical.

There were two large mortuary examination tables nearby, with a third on the far side of the room. The walls were tiled to about head height in pale celeste tiles, and some work benches and an assortment of luminous coloured chemicals ran the full length of the room.

I could have lived the remainder of my life quite happily without ever setting foot in one of these places again. Of course, it struck me that I might end up lying in one one day – but then I wouldn't know anything about that, would I?

Glancing around, I spotted a woman in her late 50s working at a computer. I assumed this was Professor

Angela Wilkins whom I'd found out was the pathologist who was going to be carrying out the post-mortem.

Then I saw that there was a body laid out on a metal gurney. With the exception of the head, it was covered in a white, surgical sheet.

It was Megan.

I glanced over at Annie who had already spotted her sister and stopped in her tracks for a second. She seemed rooted to the spot.

I whispered, 'We can leave if you want.'

'No.' She shook her head. 'I need to see her. At the moment, all I can see in my head is Meg lying on that beach. If I can see her here, lying peacefully, it might help.'

I nodded empathetically. What Annie said made perfect sense.

The underlying buzz of fans and the air conditioning added to the unnatural atmosphere. The pungent smell of cleaning fluids masked the odour of the gases.

Professor Wilkins, who was dressed in pastel blue scrubs, noticed our entrance and got up from where she was sitting.

'Professor Wilkins?' I asked as she approached.

She nodded with a compassionate expression on her face, then turned her gaze to Annie.

'It's Annie, isn't it?'

'Yes.'

'I'm so sorry for your loss.'

'Thank you,' Annie whispered.

Wilkins gestured across the room. 'Would you like to come and see Megan?' she asked gently.

Annie nodded but didn't reply.

She reached for my hand. I held it as we walked slowly towards where Megan was lying.

I could feel the tension suddenly grow in Annie's hand as we got closer.

Megan's face was so different to how she'd appeared earlier on the beach.

Under the lights of the mortuary, her skin was paler but had lost the horribly unnatural bluish tint. Her hair had been combed back from her face and tucked neatly behind her ears. Mercifully, the sheet was tucked up under her chin so that the gashes on her neck weren't visible.

Megan looked so peaceful. Almost ethereal. And at rest. It was such a poignant contrast to the surreal, chaotic horror of the crime scene at the beach. Now I could see why Annie had insisted on seeing her again. This was the image of her sister that she wanted in her head.

I was distracted by someone else opening the mortuary door. It was Dewi and Kelly. Touching Annie's arm, I gestured to them. Annie nodded but her eyes were filled with tears.

I caught Dewi's eye and pointed to the mortuary doors to signal that we should talk outside.

I crossed the mortuary and went out into the basement corridor. Then Dewi, Kelly and I took a few steps away from the doors so that our voices couldn't be heard.

'How's Annie doing?' Kelly asked. 'Stupid question, I know but …'

'She's devastated. They were very close,' I explained. 'Have you got any leads? Eyewitnesses?'

'We're talking to everyone who lives close to the beach,' Kelly said. 'We've found someone who walked their dog there at 7pm last night. Megan's body wasn't there then, so we know she was taken there after that time.'

A hospital porter came past wheeling a trolley of medical supplies. The rattling noise of the trolley wheels reverberated around the windowless corridor.

'Taken?' I noticed her use of the word. 'You don't think she was murdered at the beach?'

'No. Forensics have told us that there are significant footprints in the sand leading from the road. We think that Megan was carried over there and placed on the sand.'

'Christ.' I couldn't help but be surprised. 'Whoever did this was taking a hell of a risk.'

'I know. I guess if it happened in the early hours of the morning, they would assume that no one would be around.'

'Do you have a time of death yet?' I asked.

'Between 10pm and midnight last night,' Dewi said in an unfriendly tone. Something was annoying him.

'I don't suppose forensics have had time to analyse anything that they found yet?' I asked.

Kelly shook her head. 'I also spoke to Megan's neighbour, Simon Bentley. Annie seemed to think he was hiding something when you spoke to him?'

'Yeah. There was definitely something off about him.'

'Definitely a bit of an oddball,' Kelly admitted, 'but he's got an alibi.'

I shrugged. It seemed that Simon Bentley wasn't a suspect for the time being. But I definitely wasn't willing to rule him out, alibi or no alibi.

Dewi gave me a stern look. 'You've put in a request to visit Keith Tatchell at HMP Wakefield. Do you want to tell me why?' he asked sharply.

Bugger. I was hoping that North Wales Police wouldn't be made aware of this.

I raised an eyebrow. 'You've been checking up on me, Dewi,' I said with a wry smile.

'Come on, Frank,' he said dryly. 'How long have we known each other?'

'Too long, I'm thinking.' I smiled sarcastically.

Kelly glanced at me. 'Listen, we understand that what's happened to Megan is devastating for Annie. And I know you both want to find out who did this and why,' she said in a placatory tone.

Dewi fixed me with a stare. 'But I can't have you taking things into your own hands, playing at being detective, going gallivanting around and compromising the investigation.'

'Gallivanting?' I snorted. I wanted to punch him in the face.

'You're retired now, Frank,' he said in a patronising tone. 'So, just let the professionals get on with the job, eh?'

I gritted my teeth. *You cheeky little twat.*

Kelly gave me a conciliatory look. 'I can see that your instinct is to get involved. That's understandable.'

'But we can't let you do that. And there'll be consequences if you do, Frank. You got that?' Dewi said in a threatening tone.

Christ, they couldn't get more 'good cop, bad cop' if they tried.

In the old days, I would have decked Dewi right there and then. And even though I was angry, it seemed that appeasement would be the most useful way forward. I took a breath to steady myself. 'I'm happy to let you guys get on with the investigation,' I conceded.

'Really?' Dewi gave me a suspicious frown. 'Putting in a request to visit a convicted serial killer whose MO matches Megan's murder is definitely not 'letting us get on with the investigation' is it?'

'Don't worry, Dewi, we'll keep out of your way,' I said with a dismissive sneer.

'Thank you, Frank,' Kelly said. 'And we'll keep you and Annie updated every step of the way.'

'Right, we need to go and have a conversation with Professor Wilkins,' Dewi said to Kelly.

Dewi then shook his head at me as they both walked over to the mortuary doors.

Prick.

The doors to the mortuary opened and Annie came out into the empty corridor.

I watched as Dewi and Annie exchanged a few words before he and Kelly went through the doors into the mortuary.

Annie approached. Even though she was upset, and her face was streaked with tears, there was also a trace of relief too.

'You okay?' I asked. 'Sorry, I seem to be asking you that every five minutes.'

'Yes, I'm OK. I needed to see Meg like that. Just for my own sanity. And I'll go and see her properly once she's been taken to the undertakers.' Then she caught herself and shook her head. 'I just feel like I'm trapped in some horrendous dream.' She glanced at me almost to check that I knew what she was talking about.

'I remember I was like that when my mum died,' I admitted.

Annie frowned. 'She was quite young, wasn't she?'

'Fifty. I'd just moved to London with Rachel. Died in a car accident.' Suddenly there was a lump in my throat, even after all these years. 'It made me sad that she never got to meet Caitlin.'

'Of course,' Annie said sympathetically. 'That's the thing with grief. It doesn't go away. You just learn to live with it. And it gets easier with time.'

'Everything okay with Dewi?' I asked.

'I told him about what happened up on Callum's ward,' she said. 'He's going to put an officer outside his room which is a relief.'

'Good. Dewi has warned us off looking into Megan's

death. He knows that I've requested to see Keith Tatchell at Wakefield.'

Annie winced. 'Oh dear. What did you say?'

'I reassured him that we would let him and Dolgellau CID get on with the investigation,' I said with a knowing expression.

She frowned at me. 'You don't mean that though, do you?'

I shook my head. 'No bloody way. I've seen too many murder cases messed up over the years. I'm not going to let that happen to Megan. Plus, there are many advantages of being a retired detective.'

'Such as?'

'I know all the shortcuts. And I'm not restricted by police protocol.'

Hang on a second …

Something had occurred to me.

Annie noticed. 'What is it?'

'Dewi was the arresting officer when they got Tatchell all those years ago,' I said, thinking aloud.

'Really? I didn't know that, but then again, why would I?'

'No wonder he was pissed off that I put in a request to visit Tatchell.'

'I'm not following you.'

'Dewi doesn't want me digging around in the case that made his reputation.'

Annie shrugged. 'He hasn't got anything to worry about.' Then she looked at me. 'Unless he's got something to hide.'

Chapter 33

It was pitch black by the time Annie got out of Frank's car. She was bone tired. As if someone had twisted her like a sponge and wrung every ounce of energy and emotion out of her. And she felt a little dizzy and light-headed.

'Are you going to be okay tonight?' Frank asked her with genuine concern.

She nodded. 'Yes, I'm fine. I just need something to eat and try to get some sleep,' she replied as if she was slightly removed from her body.

'I'll have my phone next to me all night if you need someone to talk to,' Frank said as he looked directly at her.

She didn't know how she would have handled the past few days without him. He was her rock. In another life, she should have married someone just like him.

'Thank you, Frank.'

'I can go and see Ian Goddard on my own if you want. If you're not up to it,' he suggested.

Ian Goddard was the original senior investigating officer for North Wales Police on the Keith Tatchell case back in 1996.

'No, no. That's very kind but I want to be there,' Annie insisted. 'I need to hear what he has to say.'

'Of course.'

Their eyes met, as they had done on many occasions. He gave her a comforting look as if to reassure her that he'd be with her every step of the way.

Fearing that she was about to dissolve into tears, she started to close the car door. 'Night, Frank.'

'Goodnight Annie,' he said as he sat back into the driver's seat.

Slamming the passenger door, she took a deep breath and then saw that Stephen's car was parked over by the double garage. Her heart sank. She had hoped that he was going to get back from his business trip late. Then she could have a strong drink, food, a hot shower and fall into bed without having to speak to anyone.

She walked over the gravel drive and then along the stone pathway as she heard Frank pull away in his truck. As she fished out her front door keys, she glanced up and watched him drive away.

Chapter 34

I'd just finished grooming Duke in the stables when he started to seem a little unsettled. I wondered if he sensed my anxiety. Like Jack, he could pick up on a mood or an atmosphere very quickly. I stroked his nose for a few seconds to try and reassure him.

'It's okay, boy,' I said in a soothing voice. Then I reached into my coat pocket, pulled out two carrots that I'd taken from the house, and fed them to him. 'Here you go mate.'

Jack was lying over in some hay, watching us.

I'd always found being in the stables and tending to Duke incredibly comforting. After the day I'd had it was exactly what I needed. It was so still and so peaceful out here. Just the noise of Duke crunching on the carrots. The smell of the hay and feed.

'Thatta boy,' I said, as I stroked Duke's nose again.

For a moment, the dark images from the beach flashed through my mind. Megan's haunted eyes and face. The colour of her skin. The unnatural angle of her limbs. The deep wounds across her throat. I'd seen my fair share of dead bodies and murder victims over the years, but not many as brutal and disturbing as what I'd witnessed today.

My thoughts were broken as I heard someone coming down the track.

'Hello?' called a familiar voice. It was Caitlin.

'I'm in here,' I called out.

Caitlin appeared and gave me a hug. 'Hey Dad.'

'How are you guys doing?' I asked with a concerned expression as I started to close up the stable for the night.

I'd already called Caitlin on several occasions to check on her and Sam and to explain that TJ was very likely to be held on remand until his trial.

'Sam seems okay now. He's watching football on the telly.'

'What about you?' I asked. 'How are you?'

She took a moment and then shrugged. 'I feel bloody stupid,' she sighed. 'I allowed that arsehole into my life. And Sam's. I've screwed everything up, haven't I?' She seemed upset.

'Hey,' I said as I reached out and gave her another hug. 'No, you haven't. You're a great mother. And you and Sam are safe here. That's all you need to think about now, okay?'

'Thanks Dad,' she whispered, her voice breaking with emotion a little.

'Do you want come in for a drink?' I asked, gesturing to the farmhouse.

'No thanks.' She shook her head. 'I was going to say goodnight to Mum though.'

'I assume she's gone up to bed by now.'

'Oh right. Never mind, I'll see her in the morning.' Then she glanced at me. 'I watched the news earlier. So horrible. That poor woman. And poor Annie.'

I pulled the main door to the stable shut. 'Yeah, I'm not going to lie, it's been a very difficult day.'

'Are you okay?'

'I guess.' I gave a sigh. 'I'd like to find the person responsible for Annie's sake.'

'Of course.' Caitlin gave me a comforting pat on the arm as we started to walk up the path. I switched on my torch as we went.

As we reached the annexe, she gave me a hug and a kiss. 'Right, I'm going to leave you to it then. Night Dad. Love you.'

'Love you too,' I said quietly as she wandered away.

For about a minute, I peered up at the enormous black sky. The soft edges of the honey-coloured moon had now hardened. Over to my left, the odd twinkling light of a farm or house in the far distance as if they had been scattered carelessly. The air smelled of the damp heather and fields.

Having a strong drink, a hot shower, and fall into bed without having to speak to anyone was all I needed now.

Going inside, I pulled off my leather gloves, hung up my coat and hat, and ran my hand through my silver-grey hair in an attempt to make it tidy. I went into the living room and saw that Rachel's armchair was now empty.

I strolled to the kitchen and began my evening ritual. I poured myself two fingers of Jameson's whiskey into a heavy crystal glass tumbler with a thick base. Then I placed a solitary ice cube into the glass and gave it a swirl. Then I caught the earthy, spicy fragrance of the whiskey and had a long swig. A reassuring burning sensation in my throat. *Perfect.*

Draining the rest of my whiskey, I climbed the stairs to the first floor, padded down the landing and went into the darkness of our bedroom.

The bed was empty and undisturbed.

That's strange.

I checked the bathroom.

Nothing.

'Rachel?' I called out, as my stomach tightened with anxiety.

Where the hell is she?

I checked the spare bedroom, but it was empty.

'Rachel?' I called again.

I went over to the door to James' bedroom. I'd only been in twice since he'd taken his own life in the nearby woods. I couldn't bear to go in there. It was too painful.

Opening the door, I saw that Rachel was propped up against some pillows on James' bed. She was leafing through one of his A3 portfolios from art college.

'There you are,' I said, shaking my head with a smile. 'You had me worried for a minute.'

'Did I?' she said innocently, and then patted the bed for me to come over. 'He drew such beautiful pictures, didn't he? He was so talented.'

My whole body tensed with emotion as I forced myself to cross James' bedroom and sat down on the bed next to her. It was horribly surreal.

'I'll shift over,' Rachel said as she moved over on the bed to her right.

I lay next to her, my back against James' headboard, and then looked slowly around his bedroom. Art books and novels on the shelves. A huge collage of photos of family and his friends from school and art college. Posters for bands such as *Red Hot Chilli Peppers* and *Foo Fighters*. A Wrexham FC scarf.

My eyes filled with tears. I took a deep breath and blew out my cheeks.

Jesus, I didn't know it was going to affect me this much.

Or maybe I did, and that's why I never came in here. It was just too raw.

'Look, Frank,' Rachel chirped happily as she showed me a huge landscape sketch of the nearby mountain range of Cader Idris and Rhinogs. 'It's beautiful, isn't it?'

I put my hand over to touch the paper, and traced the drawing with my forefinger. The lines and shading that had been so skilfully drawn by my son. 'Yes, it really is,' I whispered, and then I kissed her cheek.

Chapter 35

Annie opened her front door. The house was warm and smelled of garlic and wine. There was classical music playing from somewhere. *Greig's 'Peer Gynt'*. Stephen had been cooking. For a man who was so old fashioned and insensitive, he was a remarkably good cook. And he knew it. When they used to entertain and throw dinner parties, it was always Stephen who did the cooking. He'd even been to France a couple of times to do cooking courses.

Annie took off her jacket, hung it up, and saw a cream-coloured scarf that Meg had bought her for her birthday last year.

It hit her again. Her sister was dead. Her beautiful, innocent little sister had been killed in the worst possible way. The pain of that thought just swept through her and it was overwhelming.

'Oh Meg,' she whispered, as her eyes filled with tears and her whole body seemed to contort with the agony of it. The pain was just unbearable.

Blowing out her cheeks, she took a long deep breath to try and steady herself.

Then she heard someone approaching.

A figure appeared in front of her in the hallway.

Stephen. He was wearing an expensive blue Ralph Lauren shirt, jeans and navy apron.

He shook his head and then came and took her in his arms.

'I'm so, so sorry,' he said under his breath as he held her tightly.

She nodded as she wept and let herself be held. She didn't care about his ghastly behaviour and the infidelities of recent years. It seemed irrelevant. She just needed to be held. They had been married for over forty years and that counted for something.

After about a minute, Stephen stepped back and put his hands on her shoulders. He had a pained expression on his face which seemed genuine.

'I don't know what to say,' he said gently. 'What can I do?'

Annie shook her head. 'I can't believe this has happened. It just doesn't feel real.'

'Of course it doesn't,' he replied with a deep frown. 'If there's anything I can do …'

Annie sighed. 'You can make me a very strong drink.'

'Of course,' he said. 'Why don't you go and sit down, and I'll bring it to you.'

Annie shook her head. 'I don't want to be on my own.' 'If you're in the kitchen, I'll come with you.'

'I'm making chicken chasseur,' he said as she followed him down the hallway and into the kitchen. Then he turned to look at her. 'Gin?'

She nodded.

'What have the police said?' he asked, as he pulled a full bottle of Hendrick's gin from the cupboard.

'I don't think I can go through it now,' she said, speaking softly.

Stephen frowned. 'On the radio they were talking about the women back in the 90s?'

'Okay if we talk about it in a bit?'

'Of course.'

For a few seconds, Annie allowed her eyes to roam around the kitchen. Stephen was the messiest cook she'd ever known. The surfaces were covered in bits of sliced onion, garlic, mushrooms and parsley. Frankly, tonight she just didn't care.

He poured her a stiff drink and handed it to her.

'Thanks,' she said, taking the heavy glass full of gin, tonic and ice. Then she took a long swig before deciding to drain the glass. She just wanted to anaesthetise the pain inside.

As Stephen stirred a pan, Annie poured herself another large gin.

'I'll turn this off,' he said as he went over to the Bluetooth speaker.

'It's fine. Leave it on,' Annie reassured him as she drank again. The gin had already started to numb her and give her a little buzz. The smells, the alcohol, and the music were just enough to soften the horror of the day for a while.

She watched Stephen as he expertly sliced and diced a red onion. She didn't know why it took something as horrific as this to make him be civilised to her. His eyes were roaming a little around the room as he walked around the kitchen, deep in thought.

Annie didn't know if it was the gin, the smell of the cooking, the soft lighting in the kitchen, the slow dinner jazz, but she was transported back to when she and

Stephen had first moved in together. They'd been so incredibly happy then.

Finishing her gin, she walked over to Stephen and looked directly at him.

He gave her a quizzical frown.

She reached up, took hold of his shirt, pulled him towards her and then kissed him hard on the mouth.

He tasted of warm red wine.

He frowned and took a step back. 'Woah. What are you doing?'

'I don't know,' Annie admitted, but she pulled him towards her again and this time he responded.

After a few seconds, Annie was turned on. She knew that after what had happened it was weird, but she didn't care. The gin, and kissing Stephen, had numbed the terrible pain that had gripped her insides all day.

'I'm going to need you to take me to bed, Stephen,' she whispered.

He was confused. 'I'm not sure that's a good idea.'

She gave him a withering roll of her eyes. 'Really? After everything we've been through?'

However fucked up it was, she just wanted him to make love to her. She wanted to get lost and to escape.

Reaching out, she grabbed his hand and led him out of the kitchen as they headed for the stairs.

Chapter 36

Taking off my reading glasses, I cleaned them and held them up to the light to check the lenses. My eyes were starting to sting with tiredness. It had gone midnight as I sat on the sofa in the living room with the laptop open. Jack lay asleep next to me, snoring softly. I reached over, took my second whiskey of the night and finished it. I wouldn't drink any more. I needed a clear head in the morning. It was going to be a long and challenging day.

Once I'd tucked Rachel up in our bed, I'd come downstairs. I needed to do some research in preparation for Annie and my journey to visit retired DCI Ian Goddard, and then to HMP Wakefield to talk to Keith Tatchell. I was attempting to read as many articles and background information as I could. As far as I could see, the MO of Megan's murder was exactly the same as the three women who had been murdered by Tatchell in North Wales in the late 90s. That meant that either someone had decided to copy his MO in some hideous copycat killing, or he was innocent of the murders and the same killer had struck again. As far as I remembered, the case against Tatchell was pretty tight. It had to be for the CPS to even consider going to trial for murder. But miscarriages of justice weren't unknown.

Back in 1990, three men were wrongly jailed for life for the murder of a 20-year-old woman, Lynette White, in Cardiff. The sentences were later ruled unsafe and quashed. In 2003, DNA was used to track down and eventually convict the actual killer, Jeffrey Gafoor, who later confessed to Lynette White's murder. The case had damaged the reputation of Welsh policing for years. I hated to admit it, but police officers made mistakes. And sometimes they were catastrophic.

After about half an hour of searching, an article from the *Daily Express* in 2002 caught my eye – *I was a key witness in Tatchell murders but never interviewed*. The article was about a woman called Evie Dalby who was angry that she had never been called as a witness for the prosecution, even though she maintained that she had been sexually assaulted and attacked by Keith Tatchell. The article went on to say that police had described her as 'an unreliable witness' but there were no details as to why. It was something to bear in mind for tomorrow.

And then, just as I was about to fall asleep and call it a day, an article in the *News of the World* appeared in my search.

Serial killer Tatchell had an accomplice who is still free, claims police officer.

The article was dated 2009. A detective constable, Sharon Hughes, who had worked on the Tatchell case made the claim once she had retired from North Wales Police. There was very little detail, just an allegation that evidence that Tatchell wasn't working alone had been ignored by senior officers. I did remember Sharon from her time on the force, although we were never friends.

Sadly, she died from cancer only a few years after she'd retired.

However, it did pose several questions. Why had evidence that Tatchell had not been working alone been ignored? And if he had been working with someone else, were they still out there? And had they been responsible for Megan's murder?

Is that why Dewi is so rattled by me visiting Tatchell? I wondered.

Chapter 37

Annie and I sat opposite retired Detective Chief Inspector Ian Goddard who was now in his 70s. His red hair and beard were now tinged silver-grey. He had a rash across the top of his hairline. Behind his thick glasses, his eyes were flecked green and brown, and his nose crinkled at the bridge where it had clearly been broken and badly reset. One of the perks of being a copper in the 1980s.

His living room was dark, and cluttered with books and magazines. The house smelled stale, like an old library.

I sipped at my piss-weak tea, tried not to pull a face, and then put the Wales Rugby mug back down on the only tiny space left on the messy coffee table. It wasn't the sort of table that required coasters anymore. From what I'd observed, my guess was that Goddard lived in the house on his own. There was nothing to suggest a wife or partner.

'Of course I remember you, Frank,' he said with a croaky voice as he scratched nervously at the end of his nostrils. Then he leaned forward, grabbed cigarette papers and tobacco, and started to roll a cigarette.

'Yeah, we were based at St Asaph together, weren't we?'

St Asaph was the Divisional Headquarters of North Wales Police.

'That nick was always bloody freezing,' he said, as he rolled the tobacco into a cigarette and licked the paper.

There was a moment of silence.

Goddard moved forward on his armchair and looked at Annie. His maroon-coloured cardigan was unbuttoned, and I could see his large stomach spilling over his belt.

'I'm sorry to hear the news about your sister,' he said in a distant tone as he lit the cigarette, took a drag, and then blew a plume of bluish smoke up towards the ceiling. A slice of daylight was revealed by the smoke as it drifted slowly upwards.

'You were the SIO on the Keith Tatchell case, weren't you Ian?' I asked in a friendly tone. I knew that he was, but I wanted to move the conversation on quickly.

'That's right,' he said, as he picked some tobacco flakes off his bottom lip and tongue.

I raised an eyebrow. 'Do you know why we're here?' I asked.

'Of course.' He sat back in his armchair and looked at Annie. 'I had a call from someone over at Barmouth nick detailing the circumstances of your sister's murder. Terrible. Then I saw it on the news.'

Annie pushed a strand of hair around her ear and nodded. 'As far as we know, it's exactly the same circumstances as the murders that Keith Tatchell committed in the late 90s.'

'Yeah, that's what I hear,' Goddard said, shaking his head almost as if talking to himself. 'Very strange. Very strange.'

He seemed to have drifted away into thought or a memory.

'And you were convinced that Tatchell committed those murders, weren't you?' I asked.

'Of course.' Goddard was instantly annoyed. 'There was no doubt in my mind or anyone else's. Tatchell was an evil bastard.'

Hit a bit of a nerve there, didn't I?

'Because as we see it,' Annie explained, 'either someone has decided to copy Tatchell, or the person who committed the murders all those years ago is still out there.'

'Let me stop you there, love,' Goddard snorted irritably. 'The person who committed those murders is tucked away safely in Wakefield prison. How else could you explain the murders stopping?'

I didn't like to point out there were documented cases of murderers leaving long gaps before they killed again.

I narrowed my eyes. 'But you must have looked at other suspects for the murders, Ian?'

'A couple,' he admitted defensively. He blinked as he dragged on his cigarette again. He clearly didn't want to discuss it.

'Go on,' I prompted him.

'We had Tatchell bang to rights.' Then he fixed me with an icy stare. 'It's a secure conviction, Frank. You don't need to start sticking your nose in this and stirring anything up.'

'Dewi Humphries worked on the investigation, didn't he? I asked, purposefully ignoring him.

'That's right,' he snapped with a frown. 'What's that got to do with anything?'

I shrugged. 'I was just checking.'

He's definitely rattled.

Maybe Goddard and Dewi were both paranoid that there was something wrong with the case against Tatchell. I didn't know. But Goddard's reaction had been decidedly shifty and suspicious. As had Dewi's, come to think of it. Neither of them would want their reputation damaged if there had been anything untoward in Tatchell's conviction.

'A newspaper article from a few years later mentions a woman called Evie Dalby,' I said, 'but from what I can see, she was never called as a witness for the prosecution. Is that right?'

Goddard let out an irritated sigh. 'Jesus ... Yes, that's right. We considered her an unreliable witness.'

Annie frowned. 'Why did you think Evie Dalby was an unreliable witness?'

'She was a hooker,' Goddard said with a dismissive snort. 'She reckoned that Tatchell and a mate of his had sexually assaulted her. I just thought that the defence counsel would make mincemeat of her, and it might just confuse the jury.'

A mate of his? That's interesting, I thought.

Goddard's breathing was laboured as he got increasingly agitated. His growing anger and tetchiness were a little suspicious. If the conviction against Tatchell was watertight, he didn't need to worry, did he?

'Look at it from my point of view, Ian,' Annie said in a conciliatory tone. 'My sister was brutally murdered in the same way as three women twenty-five years ago. It's only natural that I would wonder if the same person did it.'

'I suppose so,' he replied unconvincingly, 'but you're wrong.'

'What about this theory that Tatchell had an accomplice?' I asked.

'Nah, that was bollocks made up by some journalist to

sell newspapers years later.' Goddard shook his head adamantly. 'I gave no credence to it.'

'You're convinced that Tatchell was working alone?' I asked just to clarify.

He didn't answer me.

There was silence as he leaned forward and stubbed out his cigarette. He clearly wasn't happy.

'I've told you everything I know,' he sneered at us. 'Tatchell murdered those women. On his own.' He glanced over at Annie. 'And I'm sorry for what's happened to your sister. Believe me. It's a horrible thing to go through for you and your family. But you're looking in the wrong place for answers. My guess is that there's some crackpot out there who read up on the case and has decided to become some kind of copycat killer. It wouldn't be the first time.'

I glanced over at Annie. Goddard was hiding something from us. I just wasn't sure exactly what.

Chapter 38

Annie and I stood in the long queue to go through HMP Wakefield's security before we could meet with Keith Tatchell. We had spent half an hour sitting in the waiting area with the relatives of other prisoners. Annie had told me that she'd only managed to sleep for about three hours. What she had experienced the day before still haunted her. Then we watched small children playing in an area with toys, a slide and a ball pit. They were so innocent but I knew, despite their age, they'd be forced to go through strict security before meeting their fathers. It wasn't a good start in life. Annie and I talked about the ongoing cycle of crime and how difficult it was to break.

Eventually we'd been called to join the queue and we inched forward slowly. Having processed the conversation with Goddard, we hadn't got much further than to agree that he had clearly been hiding something from us. He had also been very agitated at the thought of anyone looking into the case against Tatchell. And so had Dewi.

'Do you think Goddard knew Tatchell from some-where?' Annie eventually asked.

'I don't know,' I admitted. 'Why do you say that?'

'His overwhelming conviction that Tatchell was guilty,' Annie replied. 'It felt personal maybe.'

'Maybe. Or Goddard doesn't want anyone tarnishing his reputation as a good detective,' I suggested. 'And of course Dewi worked the case too.'

'Which is why he's so pissed off with you.'

'Yes. That combined with him being a total prick,' I muttered.

As we shuffled forward again and then went through security, I began to wonder what Tatchell's motivation for meeting us was? He had maintained his innocence throughout his trial and after. That wasn't a surprise. Killers like Tatchell were both narcissists and fantasists. They rarely took any responsibility for what they had done. Interviews with Tatchell's previous partners had described him as very charming and funny to start with. But as those relationships developed, he became incredibly controlling, jealous and violent. It was a pattern of behaviour that he'd exhibited since he was a teenager.

We moved along and eventually were frisked and then instructed to walk through a metal detector.

Given Tatchell's profile, we'd been told that we would be meeting him in a separate room, away from the main prison visiting area. That was a relief, because in my experience the main room could be incredibly noisy with loud chatter, kids playing and babies crying.

Annie fidgeted nervously as we waited.

'I'm not quite sure what we're going to get out of this,' she said, which was a change of opinion. I wished she'd said that two hours ago and I would have gladly come to Wakefield on my own. Annie's head was all over the place.

'I think it would be useful to hear what Tatchell has to say about the murders and his trial. I did try to see if we could talk to his defence barrister, but he's retired and moved abroad.' I rubbed my beard. 'There are only two explanations for what happened to Megan. Either she was killed by the same man who carried out the murders in the late 90s and Tatchell was wrongly convicted. Or there is someone out there who was either Tatchell's accomplice at the time or someone who is now obsessed with him and copied what he did.'

'I know,' Annie agreed. 'And I know it sounds silly, but I feel guilty being two hours away from Megan and every-thing that's going on back in Wales. I feel like I should be back there with her. Not here talking to …' She didn't finish her sentence.

I nodded reassuringly. 'If you want to go back to the waiting area, I'm really happy to meet him on my own.'

'No.' She shook her head. 'I've come all this way. I want to see him and hear what he has to say.'

After about five minutes, Tatchell was led in by a prison officer.

'You've got fifteen minutes,' the officer said to us gruffly, and then he left.

Tatchell sat down. He was small in stature and height. His hair was dark brown and streaked with grey. Behind his glasses, his eyes were blue and cold. He was wearing the prison regulation grey sweatshirt and joggers, and navy Nike trainers.

'Thank you for meeting us today, Keith,' I said calmly.

He ignored me, wiped his mouth with the back of his hand, and stared directly at Annie. 'It was your sister who they found on that beach over in Barmouth yesterday. That's what the chaplain told me.'

Annie nodded but she was taken aback by his blunt-ness. 'Yes, that's right.'

'I'm sorry.' He sniffed and rubbed his thin nose. 'That's

terrible.' His accent was definitely North Wales, but he sounded educated and articulate. However, his words also felt hollow.

Silence.

He sat back in his seat and gave a deliberate, audible sigh. 'I wondered if he would ever start again. To be honest, I thought he must have died.'

I squinted at him. 'I assume you're referring to the man who you think murdered those women in the late 90s. The murders that you were convicted of?'

'Yes, of course.' He seemed to find my question faintly amusing. 'I know you've heard all this before but I'm completely innocent. They got the wrong man.'

'Ian Goddard doesn't seem to think so,' Annie said.

Tatchell raised an eyebrow. 'Oh, you've been to see him already, have you?' he sneered.

'We saw him this morning,' I explained.

'Jesus,' he said with a withering expression. 'You do know the history between me and Detective Chief Inspector Ian Goddard?'

Annie frowned. 'No.'

'No?' he said sarcastically. 'I'm pretty sure he didn't tell you about that.'

Tatchell now seemed agitated.

'Can you tell us what you mean?' I said.

'I had an affair with Maureen Goddard in 1995. DCI Goddard's wife. He found out, and made it his mission to fit me up for whatever crime he could. When these murders took place, he decided to put me in the frame for them. And bingo, here I am twenty-five years later.'

'But that would have come out at trial.' Annie frowned sceptically. 'Your defence counsel would have flagged this up as a huge conflict of interest.'

'There was no proof.' Tatchell shook his head. 'Maureen denied that the affair had ever taken place. So, it was my word against hers and DCI Goddard's. Who do you think the jury believed?'

'I haven't seen the trial papers,' Annie said, 'but there must have been significant evidence against you for you to have been convicted.'

'Oh, don't worry, there was,' he snorted ironically. 'My DNA ended up in one of the victim's cars. And the eyewitness who saw me with Linda Simmons on the night of her murder was very convincing.'

'Are you saying that you weren't with Linda Simmons that night?' I asked.

'Yes, I am.'

Annie looked at him with wary puzzlement. 'Did you know Linda Simmons?'

Tatchell shrugged. 'Yes. We'd been out a few times the year before, but nothing serious. I hadn't seen her since then.

'What about Christine O'Malley?'

'The "eyewitness" that saw me with Linda that night,' Tatchell said, using his fingers to give the word eyewitness ironic speech marks. 'I've no idea why she went on the stand to give that evidence, but she was wrong.'

I watched Tatchell for a few seconds. He seemed incredibly calm in what he was telling us. As if he was resigned to his unswerving belief that he was innocent.

'What can you tell us about Evie Dalby?' I then asked.

'Evie Dalby?' Tatchell gave an ironic laugh. 'Not my finest hour, I grant you. But it certainly doesn't make me a serial killer.'

Annie leaned forward. 'Can you tell us what happened?'

'I'd been drinking all day with a mate of mine. And,

for some reason, we decided that we wanted the services of what I've always called 'a lady of the night'.'

'A prostitute?'

'Yes, a prostitute. We went to my mate's house. I'm not really sure what happened, but Evie got very angry and left. I think there was an argument about money. The next thing I knew, I'd been questioned about a sexual assault.'

'But that wasn't true?' Annie asked.

'God, no,' Tatchell replied adamantly. 'We didn't know what she was talking about.'

'And who was your friend?' I asked.

The question seemed to throw Tatchell off guard just for a moment. Then he regained his composure. 'I'm afraid I can't tell you that. He has a very responsible job. Anyway, the charges were eventually dropped.'

There was something about this question that seemed to have unsettled Tatchell.

I pressed on. 'There were stories in the press that suggested you had an accomplice when you committed the murders. What did you think about that?'

Tatchell raised an eyebrow sardonically. 'An accomplice to the murders that I didn't commit?' He seemed faintly amused. 'I didn't really give it a second thought. It wasn't me.' Then he shrugged. 'I know you've come a long way, but I'm not sure what else I can tell you. Because I wasn't there.

Chapter 39

'What did you think?' Annie asked as we pulled out of the busy prison car park.

'What did I think?' I scratched my head and drove the pick-up out onto the main road. 'I think that if I had been interviewing Tatchell as a serving officer in CID, I would have believed most of what he told us.'

'Really?' Annie was confused. 'He gave me the creeps.'

'I'm just going on my gut instinct, but there were a few times where he let his guard down and I began to doubt what he was saying.'

'He definitely didn't like talking about this incident with Evie Dalby. He seemed to clam up a bit and looked uncomfortable.'

'Yes, I noticed that. I found him difficult to read so maybe I'm off.'

Annie shook her head. 'You should know, Frank. You've interviewed your fair share of murderers.'

'In my limited experience, psychopaths are incredibly hard to get a handle on. But if you watch carefully, you can see where the joins are, if you see what I mean?'

'Yes, I do. I've seen a few men like that in my court over the years,' Annie said, but I could see that she had then drifted away. No doubt the grief of what had happened to Meg had overwhelmed her again.

As I followed the signs to the motorway, we sat in a comfortable silence as I allowed Annie just to feel or think whatever she needed to. I saw her wipe away the tears from her face and then pull down the vanity mirror on the back of the sun visor to check her make-up.

She looked over at me. Fragile and lost. 'Do I have eyes like a panda now my mascara has run?' she asked.

I shook my head. 'No. Not at all,' I reassured her.

'You're a good liar, Frank.' She laughed as she dabbed her face with a tissue. 'I'd like to know who Tatchell was with when this alleged assault on Evie Dalby took place.'

'Yeah, that did seem to touch a nerve.'

'A responsible job?' Annie said. 'I wonder what he meant by that?'

'If Evie Dalby reported it, it will still be on file some-where, even if charges were dropped. Maybe we can go and talk to her if she's still alive.'

'I think that would be a good idea,' Annie said with an affirmative nod. Then she glanced over at me again and sniffed. 'I'm all right now I've had a bit of a cry. It just seems to blindside me.'

'It's fine. You don't need to explain any of it to me. There's no right or wrong way, is there?'

'No,' she agreed. 'Maybe we should see if we can talk to Maureen Goddard, or whatever her name is now.'

'Might be difficult to track her down. And she may not want to rake up the past.'

Annie shrugged. 'Has to be worth a try though?'

'Yes. We can definitely try.'

'Thank you,' Annie said gratefully. Then she had a

thought. 'Actually, there's someone I think can help us. And he owes me a few favours to say the least.'

'Okay,' I said, none the wiser. 'Where are we going?'

'Corwen,' she said. 'His name is Ethan Cole.'

I furrowed my brow quizzically.

'He was the son of an old friend, but he was a bit wayward so I took him under my wing for a while. He was a bit of a whizz at computers and programming so I encouraged him to do a degree. He ended up with a first in computer science from Manchester. I'll give him a call and tell him we're on our way.'

Chapter 40

As we entered Corwen, I slowed down the truck and stopped at some traffic lights.

I turned to Annie. 'I'm wondering what a young man with a first class degree in computer science from Manchester is doing in Corwen?'

'Ethan's dad died when he was young, and his mum's not well,' she explained. He's now her carer. You wouldn't believe the change in him. When he was in his late teens, I was convinced that he was going to spend most of his life in prison.'

'I guess he must be pretty grateful that you helped him turn his life around?'

'Not always as grateful as you'd think.' Then she laughed. 'But he's a good kid.'

We parked in the centre of Corwen, a market town in Denbighshire which stood on the banks of the River Dee and beneath the Berwyn mountains. It was ten miles west of Llangollen. The town was also known for its connections with Owain Glyndwr, the last crowned Prince of Wales, who led a Welsh rebellion against the English in the early 1400s from a manor house in the area. In the centre of the town was a huge sculpture of him sitting astride a horse.

Getting out of the pick-up, I noticed that the air had become noticeably chilly. I was also stiff from the long journey back from Wakefield, so I stretched out my back and gave a satisfied groan.

'Better?' Annie asked with a bemused smirk.

'Hey,' I protested at her teasing. 'I've just spent the best part of two hours in that bloody truck.'

'Well buy something more comfortable to drive. I've lost all the feeling in my bum and lower back.'

'Rachel has been telling me to get a better car for years,' I said with a tinge of sadness. She hadn't been out in the truck with me for over six months, and now never mentioned the possibility of us buying a nice SUV that she'd always wanted.

Annie pointed to a nearby sandwich shop. 'He's above there.'

Going to a red front door to the side of the shop, Annie pressed the buzzer and Ethan let us in.

We went up the carpeted stairs and saw Ethan giving us a big toothy grin from a door at the top. He was mixed race, with short dreadlocks, hoodie, long basketball-style shorts, white sports socks pulled up, and Adidas slides.

'Hey,' he said with a serious expression as he embraced Annie. 'I'm so sorry about your sister. It's horrible.'

'Thank you, Ethan,' Annie said with a benign smile.

'I saw it on the news,' he said, shaking his head. 'Anything. Just ask.'

Annie nodded. 'Much appreciated.'

'Come in, come in,' he said enthusiastically.

'This is my friend, Frank.'

Ethan shook my hand a little too firmly. 'Hey, man.'

The flat was far neater and more stylishly decorated than I had imagined from the outside. There were a couple of framed, signed basketball shirts up on the wall. Ethan ran various accounts in the cloud for legal firms. Annie didn't really understand what that entailed but she knew that he earned good money from it.

'How's your mum?' she asked, pointing to a closed bedroom door.

Ethan shook his head. 'Not great. She would have loved to have seen you but she's out of it on pain medication.'

'Send my regards, will you?' Annie said as we followed him along the landing.

'Yeah, of course … This is where the magic happens,' Ethan explained in his slightly manic manner as he opened the door to a large room that had a multitude of monitors, keyboards, hard drives and laptops.

We all sat down around the main desk, and Ethan turned his chair quickly round to face a large monitor.

'What are we looking for?' he asked, glancing back at Annie.

'Maureen Goddard,' she said. 'I'm guessing that she lived in North Wales in the mid-90s. Probably aged between 30 and 45 at that time. So, that puts her in her 60s or early 70s now.'

'So, she's old then?'

'Hey,' Annie protested with an amused expression. It was nice to see her without the haunted look that she'd worn since seeing Meg on the beach the previous day, even if it was only for a couple of minutes.

'Kidding, obviously,' Ethan said with a laugh, and then went to work on the computer, typing furiously and using his mouse to click on various sites. It was hard to follow what he was doing or how he was making decisions about what to do next. But my computer skills were basic.

'Anything?' Annie asked after about a minute.

'Yeah. Got it.' Ethan pointed to the screen. 'Maureen Elizabeth Goodwin. Born Rhos On Sea, April 16th, 1957. Married Ian Goddard, June 12th 1979. Deceased December 5th 2021, Wrexham Maelor Hospital.'

'Deceased?' Annie couldn't hide her disappointment.

'Yeah, I'm afraid so,' he said with a shrug. 'I'm guessing you wanted to talk to her?'

Annie nodded. 'Can you find out what her last address was?'

'Maybe,' he said, as he started to type again. 'Electoral register has her at 23 Hope Road, Bala.'

Annie scribbled down the address. 'Thanks.'

'Is that it?' he asked.

I leaned forward. 'At the risk of pushing our luck, can I give you another name to work your magic on, Ethan?'

'Of course. No problem. Fire away.'

'Evie Dalby. I'm guessing the same sort of age and living in North Wales too.'

'Actually, I'd try Evelyn Dalby,' Annie suggested. 'Given the age and when she would have been born.'

'Yeah. Evelyn,' I agreed.

There was about a minute as Ethan tapped away at the keyboard frantically. Then he turned and gave us a thumbs up. 'Good news, guys. I've got an Evelyn Dalby, born in Barmouth in 1965. And from what I can see, she's alive and well and living just down the road in Maerdy.'

Annie and I exchanged a look. It seemed that we were going to Maerdy.

Chapter 41

Annie reached forward and knocked on the door. We had found the small, detached cottage in Maerdy, a small hamlet on the outskirts of Corwen. It was the address that Ethan had given us for Evie or Evelyn Dalby. I had no idea if she would talk to us given the nature of what had happened and how long ago it had been.

After a few seconds, the door opened slowly and an attractive woman in her late 50s peered out. She had auburn hair that fell in curled tresses around her shoulders, pale skin, blue eyes and fashionable glasses. She had the appearance of an actress, or possibly someone who had once been a model rather than a former prostitute.

'Evelyn Dalby?' Annie asked in a gentle voice.

'Oh God, Evelyn?' she snorted in an amused tone. 'Evie.' Then she gave us a quizzical look. 'You're not Jehovah's Witnesses, are you?'

'No, no,' I reassured her. 'Nothing like that.'

'We'd like to talk to you about something that happened to you about thirty years ago,' Annie explained.

Evie immediately seemed suspicious 'Really?'

I gestured to the front door that she was partially standing behind. 'If we could come in for a few minutes? We think you might be able to help us.'

She frowned, as if she suddenly realised what we might be talking about. Then she shook her head. 'Sorry, I don't make a habit of letting strangers into my house. And I have no interest in talking to you about something that happened thirty years ago.'

As she went to shut the door, I put my foot in the way.

'You need to move your foot before I call the bloody police,' she growled as she glared at me.

'Please,' Annie said in a pleading tone.

'Move your bloody foot!' she yelled at me as she slammed the door against my toes.

'My sister was found murdered on Barmouth beach yesterday. I'm sure you've seen it on the news or read about it. I think you might be able to help us find out who killed her.'

Evie stopped for a second. Then she let go of the door and furrowed her brow. 'I don't see how I could possibly do that,' she said dismissively.

'Please,' Annie said, looking directly at her.

Silence.

Evie wasn't convinced but she opened the door and beckoned us in. 'I'll listen to what you have to say. But I'm going out in ten minutes, and I can't be late.'

———

HAVING FILLED Evie in with some of the background detail, Annie and I now sat on a sofa across from her. The room was light and airy with white curtains, cream carpet, and framed posters advertising art exhibitions on the walls.

'I still don't know how I fit into any of this,' she said, her eyebrows raised in question.

I leaned forward. 'We understand that you were attacked by Keith Tatchell and a friend of his in the mid-90s.'

'I was sexually assaulted. They tried to strangle and rape me, but I managed to get away,' she corrected me. 'I think they would have killed me that night. And then when I saw the news about that monster in the papers a year later, I knew that they would have murdered me.'

I gave Evie an empathetic look. 'I'm so sorry.'

'I've tried to lock it away,' Evie admitted with a sigh.

Annie moved a strand of hair from her face and asked, 'But you were never called to appear at Tatchell's trial?'

'No. I thought I would be. Two detectives came to see me and took another statement after he had been arrested.'

'Why do you think you weren't called?'

'Why do you think?' she said sharply. 'I was a brass. A hooker. No one was interested in what I had to say. As far as the coppers were concerned, I was asking for anything that happened to me.'

'Did the detectives say anything else?' I asked. I was starting to formulate a hypothesis as to why Evie hadn't been called to give evidence. And it wasn't anything to do with her being a prostitute.

'The older one, Goddard, I think his name was …'

'Yes, that's right.'

'Anyway, he appeared to be very annoyed by the fact that there had been two of them. It seemed that it was very inconvenient that I'd been attacked by Tatchell <u>and</u> his mate.' She paused for a moment. 'I actually wondered if that was why I wasn't called to be a witness. Because my testimony didn't fit in with what Goddard wanted the jury to hear.'

Which tallied exactly with what I'd suspected before we arrived.

'Can you remember anything about the other detective who came with Goddard?' I asked.

'He was young. Black hair, smart suit.'

'DC Humphries?' I suggested. It sounded like Dewi when I'd worked with him.

'Could have been,' she said with a shrug.

Annie narrowed her eyes. 'And is there anything you can remember about this man that was with Tatchell?'

'He was a nasty bastard. Worse than Tatchell. Proper evil. He seemed to get off watching me in pain.'

'Do you remember his name?' I asked.

'Sam,' she said uncertainly.

'Sam?' I asked to clarify.

'Sam … or maybe Simon.'

I peered over at her. 'What else can you tell us about this man?'

'He was not bad looking, to be honest. And he absolutely reeked of aftershave. Like he'd had a bloody bath in it.'

'Can you remember anything that this man and Tatchell were talking about before they attacked you?'

Evie puffed out her cheeks and let out a long breath. 'Christ, it was a long time ago.'

'Even if you think it's not relevant, it might help us,' Annie said gently.

She thought for a second. 'They did have a funny little thing they kept saying to each other and then laughing. They said, *It's all right. He's on the square.* I guess they meant they were honest or something. It was just weird.'

On the square? I had no idea what that meant except that they were 'on the level'.

'Anything else?' I asked, continuing to probe.

'And this other one was talking about all the different places in the world he'd flown to. He said that was his job.'

I frowned. 'His job?'

'Yeah, that's what he said. I assumed that he was a pilot. He had that sort of air about him. All cocky. If his job was flying all over the world, I assumed he was a pilot.'

I immediately glanced at Annie. We were both thinking the same thing.

Simon Bentley. The man who lived next door to Megan's caravan.

Chapter 42

Even though Annie and I immediately wanted to go and talk to Simon Bentley again, we were driving through Bala, so it made sense to stop at Maureen Goddard's last known address before she died.

We soon found 23 Hope Street which was just off Bala High Street and opposite a children's playground and a car park.

Annie knocked at the door and a woman in her 40s answered. She had her dark red hair pulled back in a ponytail and wore large glasses. She had a pen in her hand and seemed lost in thought. Then she gave us a quizzical frown.

'Hi there,' Annie said. 'I wonder if you can help. We think that this was the address for a Maureen Goddard?'

The woman squinted at us. 'That was her married name. She was Maureen Goodwin for the last twenty years of her life,' she said suspiciously.

'Are you her daughter?' I asked.

The woman nodded warily. 'Can I ask why you want to know?'

'And is Ian your father?'

She snorted. 'In name only.' Then she furrowed her brow and seemed annoyed. 'What's all this about? If he owes you money …'

'No, it's nothing like that,' Annie assured her. 'We spoke to your father earlier today.'

'Good for you. I have nothing to do with him.'

Whatever had happened between them, she really didn't like her father.

Annie narrowed her eyes and said, 'And we also spoke to Keith Tatchell.'

The woman was shocked. She instantly held up her hand. 'Woah. Whatever you want, I'm not interested. Are you journalists?'

She moved defensively behind the door. If we weren't careful, she was going to slam it in our faces.

'Do we look like journalists?' Annie asked gently.

'Retired journalists then?' the woman conceded.

Charming, I thought sardonically.

'No,' Annie said in a quiet voice.

'Right, well I'm very busy so I'm going to close the door now,' she said sharply.

'It was my sister who was found murdered on Barmouth Beach yesterday. And we thought that your mother might have been able to help us with a few things,' Annie said. 'I'm trying to find out who killed my sister.'

'Aren't the police doing that?' she asked.

Annie's eyes registered a flicker of pain. 'I just want to find out what happened to her.'

The woman blinked as her manner had softened. 'I'm really sorry, but I still don't know what I or my mother have to do with this.'

There was an awkward silence. She was clearly debating whether or not to let us inside.

Then she gestured. 'Come in.'

'Thank you,' Annie said quietly.

Nice one.

We went inside the small hallway that smelled of wet dogs.

'I'm Daisy. Maureen was my mum, but she died from Covid a couple of years ago,' she explained.

'I'm so sorry to hear that,' I said compassionately.

'Thank you … I don't understand why you thought Mum could help you.'

'There were many similarities between the murder of my sister and the murders of the women who Keith Tatchell was convicted of,' Annie explained.

'What?' Daisy seemed confused. 'I don't understand.'

'Neither do we,' I said gently, 'but Tatchell claims that he had an affair with your mum in the mid-90s and that your father held a grudge against him.'

There was a long silence as Daisy seemed to gather her thoughts. She was visibly upset. My statement had clearly touched a nerve.

'Sorry,' she said, her voice choking. 'I haven't thought about all that for a long time.' Then she peered at us. 'Yes, Mum did have an affair with him.'

Okay, that's interesting.

'And your father found out?' I said, keen to keep this line of questioning going.

Daisy nodded. 'They tried to put it behind them, but they got divorced a few years later.'

I looked at her quizzically. 'But your father was the senior investigating officer on the Keith Tatchell case. It would have been a huge conflict of interest.'

Daisy shrugged. 'Dad said it wasn't relevant. I know that Keith Tatchell tried to use his affair with Mum as some kind of defence, but she denied it and said he was lying.'

I took a few seconds to process what Daisy had said. Tatchell had been telling us the truth. Did that mean that the case against him wasn't watertight? Or were his allegations that Ian Goddard had planted evidence to 'fit him up' valid? *Jesus.* Had we just stumbled on a terrible miscarriage of justice?

'Thank you for talking to us, Daisy,' Annie said with a kind expression. 'I can see that it's brought back some painful memories.'

'It's fine,' Daisy reassured her. 'I can't imagine what you're going through. It's horrific.'

'It is,' Annie admitted. 'Thank you.'

As we turned to go, I thought about the whole accomplice theory that I'd read about. I looked at Daisy. 'Just one thing before we go. Did your mum ever mention if Keith Tatchell had a friend, a man, that she ever met?'

Daisy shook her head. 'Not that I remember.'

She opened the front door for us to go out but then something occurred to her. 'Actually, we once bumped into Keith Tatchell in a supermarket. It was about six months before he was arrested. My mum was dead embarrassed. And he was with a man who I assumed was his friend.'

'Do you remember anything about him?' Annie asked.

'Not really. Except that he was wearing very strong aftershave. I remember my mum saying that he always did, and that she found it made her feel a bit sick. And then we laughed. But that's all I remember I'm afraid.'

'Okay,' Annie said. 'Thanks again.'

As we went towards the front door, Daisy stopped. 'There is something,' she said thoughtfully. 'I don't know if it's going to be any use though.'

'Anything,' Annie said. 'Please.'

'Mum had kept all her diaries in a box going way back. Sometimes it was no more than a doctor's appointment or a holiday. But sometimes she wrote a few lines about her day. I've read through them a bit and I didn't see anything out of the ordinary, but you're welcome to have a look if you think it might help. To be honest, I keep thinking I should throw them away, but I can't seem to bring myself to do it.'

'If we could borrow them, that would be very useful,' I said.

Daisy pointed to the stairs. 'They're up in the attic.'

I gestured. 'I'll give you a hand.'

Chapter 43

It was nearly dark by the time we started to drive away from Bala and towards Snowdonia. The sky above us was sauntering from the soft apricot of day to the shimmering purple and dark indigo of night. The sight of an aeroplane above drew my eyes skyward. The thin white line of its water vapour drew a neat line that dissected the lightening sky in a diagonal shape. It was heading west. I wondered where it was going. Either Ireland, or the next stop after that, which was the east coast of North America. It made me think momentarily of Simon Bentley.

'Do we think that Simon Bentley is this friend of Tatchell's?' Annie said after a few minutes of pensive silence.

'I don't know, but you just read my thoughts.' I tried to process all that we'd learned in the past few hours. 'Bentley fits the age profile. We know that he used to be a pilot, but there must be a few retired pilots living in North Wales.'

'But he has the caravan next to Meg's,' Annie pointed out.

'I know, but it's still a bit of a stretch.'

'Is it?' she asked, frowning. 'If we assume that Tatchell's friend was a pilot, it seems a huge coincidence that a retired pilot was living next to Meg when she went missing. And that she was murdered in that way.'

'True,' I conceded. 'There's one way of shaking this up to see what falls out.'

'What do you mean?'

'We just go and ask Bentley if he knew Tatchell. See how he reacts.'

Annie nodded, but she was worried. 'That seems very direct.'

'You look concerned.'

'It's just that this is all happening so fast. I'm trying to get my head around it. Yesterday I wondered if Callum had something to do with Meg's death.'

'What do you think now?'

She shook her head. 'Callum might be very selfish, but I don't think he's capable of doing that to his own mother.'

'My instinct is that we're on the right track here. I really do think that Tatchell had an accomplice. And Bentley definitely needs looking at.'

'Yes,' Annie agreed, and then stared out of the car window. 'I think you're right.' Then she turned to me and said, 'On the square?'

I frowned. I didn't know what she meant.

'That's what Evie Dalby said. Tatchell and his mate kept saying to each other. He's all right. He's on the square,' Annie recalled as if it was significant.

'Yes,' I agreed, still none the wiser.

'It's a Masonic term. My father was a mason and he used it to mean that someone else was also a mason. It's like code. Tatchell and his friend were masons.'

Then I looked at Annie. 'I don't know if this is significant, but so were Ian Goddard and Dewi.'

'What?'

'The North Wales Police had their own Masonic Lodge in St Asaph. They asked me to join in the 90s when I was there. I told them where they could stick it. But it seems a strange coincidence.'

.

Chapter 44

The Vale Caravan Park was in virtual darkness by the time we pulled in and parked up. There were no lights on in Bentley's caravan. Maybe he was out. That would be frustrating.

I got out of the truck and glanced up. The moon had been covered by a thin, wispy smudge of clouds. Over to our right, inky black clouds lay like a dark blanket over the mountains of Snowdonia. I let the cold icy air blow over my face to refresh me. The driving and pace of the day was starting to take its toll. Gone were the days where I could survive on three to four hours of sleep while working a major investigation.

As the headlights of my truck turned themselves off automatically after a few seconds, the caravan park was plunged into shadowy darkness. The only sound was the distant barking of a dog, and the wind rattling around the creaking wooden shells of the nearby caravans.

It was an eerie place at this time of year.

I took a flashlight from my pocket and turned it on.

'No lights on. And no car. I think he's out,' Annie said, gesturing to Bentley's caravan.

'Yeah.' I shrugged. 'But let's go and have a look anyway shall we?'

Annie looked at me suspiciously. 'Frank?'

'What?' I said innocently as we approached the caravan.

I could see that Annie was now staring at Meg's empty caravan next door which was also in total darkness.

'You okay?' I asked her in a virtual whisper.

She nodded. 'It's just that this is the first time I've been back here since … you know. Since Meg was found.'

I gave her an empathetic nod as we arrived at Bentley's caravan. The temperature had dropped quickly and every inch of my exposed skin was cold. My feet had started to numb a little despite my socks and boots.

I walked up the three wooden steps onto the decked veranda of Bentley's caravan. The wind came again, moving the wood panels so that they gave an uncomfortable creak. Someone nearby was burning coal, and the air was now thick with the smell.

Annie joined me and we went to the front door. I gave it a decent knock.

We stood there waiting, knowing that Bentley wasn't inside.

Nothing. No sound at all now.

I shared a look with Annie who gave a shrug as if to say we already knew that he wasn't in.

I reached into my pocket and pulled out a small black case. Inside were several lock-picking tools.

Annie raised her brows. 'We're not going to break in, are we?'

I pulled a face. 'Now that we're here, it seems a shame not to have a look around.'

She gave a withering sigh. 'You're going to get us arrested.'

I shook my head as I pulled out the tools. 'We'll be in and out in a few minutes. Trust me.'

Annie gave a little groan as I went to work.

Thirty seconds later the door to the caravan was open.

We went inside, using my flashlight and Annie's phone torch to light our way.

As we'd seen on our previous visit to the caravan, it was very neat and tidy inside.

I spotted the framed photographs of the aeroplanes on the wall again.

'What are we even looking for, Frank?' Annie whispered.

'I'm not sure until I see it,' I admitted.

Using my flashlight, I went over to a table in the living area and peered at some paperwork. There didn't seem to be anything of interest. Bank statements, savings accounts, mobile phone bills. An MOT certificate.

What I did notice was a strong smell of aftershave in the air.

'You smell that?' Annie asked.

I nodded. 'Aftershave.'

Wearing strong aftershave didn't make Bentley a killer, but it certainly fitted Evie Dalby and Daisy Goodwin's recollection of the man with Tatchell.

Working my way around, I got to the bookcase that stretched from the floor to the low ceiling. I ran my light over the spines of the books. There was a small sculpture, no bigger than my fist, of two people having sex.

'Frank?' Annie whispered.

I turned around but I couldn't see her.

'Where are you?' I asked, as I shone the light around.

She appeared, waved her phone torch at me and then beckoned for me to follow.

Leaving the living area of the caravan, I manoeuvred around furniture and then followed Annie to where I assumed the bedroom was located. It was almost the identical layout to Meg's caravan if memory served me right.

'Down here,' Annie said. 'You need to come and see this.'

As I entered the large bedroom to the rear of the caravan, I saw that she had opened the doors to the built-in wardrobe. She used her light to gesture to what was inside.

Hanging up were some smart shirts, suits and polo shirts.

Then there was a gap on the rail, followed by what appeared to be a rubber suit, and a leather garment that was covered in chains and straps. Over to the left, a small shelf with some white linen gloves.

'Kinky,' I said.

'It's more than kinky,' Annie said quietly. She then shone the torch to the bottom of the wardrobe where there were four masks made from latex and leather. 'It's plain weird.'

Suddenly there was the noise of an approaching vehicle, and then the whole caravan was flooded by the glare from headlights.

'Shit!' I hissed under my breath as I moved back towards the front of the caravan, across the living space and carefully glanced out of the window.

Bentley had parked his car outside and was helping a rather drunk middle-aged woman out of the passenger door. She gave a cackling giggle as she put her arms around him and gave him a kiss.

There was no way that Annie and I could leave via the front door.

Moving swiftly back towards the bedroom, I saw Annie peering at me nervously.

'It's Bentley,' I explained quietly. 'He's got a woman with him.'

Annie's eyes widened. 'What are we going to do?'

'There's a back door from the kitchen, isn't there?' I said, remembering the layout of Meg's caravan.

We heard the noise of Bentley opening the front door, and then drunken laughter.

'Here we go. Home sweet home,' Bentley boomed as he snapped on the lights. Even though he'd been driving, he sounded very drunk.

Shit! We both froze and glanced at each other.

I gestured to the kitchen, and very slowly we turned to make our way out of the bedroom.

'What can I get you to drink?' Bentley asked. 'I've got some white wine chilling in the fridge.'

'Oooh, check you out, Simon. A right charmer,' the woman laughed. 'That would be lovely.'

Realising that Bentley would now be heading to the kitchen, Annie and I backed up as quietly as we could, went into the bedroom, and hid behind the flimsy door.

Hearing Bentley's footsteps, I held my breath.

Annie looked at me in sheer panic.

Suddenly, the light in the bedroom came on.

Shit, he's coming in here!

My pulse was racing as I froze, and we made ourselves as small as we could behind the door.

Bentley bounded in, grabbed a bottle of aftershave, sprayed himself, then bounded out and turned off the light.

Jesus, that was close.

I listened intently as he gave a cheery whistle and busied himself in the kitchen getting some drinks.

'Put some music on if you want,' he called out.

'Okay,' the woman shouted back.

I gave Annie a knowing nod. Music would be good, and the louder the better. Once Bentley was back in the living area and preoccupied with his guest, we could make our way out with the music covering any sound that we might make in the process.

The plinky strings of *Perhaps Perhaps Perhaps* by *Doris Day* started to blast from the front of the caravan.

Through the crack in the bedroom door, I saw Bentley walk past with two large glasses of white wine.

After a few seconds, I gave Annie a nod.

Moving slowly, we went out of the bedroom and crept down towards the kitchen.

My heart was now pounding against my chest.

Reaching for the handle to the back door, I turned it slowly so as to make as little noise as possible, although *Doris Day* was providing us with a decent amount of cover.

Pushing the door, I felt it stop.

It's locked. Shit.

There was no key in the door.

Annie's anxiety seemed as if it had gone through the roof as she went to search for a key.

I pulled out my lock-picking tools and went to work. My hands were now a little shaky.

'Have you got any ice?' the woman said loudly above the music. 'I like to have ice with my white wine.'

Bentley laughed. 'Very sophisticated! I think I've got some in the fridge.'

Jesus.

We had a matter of seconds before he entered the kitchen again.

I twisted the small tool to release the lock.

Nothing.

Come on, come on.

I tried it again.

It clicked.

Grabbing the handle of the door, I twisted it, opened the door and we scuttled outside onto the decking.

As I went to close the door behind us, the wind caught it and it slammed shut with a bang.

I pushed Annie back against the wood panels of the caravan so we were flat against the wall.

The back door opened and Bentley peered out.

'Hello? Is anyone there?' he asked, sounding confused.

Silence.

'Hello?' he called again.

I held my breath.

Silence.

Then I heard the door close and lock.

Putting my hand on Annie's shoulder, I gestured for us to go across the decking to the rear of the caravan and down the wooden steps to the grass below.

As we approached my truck, I looked at Annie and pulled a face. 'Sorry.'

'Bloody hell, Frank. I've got heart arrhythmia,' she said breathlessly. 'That nearly killed me.'

Chapter 45

Annie was bone tired as she finished her plate of fresh filled pasta with grated parmesan that Stephen had made her. Her mind was still racing after her and Frank's narrow escape from Bentley's caravan.

'That was delicious,' she said distantly as she sat back and drained the last of the wine.

'No problem,' Stephen said with a little theatrical bow. Then he pointed to her empty glass. 'You want a top up?'

Annie shook her head and put her hand over her glass. It was strange and slightly awkward that they were playing at being a normal couple. As far as she was concerned, last night had been a one-off. A pity shag or mercy shag, or whatever you wanted to call it. It didn't change the years of infidelity and bad behaviour.

'I'm fine thanks.' Then she gestured to the stairs. 'I think I'm going to head up.'

Stephen gave her an expectant look as if to ask if she wanted 'company'.

'Listen,' she said gently. 'We haven't talked about what happened between us last night.'

He raised an eyebrow. 'Do we need to talk about it?'

Oh my God, he actually thinks that last night has suddenly solved all our problems. He's so deluded.

'It was what I needed last night, but I don't know if it meant anything. My head is just all over the place at the moment,' she admitted. 'But I do appreciate you being here for me.'

'Of course,' he said with an understanding nod. 'I know we've had our differences over the years. And I know that my behaviour has been far from exemplary, but I can't imagine what you're going through at the moment. So, if you need anything, anything at all, you just let me know, okay?'

'Thank you.' Annie got up from the dining table and went to take the plates.

'Leave those,' he said. 'Just go upstairs and get some sleep. In the nicest possible way, you look tired.'

'It's been a long day,' she sighed.

As she walked out into the hallway, she took the small box of diaries that Daisy Goodwin had given her.

She thought she would read through them up in bed until she fell asleep.

Stephen came out of the dining room holding the plates and gave her a quizzical frown. 'I was wondering what those were? They look like diaries.'

'They are.'

He frowned. 'Whose are they?'

'I don't have the energy to explain,' she sighed. 'I'll tell you in the morning if that's okay?'

'Of course,' he said. 'No problem.'

Annie headed for the stairs carrying the box and went up.

Chapter 46

'You look exhausted, Dad,' Caitlin said. 'Do you want a beer? I saw some in the fridge.'

'That would be great.'

She got up and wandered away towards the kitchen.

Glancing at my watch, I saw that it had gone ten. Rachel was sleeping peacefully in her armchair. I'd put a blanket over her and taken off her reading glasses. Sam sat watching a film on his phone with his headphones on. The flickering light from his phone was cast up onto his face. It was past his bedtime but I was just glad to have him here. The last few days had been chaotic for him, so routine could wait.

I'd put on a few small lamps which gave the living room a shadowy cosiness. I'd also lit an open fire that now cast a lovely orange glow, and the heat that it was throwing out was making me sleepy.

My mind went back to mine and Annie's escape from Bentley's caravan. Was Bentley really Tatchell's 'mystery' accomplice? He fitted Evie Dalby and Daisy Goodwin's recollection. He was handsome for his age, wore strong aftershave, and had been a pilot who had flown around the world. He had a strong interest in S&M. He lived on his own in the caravan next to Megan's. The police needed to take another look at him as soon as possible.

Picking up my phone, I noticed the pink post-it stuck inside that had *TAP 134 3A* written on it. I still had no idea what it meant or if it was relevant. I made a mental note to give it some thought in the morning when I had more energy.

I scrolled through my phone to check for messages. Nothing. It was more out of habit than believing there would be any. My social circle was very small to non-existent these days. I'd always been a bit of a loner and happy in my own company. A couple of male friends had moved south to be closer to their family. A couple had died. Annie was the only true friend I had now. But that was fine.

'Here you go,' Caitlin said, handing me a cold San Miguel and pulling me away from wading into self-pity.

'Well, it's been a long day. I'm bloody exhausted,' I groaned. 'Lechyd Da.'

'Lechyd Da,' Caitlin said as she raised her beer and flopped down on the other end of the long sofa from Sam.

'I'm not sure you should be gallivanting around the country, Dad. Can't you let the police get on with doing their job?'

I didn't say anything for a few seconds. 'We're just looking at something that might help catch whoever did this to Annie's sister.'

Her eyes searched my face. 'And why can't the police do that?'

'They don't think that what we're looking at is a valid line of enquiry.'

'Why not?'

'Why not?' I said quietly, as I scratched my beard and

then took a long swig of beer. 'That's a very good question. The original senior investigating officer was compromised when building a case against Keith Tatchell.'

Caitlin was shocked. 'You mean Tatchell didn't do it?'

'I'm not sure yet, but there are enough doubts for us to keep digging around. We're looking at the theory that he might not have been acting alone all those years ago.'

'That's a bit creepy,' Caitlin said with a little shudder. 'That means that person is still out there.'

'Possibly,' I replied.

'Won't you get into trouble doing all this digging around? You're retired.' Caitlin then gave me a suspicious frown. 'Unless you kept your badge?'

I gave a dry laugh. 'Don't worry, I didn't keep my badge. But yes, we might get into trouble. But given what's happened …'

'I'm no expert,' she said, as she sat forward on the sofa and sipped her beer, 'but why didn't the police suspect that there was more than one killer all those years ago?

'The police ignored the testimony of a woman who was attacked by Tatchell and another man but she managed to escape.'

'What? Why would they ignore that?'

'Two reasons. She was a sex worker,' I explained.

'What, so she doesn't count?' Caitlin asked angrily.

I shrugged. 'Those murders took place twenty-five years ago. It was a different world back then.'

'That's true,' she said emphatically.

'I also believe that the SIO had a vendetta against Tatchell because he slept with his wife. And that SIO didn't want this woman's testimony to interfere with the case they had against Tatchell as a lone killer. If it had come out that there was a suggestion that he wasn't working alone, it would have weakened the case against him. His defence could have argued that the murders had been carried out by this accomplice, and even that Tatchell had been coerced into being there.'

'Jesus, Dad,' Caitlin said with a sigh. 'Do you know who this other person might be?'

'We've got an idea, but nothing concrete yet.'

We sat in a comfortable silence for a while, and then Caitlin reached for the remote control and pressed a button.

Beetlebum by *Blur* began to play quietly on the Bluetooth speaker.

I smiled over at her.

'You remember this?' she asked with a grin.

'Of course.' I laughed. 'How could I forget this? You and James played this album to death on that holiday to Menorca.'

'You said that you liked this song because it sounded just like The Beatles.'

'It does,' I said. 'Or it could have come off Lennon's early solo albums.'

'When was that holiday?' Caitlin asked with a frown.

'1997?' I suggested.

She nodded. 'Sounds about right.'

'Great holiday,' I said as I thought back to Rachel, Caitlin, James and I splashing around in the communal pool, reading books, and going out for dinner in the evenings.

Caitlin chortled. 'We were the Fab Four.'

'We were,' I said. I was overwhelmed as I thought back. 'You take all that for granted, don't you? You think that there will be countless more holidays like that. But those moments are just more precious than you ever think they are.'

Silence.

'I really miss him,' Caitlin said, looking teary.

'So do I,' I whispered as a lump came to my throat.

We listened to the music for a while.

Caitlin then smiled. 'I'd never seen Mum as happy as she was on that holiday.'

'Except when she found out that calamari was fried squid,' I joked.

Caitlin roared with laughter at the thought of it. 'She went mental. She'd nearly finished a whole plate of it before you told her.'

'I know. And she blamed me for not telling her sooner.'

Caitlin shook her head and smiled. 'I'd like to take Sam away somewhere nice.'

'Has he ever been abroad?'

'No, never. We've never had the money.'

'We'll go,' I said quietly. 'When all this has settled down, we'll take him away somewhere. You've both been through a lot.'

'Yeah, that would be nice, Dad.' She gave me a lovely smile, then pointed towards the kitchen. 'Got any cheese?'

'Yes.'

'Welsh rarebit?'

'Perfect,' I sighed with a smile.

As Caitlin hurried off to the kitchen, I stood up and made my way over to the large bookshelves on the other side of the room.

I ran my forefinger over a line of books. Everything from the classics, such as Dickens and the Brontes, to chick lit and biographies. I remembered I had an old book on Freemasonry from decades ago. I wanted to have a look at it.

There it is.

My eyes paused on the spine of the book – *The Brother-hood* by *Stephen Knight*. It was an expose of Freemasonry from the 1980s. I vaguely remembered reading it. As a police officer, I'd always frowned upon the shady relationship between the police, especially the London Met, and Freemasons.

Given Annie's recollection that *on the square* was a masonic term, I pulled out the book. The cover featured two hands shaking. An image of the infamous *Masonic handshake.* The hands in the photograph were both wearing white linen gloves.

Jesus. White linen gloves!

My pulse quickened. Bentley had a pair of white linen gloves in his wardrobe.

I reached for my phone and dialled Annie's number.

'Hello Frank?' she said, sounding tired. 'Everything okay?'

'Bentley is a mason,' I blurted out.

'What?'

'He's got a pair of white masonic gloves in his wardrobe.'

Chapter 47

There was loud knocking on the front door of our farmhouse. It startled me as I sat bolt upright and took in my surroundings. I'd fallen asleep on the sofa in the living room and the television was still on. I took a breath and then stood up feeling disorientated.

There was another knock at the door. It sounded urgent. My instant thought was of Caitlin and Sam.

Breaking into a slow jog, I headed to the door, aware that my legs weren't working fully and that I was still half asleep.

I opened the door and saw Dewi was standing on the doorstep. It was hammering down with rain. His raincoat was glistening wet and his hair slightly matted.

'This isn't a social call, Frank,' he said with a serious expression.

I gave him an ironic smile. 'I didn't think it was. Is this about our trip to Wakefield?'

He frowned. 'You went to see Tatchell?'

I shrugged. I wondered if it was the right time to tell him all that we'd found out about Simon Bentley. As far as

Annie and I could see, the masonic link was significant. If Dewi and Ian Goddard had bothered to interview Evie Dalby twenty-five years ago, that would have been vital evidence. Did Goddard and Dewi's membership of the St Asaph Masonic Lodge prevent me from revealing this evidence? Possibly.

Before I could decide what to divulge, Dewi gave me a dark look. 'It's not about that. We've finally found Megan's car.'

'Okay,' I said. I couldn't work out why he was wearing such a severe expression on his face. 'Where was it?'

'It was abandoned in a field close to Llanfachreth.'

Llanfachreth was a tiny hamlet about three miles north of Dolgellau.

'Someone poured petrol inside the car and tried to torch it,' Dewi said. 'They must have left the scene before the fire took hold because it didn't catch.'

'Any idea why the car was abandoned over there?' I asked.

'At first, I thought it might have been stolen by kids,' he replied. 'We get a few of those around here, as you know. Teenagers stealing cars, dumping them and setting them on fire.'

I gave him a dubious look. 'Why don't you think it was kids?'

'I got a call from traffic a few hours ago. They got an ANPR hit on the registration plate. Megan's car was recorded at the traffic lights a mile outside Dolgellau going north on the A470.'

'When was this?'

'The day before Annie reported her missing.'

My stomach tightened. 'I don't suppose you've got any idea who was driving the car?'

Dewi gave a sigh as he tapped on his phone and turned

to show me the screen. 'Megan's car stopped at those traffic lights and there's a CCTV traffic camera there. You can clearly see who's driving her car.'

The CCTV image clearly showed a man sitting in the driver's seat.

It was Callum.

Chapter 48

Having napped on top of the bed for a while, Annie had stirred to find she was still fully clothed. For a second or two, she tried to remember why she was lying on the bed. And in those blissful milliseconds, she was completely unaware of anything that had happened in the previous few days. And then it came thundering back to her like an express train that took her breath away. Her beautiful sister had been murdered and left on a beach. The horrific image of her face under the white forensic tent was imprinted on her mind and would be there forever. For whatever reason, Annie had needed to see her sister at that moment. She needed to know how she had been in the final few seconds of her life, however horrific and traumatic that might be.

Annie sat up and let her legs and feet dangle over the side of the bed. But then the overwhelming pain of grief and loss swept through her. Burying her head in her hands, she sobbed uncontrollably. After about a minute, she tried to get her breath back. She wiped her face with the palms of her hands and sniffed. Then she blew out her cheeks.

The outpouring of grief had left her utterly exhausted and breathless.

Padding across the thick carpet in her bare feet, she went into the en suite bathroom and peered at her reflection. Her eye make-up had run – again. She splashed her face with cold water and wondered when the pain of her loss would end. Or at least become more manageable.

She then gazed at her reflection again in the mirror. The deep crow's feet around her eyes that had just crept up on her over the years. The saggy skin around her neck. She had friends who had paid for 'work' to be done, but that wasn't Annie's style. She wanted to look the age that she was. It seemed ridiculous to try and reverse the ageing process. And some of those friends just looked like they'd had Botox, fillers, lifts or tucks.

She took off her make-up, cleansed and moisturised her face, and cleaned and flossed her teeth. Her mind then turned to the events of the day, and Frank's late phone call about Bentley being a mason. She had taken a cursory glance at some of Maureen Goddard or Goodwin's diaries. Her daughter Daisy had been right. Most of them had proved to be no more than appointment reminders. School term dates, doctors, dentists etc.

Popping on her pyjamas and a thin dressing gown with a Japanese print on it, Annie went out of the bathroom and back over to the bed. She felt refreshed. Her sobbing seemed to have purged the grief from her for the meantime.

Sitting and thinking, she took the diary from 1995. As she turned each page carefully, she saw the initials KT written with a ? beside a date – 13th February. She assumed that KT stood for Keith Tatchell, and wondered if that was the date when Maureen's affair with Tatchell had started. The initials KT were written in several more times. Then on June 6th, she had written *KT to Brighton.*

Her phone buzzed next to her on the bed.

It was Frank.

It was 1.08am which meant that whatever he needed to talk to her about, it was important. And that made her feel anxious.

'Hello?' she said cautiously.

'Hi Annie,' he said in a calm but serious tone.

'Hi Frank.'

'I've just had Dewi here. They've found Meg's car abandoned in a field close to Llanfachreth.'

'Llanfachreth?' Annie didn't understand. 'Did someone steal it? Or was it …' Then her voice trailed off. Was it taken and dumped by the person who had murdered Meg?

'They've got CCTV of someone driving the car the day before you reported her as missing. They were driving the car out of Dolgellau and heading north towards Llanfachreth.'

'Okay,' Annie said, sounding uneasy. It was as if Frank was hiding something from her.

Silence.

'It was Callum driving the car, Annie. I'm really sorry.'

Chapter 49

Annie and I approached the small remote lane in Llanfachreth. We didn't need satnav to find it, as the dark rainy sky was lit with the flashing blue strobes of two police patrol cars that blocked the narrow road where the field was located. The rain continued to hammer on the roof of my pick-up as we slowed – a fierce, relentless drumbeat.

Annie had been insistent that we travel over to where Megan's car had been found. I had explained that we might not be allowed anywhere near as it was now a crime scene. But she was determined, and I'd seen how forceful she could be when we had visited the beach that day over at Barmouth.

Annie had spent the journey turning over the idea that her nephew Callum was responsible for Meg's murder. It didn't make any sense. And it didn't explain the similarities with the Tatchell murders of the 1990s. Had Callum really murdered his own mother using the same method as a serial killer from twenty-five years ago? Annie just couldn't believe it. Or she didn't want to believe that he was capable of such a thing. I wasn't sure, but I was keeping my counsel. It seemed wise to wait and see what the police and SOCO team found in the abandoned car. Although it seemed highly unlikely, Callum driving Meg's car, dumping it and then trying to set it alight might not be related to her death. My dark instinct was that it was too much of a coincidence for the two not to be connected, but I still had a nagging doubt too. I'd been convinced that Simon Bentley was our 'prime suspect'.

I pulled the truck over to the side of the road and up onto the muddy grass verge. As we got out, I pulled my baseball cap low over my head as the rain slapped noisily against the metal of my truck and the road surface. Annie unfolded a large golfing umbrella and held it over her head.

As we made our way down the road towards the police cordon, there was a deep rumble of thunder that sounded like it was pretty close. The wind picked up a little and blew the icy rain into my face. I wiped it from my eyelashes and blinked.

A young female police officer was standing by the blue and white police evidence tape which flapped noisily in the wind.

'Hi there,' I said, squinting at the officer through the pelting rain. 'We're here to see DCI Humphries. Frank Marshal and Annie Taylor.'

She glanced down at the clipboard and nodded. 'Yes, DCI Humphries asked me to look out for you.'

Annie gave me a look as if to say 'I told you so'.

The officer pointed to a large, rusty iron gate that was open and clearly led to the field where the car had been found. 'He's just in that field there.'

There was the sudden juddering noise of a portable generator's engine, and the air became almost instantly thick with diesel fumes.

As Annie and I came off the road and into the field, we saw that the SOCO team had erected huge halogen arc lights over Meg's car. There were about half a dozen SOCOs in full white forensic suits, hats, masks and rubber boots making a forensic examination of the car, which had all four of its doors open and its hatchback up in the air.

'Do you want to stand under this?' Annie asked, gesturing to her umbrella. 'You're getting soaked.'

'There's nothing getting through this,' I said, pointing to my Berghaus climbing waterproof, 'but thank you.'

Two figures approached and came out of the haze.

It was Dewi and Kelly.

'Annie,' Dewi said over the noise of the generator's engine. 'I suspected you'd want to be here when we were examining the car.'

'I do,' she said. 'So thank you for letting us know.'

'No doubt Frank's told you that we've got CCTV of Callum driving this car the day before you reported your sister missing?' Kelly asked gently.

Annie nodded with a sombre expression. 'It doesn't mean that he killed her though does it?'

'No, it doesn't,' Kelly agreed.

Dewi raised an eyebrow. 'But I'm afraid it is very suspicious.'

He sounds certain already.

Dewi was more fidgety than usual. He scratched at his nose.

Is it pure coincidence that as Annie and I circled in on Simon Bentley, this evidence against Callum appeared?

My eye was drawn to some activity over by the boot of the car. A SOCO was leaning inside the back of the car and using a torch to look at something.

'DCI Humphries?' one of the SOCOs called over.

'Better go and see what they've found,' Dewi said as he turned and walked towards the car.

Annie shot me a concerned look.

A few seconds later, the SOCO held up a clear plastic evidence bag for Dewi to inspect.

Using a torch, he peered at whatever was inside very carefully. Kelly walked over to join him.

'What is it?' Annie whispered anxiously to me. 'What have they found?'

I patted her arm. 'I'll go and find out.'

'Please,' she said. Her breathing was quick and shallow.

'I'll be back in a minute,' I reassured her.

Cowering from the rain, I made my way across the muddy field, and for a second my boot slipped and I nearly lost my balance.

Steadying myself, I saw Dewi glance over at me suspiciously. He was deep in conversation with who appeared to be the chief forensic officer.

Once Dewi had finished, he and Kelly walked towards me.

'What is it?' I asked, gesturing to the boot of the car.

'A hammer.' Dewi then looked directly at me. 'It's got blood stains on it.' He looked almost relieved.

'Obviously we'll do all the tests, but it could be the weapon that was used to attack Megan,' Kelly pointed out.

Dewi shrugged. 'It fits the profile of the weapon that Professor Wilkins and the forensic team suspected was used.'

Callum just left the hammer in the boot of Megan's car?

'Jesus,' I said under my breath, hiding my growing instinct that something wasn't right.

As I turned to walk back to Annie, who was staring over at me quizzically, there was another raised voice.

'DCI Humphries?' called the same SOCO as before. 'You need to see this, sir.'

I turned back. The SOCO team had found something else in the car boot and it sounded like it was significant.

Dewi went back over and started to have an animated conversation with the team again.

I glanced back at Annie. She looked so lost and vulnerable standing on her own, the rain thrashing down on her umbrella as she waited for answers to what had happened to her sister. It brought out every protective instinct in my body. I wanted to shield her from the discovery of the hammer and whatever else had been found. Despite my uncertainly, the idea that Megan might have been brutally murdered by her own son – Annie's nephew – was just going to compound the misery and pain.

'Frank?' said a voice.

It was Kelly approaching again.

'It's not good news for Annie, I'm afraid,' she said with a dark expression.

'Why? What is it?' I asked.

'There was a length of piano wire hidden under the spare tyre in the boot.'

That seems convenient, doesn't it?

'As you can imagine, this means that we are going to have to arrest Callum on suspicion of Megan's murder,' she announced. 'Whether or not he has some form of amnesia is neither here nor there, I'm afraid.'

'Yes, I understand.' Then I looked at her. 'Are you going to arrest him right away?'

She nodded and shrugged. 'I don't think we have any choice. Unless his doctors advise us against it.'

Then I glanced at Annie. 'You think we could follow you to the hospital when you go to pick him up? Annie's looked after him most of his life, so whatever he's done, she'll feel that she should be there.'

'No problem. I'll give you the heads up when we're leaving here.'

'Thank you, Kelly,' I said gratefully, and then I made my way back over to Annie.

As I approached, her eyes widened in fear.

'What is it?' she asked in a terrified voice.

'I'm so sorry,' I said, as I put a comforting hand on her shoulder.

Chapter 50

Annie and I drove towards Glan Clwyd Hospital in silence. I didn't know what to say to ease her pain at what we had discovered. Even though I had the heater on to almost full blast, the steering wheel felt cold under the palms of my hands.

I glanced over at Annie. She sat shivering a little, even though she was now wearing the extra puffer jacket that I kept in the cab of the truck. She had turned the collar up, and her hands were hidden inside the big sleeves as if she were a child. She sat still, silent, remote and lost. Her chin tilted upwards, with her eyes locked on the big moon that dominated the night sky. She hadn't shed any tears since we'd started driving.

'I wonder if she's up there looking down,' she said very quietly.

'I think she is,' I said, and then took a moment. 'I've always consoled myself that we go somewhere afterwards.'

Annie nodded. 'I want to ask her what the hell happened to her. If only she could answer me. I want to ask her, 'Who did this to you, Meg?' She looked over at me. 'Isn't that strange?'

'Not really,' I reassured her. 'She's the one person who could give us the answers we're looking for.'

Annie sighed and then furrowed her brow. 'Do you really think Callum could have done this?' she asked in bewilderment, almost as if she was talking to herself.

'I wish I could give you an answer to that, but I don't know him.'

'I do … It doesn't make any sense to me,' she said as her eyes filled with tears. 'Maybe if there had been a fight and some kind of accident. But this is so cold and evil. I just can't get my head around Callum doing that to her and then taking her to the beach like that.'

Silence.

'But the evidence is overwhelming, isn't it?' she asked, as if seeking confirmation.

I took a few moments to respond.

'It is,' I said uncertainly as I ran my hand over the surface of my beard.

Annie looked over at me. 'What? It feels like there's a 'but' coming, Frank?' she said searchingly.

She was right. There was a 'but'.

'My gut instinct is that it's all too neat.'

'How you do you mean?'

'The police believe that Callum drove Megan's car up to the field, put the hammer and wire he'd used to kill her in the boot, and tried to torch the car but failed. Now they've got him bang to rights.' Even as I said the words, it sounded implausible.

'And you're wondering why would he take that risk? Why be that careless?'

'Exactly,' I agreed. 'The hammer and wire are metallic. There's no guarantee that they'd be destroyed in a fire.

Why would Callum just leave them there? He could have buried them in the middle of nowhere or thrown them into a river or a lake.'

'Which means that you think someone else might have put them there?'

'Maybe,' I said. 'I can't be certain. But it feels too easy, too simple, doesn't it?'

'It does. But who would plant evidence?'

'I just don't know.'

'I really thought we were on to something with Simon Bentley,' she said softly. 'Or at least that Tatchell had some kind of accomplice working with him.'

'So did I.'

'What can we do?' Annie said anxiously.

I sighed. 'I don't think there's anything we can do tonight.'

'But they're going to arrest Callum for Megan's murder.'

'He'll be on remand for months. If there's something suspicious, we'll find it. I promise you.' Then I glanced over at her. 'But I also need to point out that I might have got this wrong. If Callum was drunk or high … I just don't know.'

Annie nodded to show she understood there were no easy answers. She stared out of the passenger door window.

For the next twenty minutes we drove in virtual silence. Small talk and chatter just didn't feel appropriate. We were going to the hospital where Annie's nephew was about to be arrested and charged with his mother's murder. Things didn't really get bleaker than that.

Taking the turning to the hospital, I slowed as we pulled into the vast car park. Given that it was now the early hours of the morning, it was almost empty.

As we parked close to the main entrance, I spotted Dewi, Kelly and two uniformed officers getting out of their cars.

I turned off the ignition and then looked at Annie.

'Are you going to be all right doing this?'

She nodded. 'He's not going to understand what the hell is going on, is he?'

'No, not if he still has amnesia.'

'And that means he's going to be terrified.' Annie sighed. 'Isn't it awful? Despite what Callum might have done, there's still a little part of me that just wants to protect him.'

I gave her an understanding nod. 'He's your nephew. You've known him since he was a baby. It's instinctive to want to protect him.'

We got out of the truck and then wandered across the car park to where Dewi and the other officers were waiting.

Dewi was on the phone. He furrowed his brow as he looked at the other officers. 'Anyone heard from PC Brannigan?'

There was a collective shake of heads.

'That's weird,' he said, looking up at the hospital building. 'He's not answering his phone.'

I assumed that Dewi was referring to the uniformed police officer who had been assigned to protect Callum while he was still in hospital.

'Piss break, coffee?' one of the other officers suggested.

Dewi put his phone away and rolled his eyes. 'More likely the vending machine.' He then looked at me. 'PC Brannigan is, as my mother used to politely say, no stranger to a fish supper.'

The officers chortled at the implication that PC Brannigan was fairly overweight, but soon stopped as they realised that this wasn't appropriate given Annie's presence.

'At the moment, Callum doesn't even recognise me,' Annie said to Dewi and Kelly, 'so he's not going to understand what's going on when you arrest him.'

Kelly lightly touched Annie's forearm. 'We'll do our best to keep his arrest calm and civil. But I do fear that he might need to be restrained.'

The quiet of the car park was broken by the sound of shouting. I couldn't work out where it was coming from.

I scanned the car park carefully.

Nothing.

Then more shouting.

Who the hell is that?

As the shouting became more urgent, Dewi and the officers exchanged concerned looks.

The voices were echoing, as if the shouts were coming from high up.

My eyes were drawn upwards toward the higher floors of the hospital building.

Suddenly, breaking glass exploded on the road about twenty yards away from us with.

The noise made everyone jump.

What the …!

'Jesus Christ!' Dewi cried.

'What's going on?' Annie asked me nervously.

'No idea.'

Taking a few steps backwards, I glanced up. It looked as if the glass had fallen from above us. Maybe a window had been smashed.

Then there was a terrifying scream.

My eyes locked on to something falling from one of the windows.

It was a person.

Bloody hell!

Before I could react, the person hit the road in the same place as where the glass had fallen and smashed.

There was a sickening noise as the body bounced off the road and then twisted over.

'Oh my God!' Annie screamed.

I joined Dewi, Kelly and the other officers and we raced over.

Even though the man's face was streaked with blood, I instantly recognised him.

It was Callum.

Glancing up, I saw someone looking out from where he had fallen.

A person wearing a black balaclava peered out before quickly disappearing back inside.

Without thinking, I sprinted towards the automatic double doors at the hospital entrance. I wasn't going to let him get away.

The doors opened and I raced into the hospital lobby. It was empty.

Looking around, I saw a nurse waiting for the lifts to my left.

A killer in a balaclava wasn't going to risk using a lift to make his escape.

Looking to my right, I saw the door for the staircase to the fire escape.

Callum's room had been on the second floor.

Swinging open the fire exit door, I stopped and listened.

Nothing. No footsteps. Silence.

I started to mount the stairs two at a time but I was out of breath by the time I got to the first floor.

Jesus. I was panting.

I stopped again and listened.

Nothing.

I climbed the next flight at a slower pace.

The door to the second floor came into view.

I tensed as I moved cautiously towards it.

Suddenly, it flew open and hit me full against my shoulder and body.

It knocked the wind out of my sails.

I lost my balance and fell to the floor.

Looking up, I saw the balaclavered man take a step towards me.

Then he kicked at me.

Instinctively, I put my arms up to block him, and his foot smashed into my forearms.

I winced in agony as I tried to scramble to my feet.

Protecting my head with my arms, I steadied myself for him to attack me again.

But he didn't.

Turning, I saw that he was now standing still and aiming a Glock 17 handgun at my head.

Oh shit!

My heart was thundering against my chest.

I stared into his eyes that were visible through the black fabric of his balaclava. He looked almost amused.

'Bloody hell, grandad, you're starting to piss me right off,' he snorted. It was the same voice as the man I'd seen getting into the lift two days earlier. A member of Finn's gang.

I wasn't about to stand there and let myself get shot in the head.

'I normally draw the line at shooting pensioners, but I'll make an exception for you,' he said with a cocky smirk.

I put my hands up to signal my defeat, but in the split second that he was distracted I leapt forward.

Grabbing the wrist of the hand that was holding the

gun, I pushed him backwards.

BANG!

The gun went off.

I felt the bullet zip past my ear.

Jesus that was close!

Still holding his wrist, we wrestled each other towards the banisters.

He swung a punch that hit my jaw.

I saw stars but kept my grip on his wrist.

Kneeing him in the stomach, I smashed his arm on top of the hand rail.

The Glock 17 flew out of his hand and fell down the stairwell with a metallic clang.

'For fuck's sake!' he growled, as he threw me back and punched me again.

Staggering back in a daze, I felt his gloved hands around my throat.

He pushed me back against the wall, squeezing my windpipe.

I couldn't breathe. I was trying to suck in air.

He had me in an iron-like grip.

I was starting to lose consciousness.

Don't pass out or he'll kill you.

With every ounce of strength that I had left, I stamped down on his instep.

'Jesus!' he gasped, letting go of my throat.

There was shouting and footsteps echoing up the stairwell.

'Frank?' yelled a voice.

Sounds like back up, I thought as I took a series of deep breaths.

The balaclavered man looked anxiously over the banisters.

Then he looked over at the door leading back onto the

second floor.

'Out of my way,' he snarled.

I shook my head defiantly. 'No chance.'

Without hesitation, he charged at me, slamming me back into the door with a shoulder-barge.

I fell backwards through the door. It winded me.

The man sprinted away down the corridor.

The adrenaline was pumping.

I cleared my head and took off after him.

From outside, I could hear the wail of sirens.

A nurse screamed as the man knocked her flying as he ran.

He then disappeared around a corner at the end of the corridor.

My lungs were burning with the effort of running.

I pushed on, ignoring the pain, pumping my arms as I ran.

As I turned the corner, I saw that the corridor was eerily quiet and empty.

Where the hell did he go?

Gasping for air, I looked around.

I saw a door to my right with a sign that read *Radiography*.

Pulling down the handle, I opened the door slowly.

Inside was a small office, a desk, chair and computer monitor.

Beyond that, a room that had what looked like an x-ray machine.

Is he in here?

Moving forward warily, I made my way through the office, listening intently for the sound of any movement.

I stepped into the empty x-ray room.

Nothing.

My pulse was thumping in my eardrum.

I scanned the room.

Out of the corner of my eye, I spotted a dark shape standing behind the light blue curtain on a rail to the side of the x-ray machine.

I glanced around nervously, looking for some kind of weapon.

I couldn't see anything.

He then stepped from behind the curtain.

I locked eyes with him for a moment.

He had that stupid cocky smirk again.

'End of the road for you I'm afraid grandad,' he said.

Then I saw that he was holding a large hunting knife.

Shit.

I took a step backwards.

He moved quickly towards me, jabbing with the knife.

As I turned and stepped back into the small office, I felt a hot, piercing pain in my back just above my hip.

He'd stabbed me.

I staggered as I clasped my back and felt dizzy.

The man shoved me to the floor. 'Get out of my fucking way.'

He left through the door.

I collapsed to the floor.

Putting my shaky hand to my side where I'd been stabbed, I saw that there was a lot of blood on my fingers.

Jesus. This isn't good.

I tried to pull myself across the floor towards the door. I'd lost the use of my legs.

If I could drag myself out into the corridor, someone was bound to find me.

My head was starting to swim as I pushed my palms against the cold floor.

My vision started to blur.

Then everything went dark.

Chapter 51

I blinked and then opened my eyes fully. I could hear some kind of monitor beeping and the sound of talking and movement. Then I remembered that I'd been stabbed.

As I tried to sit up, I got a piercing pain in my side.

'You're a bloody idiot, you know that,' growled a voice.

I glanced over to my right.

It was Caitlin shaking her head at me. 'I love you Dad, but you're a bloody idiot.'

'Hi Caitlin,' I groaned as I sat up. 'Nice to see you too.'

I surveyed the room. There were three beds opposite with other patients.

There was a canula coming from my left arm, and then linked up to a bag of blood plasma.

'How did I get here?' I asked Caitlin, trying to piece everything together.

'The radiographer found you unconscious in her office. If she hadn't, you'd probably have bled to death.'

'Oh right,' I mumbled as I propped myself up on a thin pillow.

'Oh right?' she repeated indignantly. 'I would have

been without a father. Sam would have lost his Taid. And what about Mum? You're seventy, Dad! I've told you already, you can't go gallivanting around like you're John Bloody Wayne.'

'Okay, I get it.' I held up my hand to acknowledge her concern. 'I actually prefer Clint Bloody Eastwood,' I quipped.

'It's not funny, Dad,' she snapped. 'I've been worried sick.'

'I know.' I sighed. 'How long have I been in here?'

'Three hours.'

'Where's Annie?'

'She rang to tell me what had occurred. I can't believe that happened to her nephew. It's all over the news.'

'Yeah, it was horrific.' I thought back to watching Callum's body falling and landing close to where I'd been standing.

Caitlin raised an eyebrow. 'Do you really think he killed his mother?'

I took a breath. 'I don't know. The evidence seems to suggest that.'

'But you're not convinced?'

'No. I'm not sure that I am.'

Before we could continue, a young male doctor approached.

'Mr Marshal, how are you feeling?' he asked, as he took the clipboard from the end of my bed and looked at the notes.

'Good. Fine. Ready to go home,' I said as brightly as I could. I pointed to the blood plasma. 'Once that's finished.'

The doctor gave me a quizzical look. 'Yeah, I'm not sure that going home today is a good idea.'

Caitlin looked at the doctor. 'It's all right. I've already lectured him about being an idiot.'

The doctor chuckled.

'Do I really have to stay here overnight?' I groaned.

'Given your age and the amount of blood you lost, yes. I'd like to keep you in overnight for observation.'

My age? Why does that still surprise me?

Caitlin gave me a sarcastic smile. 'It's okay, doctor, he's not going anywhere.'

Chapter 52

Annie was sitting at a table in a meeting room on the ground floor of Dolgellau nick. Opposite her was Dewi, Kelly and Superintendent Lisa Colwill, the highest ranking officer in the area. She was in her 50s, with short greying hair, dark eyes and a small, slightly turned up nose. She was dressed in her formal black uniform.

It had been nearly thirty-six hours since Callum had been thrown from the window of his hospital room by an unknown assailant. There was no doubt in anyone's mind that it was a hit organised by Finn as revenge for Callum stealing his drugs. There was no way that a man like Finn would allow someone to do that without serious consequences.

'Obviously you've seen the press coverage of what happened to Callum,' Colwill said quietly.

Annie nodded, but she had done her best to avoid looking at newspapers, the television or news online. It was too much for her to bear after Megan's death.

'I want to assure you that there will be a full inquiry

and that we have turned the matter over to the IOPC,' Colwill said.

'What about the original Keith Tatchell investigation?' Annie asked.

Colwill nodded. 'Yes. They will be looking at that again.'

The Independent Office for Police Conduct was a non-departmental body in England and Wales responsible for handling complaints made against police forces or individual officers. In cases like this, a force could call in the IOPC to investigate to ensure there was full transparency about an incident.

Annie glanced over at Dewi to see his reaction. If her and Frank's suspicions were true about DCI Ian Goddard and Dewi cutting corners in the original Tatchell investigation, then Dewi would lose his job or even face criminal charges.

Dewi was stony faced and avoided her stare.

'How is PC Brannigan doing?' Annie asked. PC Brannigan had been knocked unconscious while outside Callum's room.

'Severe concussion,' Kelly replied, 'but as far as we know, no lasting damage.'

'Thank goodness,' Annie said.

Colwill leaned forward and looked at her. 'It's very difficult to know what to say to you after everything that has happened in the past week. I can't imagine what you're going through. But I can assure you that I will personally oversee any inquiry.'

'What about my sister's murder?' Annie asked, her voice faltering a little.

Colwill looked over at Dewi, indicating that he should respond.

'As you know, we found significant evidence in Megan's

car when it was discovered at Llanfachreth.' He took a folder that was in front of him, then opened it and turned it to show Annie. 'Plus, when we looked through some of Callum's possessions, we found these.'

There was a photo of various items. A book entitled *In Cold Blood – the true story of the Keith Tatchell murders.* There were also other true crime books on Dennis Nilsen, Peter Sutcliffe and Harold Shipman.

Annie took a visible breath as she looked at the photo. She was shocked.

'We think that Callum already had an unhealthy interest in serial killers,' Dewi told her. 'For some reason, he made a decision to kill your sister. We will never know why, but my belief is that it was to get the money from the deposit that Megan had paid on the caravan they lived in. According to the toxicology report, Callum had crack cocaine in his system, so I'm assuming that he had become addicted to that drug. He needed money to fund his habit.' Dewi pointed to the photo of the books. 'He decided to copy and mimic the murders that were carried out by Keith Tatchell in the 1990s.'

Annie looked despondent and shook her head. 'Why?'

'Maybe he thought that it would remove any suspicion that he'd been involved in Megan's death,' Dewi suggested. 'He must have known that he would be a suspect. But he calculated that if a copycat serial killer had attacked and murdered Megan, that would remove any suspicion from him.'

Annie could see the warped logic, but she was still finding it difficult to come to terms with. She bit at her lip and then looked over at Colwill and Dewi. 'I know that all the evidence points to my nephew. But I just can't believe he'd kill her and go to all those lengths for £2,500.'

Dewi gave Annie an empathetic look. 'You were a

High Court Judge. You've seen what addiction can drive people to.'

Annie knew that what Dewi was saying was true. She'd seen addicts who would sell their own children just to get more heroin or crack cocaine. And she'd presided over the trials of alcoholics who had committed murder in a blackout, only to wake up in a cell with no memory of what they'd done.

Annie sighed. 'It's just so hard to accept when it's your own family.'

'Of course it is,' Colwill said gently.

Then Annie thought of all the investigating that she and Frank had done in recent days. And their conviction that Simon Bentley was somehow mixed up in Meg's murder. They'd got that all so wrong. Wasted so much time.

'And I assume that you will now work with the CPS and the relevant judge to come to a verdict on my sister and nephew's deaths?' Annie asked.

'Yes,' Dewi replied. 'I'm afraid it's going to be a fairly protracted process, but I don't need to tell you that. We will keep you informed every step of the way.'

Annie nodded. 'Thank you.'

One week later

Annie and I arrived early at St Mary's Church in Dolgellau for Megan's memorial service. The church was a Grade II listed building that stood on the site of the original medieval church that dated back to 1254. The only part of the 13th century building that still remained was the font.

Annie wanted to visit the graves of her *nain* and *taid* who were buried at St Mary's to lay some flowers. She told me stories of how when she and Megan were little they had helped her *nain* make jam. They had secretly eaten so much that it had made them both sick.

Crouching down by her *nain's* headstone, Annie swiped away leaves and some dead flowers before laying down the irises that she had brought with her. They had been her *nain's* favourite flower.

'Look at that,' she said quietly. 'She was born in 1904. Such a long time ago.' Then she looked up at me. 'We all end up here, don't we?'

'We certainly do,' I replied. 'It comes to us all. I find that acknowledging my mortality is actually liberating. I have a running clock so I don't want to waste a single day.

And I want to cherish the things that are important. Not worry about the things that aren't.'

Annie gave a contemplative look. 'That sounds very wise. It makes me think about me and Stephen and how much of our lives we've wasted being unhappy.'

'Maybe it's time for a change.'

'Maybe it is,' she agreed as she stood up from where she'd been crouching. 'I don't want to be lying on my death bed regretting anything.'

'No,' I said with a wry smile. 'It might be too late by then.'

We began to make our way across the graveyard towards the entrance to the church.

For a few seconds, I slowed and savoured the stillness of the afternoon. The spectre of Megan and Callum's deaths still hung over everything like a dark cloud. But the memorial service was the first tiny step forward to finding some kind of peace, and a way through all the pain and grief.

The autumnal air was heavy with the earthy smells of fallen, decaying leaves and wet soil. A wood pigeon's call echoed in the distance. It sounded urgent, anxious even. As we continued down through the graveyard, I looked at the faded grey monuments and the fallen headstones now covered in green moss and yellow lichen.

The church was over to our left. Ivy had covered a lot of the lower part of the flank wall. The sky above us was bright blue and empty of clouds.

We finally joined the gravel footpath and followed it to the corner of the church itself.

Outside the entrance, dozens of mourners dressed in black had assembled. Some were talking quietly in huddles. Others were filing inside in subdued solemnity.

I looked at Annie. 'Shall we go in?' I asked.

She nodded. 'Yes.' Then she looked at me. 'Can you sit at the front with me?'

'Of course.'

Chapter 54

Annie stood on the gravel at the back of the garden to the rear of her house. She had found an old steel bin. Packing the bottom full of wood, she poured in some petrol from the red, metal petrol can her gardener used. Lighting a match, she tossed it in and marvelled at the small explosion of flames as the petrol fumes ignited.

By her feet was a clear plastic bag that the police had given her. It was some of Callum's possessions that they'd removed from the hospital or from the bedroom he'd been using at Bryn's house. She wanted them gone, and burning them seemed to be the best way of disposing of them.

Annie had presided over the memorial service for Meg that afternoon at St Mary's church in Dolgellau. Frank had been there for moral support – as he always was. And Stephen had read a poem that Annie had chosen. The service had ended with *Monday Monday* by *The Mamas and Papas*, which Annie knew to be one of Meg's favourite songs when they were growing up together.

'Everything all right?' asked a voice.

Annie looked behind her. It was Stephen giving her a puzzled look.

'Just a bit of housekeeping,' she said by way of a vague explanation.

Stephen looked none the wiser. 'Okay, I won't ask.' Then he gestured to where the cars were parked. 'I'm popping out. Committee meeting at the golf club. Shall I pick us up an Indian on the way home?'

Annie nodded, hiding her ongoing surprise at Stephen's civility. 'Yeah, that would be nice.'

'Great,' he said in an almost chirpy fashion. 'I'll see you later.'

Annie watched him go with a curious look. Ever since Meg's murder, Stephen had transformed before her eyes, returning to the kind, thoughtful and supportive man that she had met all those years ago. It seemed a shame that it had taken something as tragic and awful as Meg and Callum's deaths for him to change his often selfish behaviour. But if there could be anything positive to take out of the tragedy, she would gladly accept it.

Reaching down, she started to pull some of Callum's possessions from the bag – magazines, old clothes, a mobile phone case – and tossed them into the dancing orange flames.

She couldn't even begin to articulate her feelings about Callum and his murder. With Meg, it was just heartbreaking, excruciating grief that sometimes subsided. But Callum was a different matter. There were hours where she would be so angry about what he'd done to his own mother that she could hardly bear it.

But then there were other moments when images and memories of him as a boy just popped into her head. The night that he had snuck into her bed when he was only about seven years old while staying over because he was scared of a thunderstorm. The morning she had watched him play football for Dolgellau Under-10s and he had won the 'Man of the Match' trophy. The beaming smile across his face as he sprinted over to the touchline to show her.

Why hadn't she been able to address his worsening behaviour? Could she have done more to help her sister deal with his addiction and destructiveness? What had turned him into the young man that he'd become? Abandoned by his father at birth. A slightly batty, disorganised mother who had a string of inappropriate boyfriends and often left him alone from an early age to fend for himself, claiming it would be good for his confidence and self-esteem. Annie was always happy to have him to stay over, but her work as a judge sometimes got in the way.

Nature or nurture? Which was it? Was Callum born to become a killer? A genetic abnormality that predestined the events of the past ten days. Or was the neglect and chaos of his childhood a major contributing factor? Annie didn't know, and she was driving herself mad just thinking about it.

She reached down and pulled out the book that she had seen on the photo that Dewi had shown her – *In Cold Blood – the true story of the Keith Tatchell murders.* It made her feel sick to even look at it. In her anger, she ripped pages from the book and tossed them into the inferno.

Flicking through the book, she saw the thicker white pages at the book's centre that contained photographs. Pictures of Keith Tatchell as a child. His parents. Where he had grown up in North Wales. DCI Ian Goddard, the lead detective who she and Frank had met only days earlier.

And then a photograph of Tatchell sitting in a pub watching a local band playing. At first, she was drawn to looking at the members of the scruffy-looking band.

But then her eyes moved over to the table where Tatchell was sitting.

A man sitting next to him. Grinning.

The man had swept-back hair.

Oh my God.

It was Simon Bentley.

Chapter 55

It was late afternoon as I made my way from the kitchen to the living room. I was carrying a tray with thick-cut ham sandwiches, cheese and onion crisps, and a mug of strong tea on it. Rachel had always joked that if she was on Death Row, that would be the choice for her last meal. I always teased her, saying that it was too bland. My choice for my last meal on planet earth would be a huge steak, fried mushrooms, fries and a pint of mild.

'Here you go, love,' I said, as I gently placed the tray down on her lap.

'Thank you,' she said with a laugh. 'You are a dear.'

'I am a dear, you're right,' I replied again.

Caitlin, who was sitting over on the sofa with Sam, laughed. 'Gosh, how long have you two been doing that for?'

'Since 1978 at a guess,' I replied.

Sam glanced at us both and looked confused. I didn't think that it was worth explaining.

I sat down at the far end of the sofa and let out a sigh.

Caitlin looked over at Rachel. 'That all right, Mum?'

'Perfect,' she replied in what sounded like a Norfolk accent. Then she looked over at us. 'Frank, who used to talk like that? Perfect,' she asked, repeating the accent.

'I don't know,' I said with a shrug, but it was nice to see Rachel so lucid and chatty. She had definitely perked up since Caitlin and Sam's arrival at the house. 'Was it Pam Ayres?'

Rachel shook her head. 'She had a country bumpkin accent, but not Norfolk.'

'Right. What about that bloke from *Open All Hours*? David Jason?'

'Bloody hell, Dad,' Caitlin chortled. 'That was set in Yorkshire.'

'Was it?' I asked.

'Yes, yes,' Rachel agreed with a grin. 'Arkwright was his character's name, and it was set somewhere like Doncaster.'

I gave Caitlin a knowing look as if to say that when Rachel was recalling stuff from her long-term memory, she was lucid and sharp.

'Well remembered, Mum,' she said encouragingly.

I was aware that my phone had been buzzing in my pocket about a minute earlier. I took it out to see that there had been a missed call from Annie.

The small post-it that I'd taken from Meg's caravan floated out of my phone wallet and landed on the sofa. It had *TAP 134 3A* scribbled at its centre.

Caitlin picked it up and looked quizzically at me. 'Phone number of your girlfriend, Dad?' she teased.

'Oh your dad's got girlfriends queuing around the block,' Rachel chortled.

Caitlin raised an eyebrow suspiciously. She had always been fiercely protective of her mother, especially since she got ill. 'Has he now?' Then she looked at the post-it properly. 'Yeah, it's a flight number actually.'

I raised my brows in a show of surprise. 'How do you mean?'

'Remember I've worked as a travel agent for a decade, Dad,' she reminded me. 'TAP is Air Portugal.'

'Okay,' I said, wondering why Meg had a flight number written down on a post-it note. It was probably nothing.

'And the 3A is a seat in business class.'

'Is it?' I asked, a little confused. I knew that Meg certainly didn't have the money to travel anywhere business class.

'Why, what is it?' Caitlin asked.

'I found this note at Megan's caravan a few days ago.'

'And she travels business class, does she?'

'I doubt that,' I replied.

'You know what date the flight was?'

I pulled a face. 'No.' Then I thought about it. 'What about Sunday 21st August?' It was the day before Annie had reported Meg missing.

Caitlin took her phone and started to tap on it.

'What are you doing?' I asked.

'I'm checking to see if that flight was on that date.'

'And was it?'

'Hang on … Yes. Flight TAP 134 flew into Manchester from Lisbon at 10.25am that morning,' she announced with an element of pride that she'd been helpful to me. Then she gave me a knowing look. 'Do you want to see if Meg was on that flight?'

'She won't have been,' I said, shaking my head.

'Okay.'

I thought for a moment. 'Can you do that?' I asked, my interest now piqued.

'I can get the passenger list.'

'Is that legal?'

'No, of course not. But what are they going to do? Sack me?' She shrugged her shoulders. 'I quit and live up here now.'

'No, I suppose they can't do that now,' I agreed.

She continued tapping on her phone. I wondered what the hell I was going to do if Meg had been on a business class seat on a flight from Lisbon the day before she officially went missing.

Caitlin stopped and then looked over at me. 'Okay, I don't know what this means, but Megan was sitting in that business class seat on that flight that morning.'

'What?' I was shocked. 'Can you see who was sitting next to her?'

She peered at the screen again. 'Oh, actually I can't. It's a comped seat.'

'I don't know what 'comped' means?'

'Either the passenger had some frequent flyer upgrade scheme,' she explained, 'or they're staff.'

'Staff?'

'Yeah, you know? Cabin crew, pilot, that sort of thing.'

My mind was now racing. 'Do staff normally get benefits once they have retired?' I immediately had Simon Bentley in my thoughts. I knew that everyone was convinced that Callum was Megan's killer, but I had to rule out Bentley, however much of a long shot it was.

'Yes, it's normally a lifetime benefit. It is on airlines like BA.'

'Can you bypass that and get to see who Meg was sitting next to?' I asked with a growing sense of urgency.

She hesitated.

'Please, this is really important.'

'It's going to take a while.'

'How long?'

'Half an hour. And it is very dodgy to start playing around with passenger lists and security. It sends up red flags.'

'If there's any problem, I'll say that I forced you to do it,' I said. 'I'm looking for the name Simon Bentley.' Then I pointed to my phone. 'I've got to make a quick call, okay?'

I dialled Annie's number, my head spinning from what I'd just discovered. Was it really Bentley sitting next to Meg on that flight from Lisbon? And what did it mean? They lived next door to each other, so some kind of romantic liaison wasn't beyond the realms of possibility. But Bentley had lied to our faces when we told him that Meg was missing. Wasn't that incredibly suspicious?

'Frank?' Annie said, sounding as if she had something pressing to tell me.

'I've got something to tell you,' I babbled. 'It's really strange and I don't know what to make of it.'

Silence.

'Annie?'

'Yes, so have I,' she said, sounding confused.

'You go first,' I insisted.

'Okay. By complete chance I looked through a book on Keith Tatchell. In one of the photos that was taken in 1995, Tatchell is sitting next to Simon Bentley in a pub. It looks like they were definitely friends at that time.'

'What?' I said in astonishment. 'So, now we have a direct link between Tatchell and Bentley.'

'Exactly. I knew we were on to something, but maybe Bentley was just friends with him. It's a small world. And I'm not sure it helps us.'

'No, it does,' I assured her. 'I've just found out what

that post-it note that we found in the caravan means. Caitlin did some digging. Meg flew business class from Lisbon to Manchester on the morning of Sunday 21st August.'

'Jesus, Frank! Are you sure?'

'Yes. We've seen the passenger list.'

'But that doesn't make any sense does it? Business class? Who was she with?'

'We're not sure, but we know that the person sitting next to her either had some kind of frequent flyer card or they were cabin crew *or a pilot.*'

Silence.

I could hear Annie's breathing had become shallow. She was getting upset.

'Sorry, I just needed to tell you all that.'

'Don't be silly. Of course you did. I can't believe that we're saying that Meg might have been in some kind of relationship with Bentley.'

'I've just thought of something,' I said.

'Go on.'

'That car was sitting outside the caravan. And we know that Bentley continually looks out of his window to see what's going on.'

'You think he might have planted it? I know for a fact that Megan never left her car unlocked. I told her that it would get stolen one day.'

'It's a long shot, but there is definitely something very strange going on.'

'Shall we do this face to face, Frank?'

'Yes. That'll be easier,' I said. 'I'll be with you in fifteen minutes. I won't be long.'

I ended the call feeling the anxiety in my stomach as I went down the hallway towards the front door.

Giving a little whistle, I saw Jack appear from the

kitchen and trot to my side. 'We're going out for a bit, mate,' I told him as I ruffled the hair on the back of his head.

I opened the front door and felt the blast of cold air against my face. Was Bentley really the killer? Had he helped Tatchell kill those women twenty-five years ago? I remembered what Evie Dalby told us about the man who had been with Tatchell the night she had been attacked and sexually assaulted. She thought his name could have been Sam or Simon. He was attractive and arrogant. He boasted of flying around the world, so she guessed that he'd been a pilot or cabin crew. Everything fitted. Didn't it?

As Jack and I walked across the gravel towards the pick-up, I continued to piece it all together in my head. Bentley had become involved in a relationship with Meg. He'd flown her off to Portugal business class. Then something had gone wrong. After years of not killing, he snapped and murdered her. Knowing that Callum and Meg shared a car, he'd waited for the right moment, creeping out from his caravan to plant the hammer and piano wire, hoping the police would eventually find them.

'Dad?' called a voice urgently.

I turned to look, and saw Caitlin jogging after me.

'Yeah, it didn't take as long as I thought to find out who was sitting in that seat after all.'

'Oh, right. Good,' I said with a growing sense of expectation.

'You were looking for Simon Bentley, weren't you?'

'Yes, that's right.'

Silence.

Caitlin gave me a strange frown and shook her head. 'Yeah, it wasn't him. It's not his name on that seat.'

I don't understand, I thought. I'd been 99% certain that's what Caitlin was going to discover.

'Well, what's the name on the list?' I asked.

'It's really weird,' she said. 'It says Stephen Taylor on it … but isn't that Annie's husband?'

My eyes widened as I grabbed my phone and called Annie.

Chapter 56

Annie held her phone. She was trawling through social media, seeing what she could find out about Simon Bentley. Very little so far. The doorbell rang and she made her way out of the kitchen, wondering who was ringing. She knew that it couldn't be Frank as she had just spoken to him. And Stephen was at the golf club.

Still holding her phone, she padded down the hallway and saw a figure standing outside on the doorstep.

Maybe it was a package that needed to be signed for? Something Stephen had ordered and forgotten to tell her?

As she opened the door, she saw a man whom she didn't recognise looking back at her.

Then she saw that he was carrying some dry cleaning in clear plastic wrapping. It looked like some of Stephen's suits and a few of her jackets that she'd dropped in a few weeks earlier.

'Oh great, thanks,' she said to the man as he handed over the dry cleaning.

'Here you go,' he said politely. 'It's on your account is it?'

'Yes please,' she replied as she gave him a kind smile and closed the door. She was finding it hard to concentrate given what she had discovered and what Frank had just told her about her sister being on a flight from Portugal. None of it made any sense or added up.

The dry cleaning was heavy and cumbersome. Putting her phone down on the hall table, she went up the stairs clutching the clothes. Her head was a whirling mess.

Going into the master bedroom, she plonked the clothes down on the bed and walked over to the enormous built-in wardrobes that went down the far side of the room.

Pulling off the thin plastic wrapping, she took one of Stephen's suits and went over to hang it up. It was a lovely fitted navy suit. She checked the label. *Paul Smith.* Stephen was never one to scrimp when buying clothes.

Taking a step back, Annie looked at the row of suits that hung in a line.

Jesus, she thought. *Stephen's had some of those suits for thirty years!*

For a moment it seemed to be so strange doing something so mundane and ordinary as putting away a few bits of dry cleaning. But in some ways the normality and familiarity of the task felt reassuring.

Annie pulled a couple of the older suits out of the wardrobe, resolving that she would insist that Stephen take them to the local cancer research shop to make more room in the wardrobe.

She got an overpowering waft of aftershave from the suits. It was thick and intense. It was redolent of the times when she and Stephen were first together. That's what she always remembered about him in the old days. He always smelled of strong aftershave. In fact, people used to comment on it.

For a moment, Annie stopped.

Aftershave?

She put the thought out of her mind.

'Having a clear-out?' said a voice.

Jesus!

She gave a little squeal as she almost jumped out of her skin.

It was Stephen.

He was holding her phone.

'Bloody hell, Stephen! You scared the life out of me,' she cried.

'Sorry,' he said with an apologetic expression. 'Two of the committee members cried off with some flu thing that's going round. So we decided to try again in a few weeks.'

Annie nodded and then gestured. 'What are you doing with my phone?' she asked.

Stephen held it up. 'It was on the hall table. It kept buzzing.' He handed it to her. 'Looks like Frank is very keen to get hold of you for some reason.' He couldn't help but sound a little pointed as he said it. He always used that tone when Frank was mentioned.

In that instant, Annie's phone rang in her hand. It was Frank.

Stephen frowned. 'Aren't you going to answer it? It might be urgent.'

Annie nodded as she pressed the answer button.

'Hi Frank,' she said.

Stephen held up one of his old suits with a wry smile. He was standing between her and the door out to the landing. 'You're going to tell me to take these down to the charity shop, aren't you?' he chortled.

'Annie,' Frank said with a sense of urgency. 'It's Stephen.'

Silence.

'Sorry,' Annie said, but she was gripped by a sudden sense of panic. What was he talking about?

'Oh okay,' she said in as nonchalant a tone as she could muster.

'Stephen was on the seat next to Meg on that plane from Portugal.'

Annie felt her stomach lurch.

'My guess is that they were having an affair,' he continued.

I think I'm going to be sick, Annie thought as she started to shake a little.

She forced an amused sigh to cover her terror. 'Oh I see. Never mind.'

Silence. She gripped the metal of the coat hanger tight.

She had her eyes locked on Stephen who was inspecting his old suits.

'Is he there?' Frank asked in a hushed tone.

'Yes, that's right,' Annie said, trying to sound amused, but her breathing was quick and shallow.

'Right, I'm on my way now.' Frank ended the call.

Annie just didn't know what to do. She felt frozen to the spot. She continued to hold the phone to her ear as her heart thumped against her chest.

'No problem,' she said, trying to catch her breath. 'Yes. Okay, I'll see you tomorrow. Bye.'

She hung up.

Stephen held up one of his old suits with a bemused smirk. 'I think this suit is now back in fashion. It's cyclical, isn't it? Fashion?'

Annie nodded, but she was finding it hard to focus. Was Stephen really the man who had killed Meg, or were they just having an affair behind her back? Then she remembered what Evie Dalby had told them. An attractive man whose name began with an S. Simon or Sam.

Or Stephen!

He was arrogant but charming, and flew all around the world on business back in the 90s. Then there was the aftershave.

Oh my God, it's him. Has it been him all along? she wondered as she watched him giving her a curious frown.

'Everything all right?' he asked her.

She had just realised that her husband might be a serial killer who had murdered her sister. How could anything be all right ever again?

'You're shaking,' he said, coming towards her and putting a comforting hand on her shoulder. She recoiled from his touch. 'What's the matter?'

'Nothing,' she said, trying to hold it together as she made for the door. 'I'm just feeling a bit dizzy. Sugar crash or something.'

He stood in front of her. Did he suspect that she knew something? Or was she just being paranoid?

Annie could feel her palms were sweaty as she took a nervous gulp.

'Get out of my way, Stephen,' she said through gritted teeth. She couldn't help herself. He'd murdered Meg. She knew he had. Part of her just wanted to run and get away from him. Part of her wanted to attack him and rip his eyes out.

'Not until you tell me what the hell is going on,' he snapped. She saw the sudden rage underneath the veneer.

Annie tried to push past him. 'Get out of my way!'

Stephen tried to restrain her, putting his arms around her shoulders.

Reaching down to a nearby bedside table, Annie grabbed a reading lamp. With an almighty swing, she smashed the lamp into the side of his head.

'Jesus!' he cried, holding his head before he fell onto the carpet.

'You killed her, you bastard!' Annie screamed as she tried to hit him again. She wanted to kill him. 'You killed Meg. You lying fucking psychopath.'

Stephen looked up at her as he cowered. The side of his face was covered in blood.

'I don't know what the hell you're talking about,' he yelled as she tried to hit him again. 'For God's sake, Annie. What's got into you? Are you insane?'

For a millisecond, Annie stopped in her tracks. Stephen's words seemed to ring true.

Jesus, what if I've got all this wrong?

'You were sleeping with Meg and then you killed her!' she screamed.

In a flash, he reached up, grabbed her arm and pulled her off balance. He lifted his leg behind the back of her calves so that she fell backwards over them and then crashed onto the carpet.

For a moment, Annie was winded and disorientated.

Then suddenly Stephen was on her. Holding the electrical cord of the lamp in his hands, he turned her onto her front.

She tried to struggle, but the fall had taken all the wind out of her.

Grabbing her hands roughly, he wound the electrical cord around her wrists tightly so that her hands were tied behind her back. The cord dug into her skin.

'What the hell are you doing?' she screamed. 'Get off me!'

Pushing her over onto her back, Stephen sat down on the edge of the bed and looked down at her. He was panting, trying to get his breath.

Annie glared at him.

There were a few seconds of silence as he composed his thoughts.

'What have you done, Stephen?' she asked under her breath in utter horror.

He ran his hands through his hair and took a long deep breath. Then he brought his eyes over to hers.

'What have I done?' he asked in a calm but icy voice.

He seemed to have suddenly become completely detached from what was going on.

'Did you kill her? Did you kill Meg?' Annie asked him as the tears stung her eyes. She needed to know, but was terrified of the answer.

Silence.

'Yes,' he said finally without a glimmer of emotion or remorse. It was as if he'd been asked something as trivial as if he was wearing socks.

Annie felt the pain and shock surge through her body. 'Why, Stephen?' she sobbed. The tears fell from her eyes and trickled down her face. She couldn't wipe them because her hands were tied behind her.

'Why?' Stephen said, ruminating. Then an expression of remembered elation came over his face. 'Well … it's the greatest rush known to man. I've taken pure cocaine and it's not even close. The high lasts for days, weeks even. So it becomes totally addictive. I want to experience that rush again.'

Annie screwed her face up and cried out, 'Jesus Christ, Stephen!'

'I can't help it.' He shrugged. 'Your brain is coded for compassion, for guilt, for empathetic pain when you inflict pain on another person.' He looked at her. 'I have none of that. I don't know why. When I was twelve, I broke the neck of our family cat because she scratched me. My parents and my sister were devastated, whereas I felt nothing. In fact, I enjoyed it.'

Silence.

'Why Megan?' Annie whispered. 'Tell me why. I need to know.'

'Megan had served her purpose just as the others had done,' he responded, as though this made perfect rational sense. His tone was that of a doctor explaining a diagnosis to a patient. 'I need to feel complete control. And see their pain. That's what I enjoy. And then ultimately I need to see them die.' He looked at her and shrugged. 'It's what I need. As I said, I just don't know why.'

'She was my sister,' Annie wept. 'Didn't that mean anything to you?'

Silence.

'No,' he said coldly. 'I know that sounds strange, but I don't feel anything. I don't feel empathy or compassion. I never have done. I'm aware that there is something terribly wrong with me. I've just become incredibly skilled at masking it.'

The cord was digging into her skin. Annie tried to roll over onto her side. Then she shook her head as she looked at him in utter disbelief. 'I've spent my whole life with you. How did I not see what you were?'

Stephen sighed pompously and crossed his legs. 'I'm afraid that deep down you're emotionally very needy and weak, Annie. You crave outside affirmation which makes you very easy to manipulate. It's why you became a High Court Judge. Status, power, kudos.'

'You're a monster,' she hissed at him as she wriggled on the carpet. Having her hands tied behind her back was hurting her shoulders.

He nodded. 'For want of a better word, I am,' he agreed

in a composed tone. 'We flew back from Portugal after a lovely long weekend in Lisbon. I actually wondered if it was going to be different this time. But as we stood out at the back of her caravan, I caught myself thinking again. My old thoughts.' He rubbed his face and then frowned. 'And then I just looked at Megan's pathetic little face and I knew what I needed to do.'

'So you just killed her?' Annie asked in utter disbelief.

'Yes,' he replied. 'And I watched you all on that beach when they found her.' He paused, deep in thought. 'Megan kept her car unlocked, so it was easy just to place those things in the boot. I knew they'd be found and that would lead the police to Callum.'

Annie fixed him with a hateful stare. 'Frank knows it's you and he's on his way.'

He smiled. 'I know that. Your reaction to his call was far too extreme for it to be anything else. You're not a very good actress.' Then he stood up.

'Keith Tatchell?' Annie said with a furrowed brow.

'Yeah, poor Keith.' Stephen uncrossed his legs and sat forward on the edge of the bed. 'He was my little helper. My hanger on. It was a very pleasant surprise when he was arrested and convicted. Things died down after that. And that overwhelming compulsion just seemed to go away for such a long time. I'd hoped that it had gone forever. But clearly it hadn't.'

Annie didn't know what to say. It was as if she was trapped in some terrible, horrific nightmare that she was going to wake up from any second now.

'I'll be back in a minute,' he said.

Annie struggled on the carpet as Stephen headed across the bedroom and out of the door.

He looked at her from the doorway. 'Don't worry. I'm coming back,' he said in a detached tone.

Pulling and twisting, Annie tried to loosen the electrical cord that was around her wrists.

For a second, she thought that she'd created enough space to pull out her right hand. She could feel that the cord was getting stuck on the bone that was just below the base of her thumb.

She yanked at it with all her strength until she thought that she was going to break the bones in her hand. It was agony.

Stephen appeared again at the door and came in. He was holding a small glass of what appeared to be water – or at least it was clear liquid.

He approached and then crouched down next to her. 'I've brought you a drink, and I'm going to need you to drink it all.'

Annie shook her head in fury. 'No.'

He shrugged as he moved the glass towards her face.

'No!' she screamed, and then pushed her lips together. He would have to kill her before she opened them, she told herself.

'Annie, there is an easier way of doing this.'

She shook her head.

In a flash, he reached over and pinched her nostrils closed with a vice-like grip. It was so forceful that she feared he was going to break her nose.

As he pushed the glass against her mouth, she moved her head away and then back the other side, desperate not to drink whatever was in the glass.

Her lungs were starting to burn with the lack of oxygen from not breathing.

No, no, don't let him do this. If you open your mouth, he's going to drug you and then he's going to kill you.

It was no use.

She let out a gasp as she sucked in air, her head now dizzy.

He gripped her face and jaw and poured the liquid into her mouth.

She spat it out, feeling it running down her chin, but the liquid kept coming.

Starting to choke, she struggled and thrashed. *No, no.*

'Get off me!' she screamed.

But then she tasted the foul liquid, and her reflexes made her swallow some of it. It had a strong metallic taste.

Stephen stood up and then sat on the edge of the bed and watched her.

'It'll take about a minute, but then you're going to feel very cold and then you're going to be unconscious,' he told her.

Annie fought with everything she had to stay conscious. She dug her fingernails into her skin trying to delay the inevitable.

Her eyelids were starting to close.

No, no, no.

Then blackness.

Chapter 57

I pulled up on the driveway at Annie's house. I parked and jumped out of the truck. My immediate concern was for Annie. I gave a quick whistle. Jack leapt from the back of the pick-up. I jogged over to the front door and went to ring the doorbell. The door wasn't quite closed, as if someone had left the house in a hurry. However, Stephen and Annie's cars were both on the drive.

Walking into the hallway, I couldn't hear anything.

Silence. My pulse was racing, my stomach tight.

'Hello? Annie?' I called out. 'It's Frank.'

More silence.

'The front door was open so I came in,' I called.

Starting to feel very uneasy, I signalled to Jack to follow me. I made a very quick search of the rooms downstairs – kitchen, study, dining room, living room.

Nothing.

This is not good. Where are they?

Jogging up the stairs, Jack and I moved from bedroom to bedroom.

Reaching what appeared to be the master bedroom, I

saw a lamp lying on the carpet, its black cord stretched out behind it. The bedside table had also been moved out or bumped into.

Shit!

My heart was pounding. Something had happened in here. Some kind of struggle.

'Annie? It's Frank,' I shouted with a sense of urgency.

Then I noticed a few damp patches in the middle of the carpet. Has someone spilled a drink?

Crouching down, I looked at them. Then I dabbed my forefinger in one patch and sniffed it. It smelled of chemicals and a metallic smell that I recognised.

Chloroform.

Bloody hell! He's drugged her.

Standing up, I took a few seconds to compose myself.

There had been a struggle of some kind in the bedroom and Stephen had used chloroform to sedate Annie.

I needed to find out where he'd taken her. And quickly.

The cars were still on the drive. They had to be here somewhere.

Jack and I jogged back along the landing and down the stairs to the hall.

Was there a cellar in the house? I didn't remember seeing one.

Then I had a vague memory of there being a door under the stairs.

Moving swiftly towards the kitchen, I spotted a door that was flat against the cream wooden panels of the staircase.

It had to be the door to a cellar.

As I approached, to my frustration I saw a silver padlock hanging from the lock on the door.

There was no way anyone could be down there if the padlock was still on.

To be on the safe side, I went over to the door anyway.

'Annie? Annie? It's Frank,' I shouted, and then froze, listening for the faintest sound or movement.

Nothing.

I glanced down at Jack who had ignored the door completely. If there was any kind of scent, he hadn't picked it up.

We went outside.

It was raining hard.

If Stephen had drugged Annie then they couldn't have gone far. Annie was petite and didn't weigh a lot, but it still narrowed down where Stephen could have taken her.

We ran around to the drive where the cars were parked.

The rain had started to come down in sheets, and the moon had been smothered in blackness.

Then out of the corner of my eye, I spotted something.

A tiny sliver of light coming from the outbuildings to my right.

Moving to the back of my truck, I pulled back the tarpaulin, grabbed the shotgun and checked it. It was still loaded.

I ran across to the entrance of the outbuildings.

Jack and I stopped for a moment.

The only sound I could hear was the rain battering down on the ground around us.

Jack gave a little whine and looked agitated. Either he had picked up on my anxiety, or there was something inside the buildings that had spooked him.

'What is it, boy?' I whispered.

We went to the door that clearly led inside.

It was painted black.

Giving it a push, I could feel that it was locked.

There was a brass-coloured yale lock at eye level.

Reaching down, I took my knife from the sheath on my ankle. I wedged it carefully between the door and the door frame at the same level as the lock.

With a quick flick, I moved the yale lock to the left and the door opened slowly.

I replaced the knife and listened intently.

The noise of rain battering down on the roof and windows masked any other sounds.

I opened the door and went inside.

I gave Jack another look and wondered if he'd pick up a scent.

Taking careful steps so as not to alert Stephen to our presence, we made our way along a long wood-panelled corridor. The walls were lined with sports memorabilia – signed photos of cricketers, golfers etc.

Pushing open a door to our right, I stuck my head in very slowly.

An enormous empty snooker room with dark leather Chesterfield sofas and armchairs, and burgundy-coloured walls.

Turning around, I saw that Jack had moved further down the corridor. He was sniffing at the bottom of another black painted door to our right.

He put out his paw and gave the wood a scratch. Then he looked at me and whined.

He can smell something.

I nodded to reassure him.

With a gentle push, the door opened.

There was a wooden staircase with a single rail going down into what must be a basement or cellar.

There was light coming from somewhere.

Then a noise or movement.

Someone's down there.

Taking a slow, deliberate step down, I felt the wood wobble. It gave a little creak as I put my whole weight down.

Shit!

I froze.

'Hello?' said a voice from the basement in a quizzical tone.

It was Stephen.

'Frank,' he called out. 'You'd better come and join us now that you're here.'

The sound of his detached voice was unsettling.

As Jack and I moved down the steps, I began to see a vast cellar. It was out of keeping with the rest of the property. The ceiling tiles were stained and the walls needed painting.

Over in the corner, I saw a huge wooden table.

And a figure lying motionless on top of it.

Annie. Oh my God.

Putting the shotgun into the nook of my shoulder, I continued to walk carefully down the wooden steps.

Stephen was nowhere to be seen.

I strained to listen but I couldn't hear anything.

Jack was close to my calves, sniffing.

Then I heard a little moan.

I spotted Annie's leg move over on the table.

Then another moan, as if she was being roused from a deep sleep.

Looking left and right, I put my finger onto the cold metal of the shotgun.

Where the hell is he?

We got to the bottom of the staircase.

I took a couple of careful steps towards where Annie was lying.

Stephen had to be hiding away somewhere.

I scoured the basement, gripping the shotgun, poised to shoot him if he attacked.

Jack gave an unsettling growl.

I froze again. Looked down.

Jack had turned around.

Someone was behind me.

Shit!

I went to spin around but it was too late.

Something hard and metallic smashed into my head.

I saw white. Dizzy. Unsteady.

As I staggered, I dropped the shotgun on the floor.

Then another blow.

Jesus.

Jack was barking and snapping at Stephen as he tried to launch another attack.

I lurched sideways.

Come on, Frank. Fight.

Another blow from the hammer.

My legs gave way and I sank to my knees.

I felt an arm jam against my throat. The crook of an elbow clamped against my windpipe. A sleeper hold.

I couldn't move.

Head spinning, dipping in and out of consciousness.

Jack was snapping and biting at Stephen, but he wasn't giving up.

The arm moved from my throat.

I gasped, sucking in air.

Suddenly, I felt something wrapping around my throat. It was thin and sharp.

It cut into my skin, drawing blood.

Piano wire.

I tried to clutch at it and pull it away but it was too taut against my skin and neck.

More barking and snapping.

Jesus, I can't breathe.

With my right hand, I slowly reached back down to my ankle.

Wrapping my fingers around the handle of my knife, I pulled it out and went to stab wildly at Stephen who was behind me.

I felt a blow against my hand, and the knife tumbled onto the floor.

That had been my one chance. It was gone.

Gasping desperately, I could feel myself slipping into unconsciousness.

This was it. I was going die.

I tried to prepare myself.

Thoughts of Rachel, Caitlin, Sam, Annie and Jack shuffled in my mind's eye – life flashing before me as it also slowly ebbed away.

Then suddenly the pressure on the wire lessened and slackened off.

What's going on?

I immediately grabbed the wire which was now loose and pulled it from my throat.

I sucked in air with everything I had. Breathing. Trying to get oxygen into my lungs.

Stephen stumbled forwards and then collapsed onto the floor in front of me.

I looked at his face as he gurgled and coughed blood.

What the hell just happened?

Then I saw something protruding from the side of his neck.

My knife.

I turned around and saw Annie standing just behind me.

Our eyes met.

'Oh my God, Frank,' she cried as she put her arms around me.

'It's okay,' I reassured her as I tried to get to my feet.

Chapter 58

I sat in the back of an ambulance that was parked up on Annie's drive as a paramedic tended to the cuts on my neck and the gash to my head. Even though he had suggested that I needed to go to hospital to check for concussion, I knew that I wasn't going anywhere.

As I looked across the driveway, I noticed that Annie was no longer sitting in the back of another ambulance. She had been checked over by a paramedic who then put a dark blanket around her shoulders. But she had disappeared somewhere.

I glanced up. The whole sky seemed to be ablaze with the strobing blue lights of patrol cars. A SOCO team had moved in to take forensic evidence from the basement and from Stephen's body. The air was full of the sound of various police Tetra radios crackling with voices from dispatch or attending officers.

I saw a figure approaching, wearing blue forensic gloves and white shoe covers.

It was Dewi.

He shook his head as he looked at me.

'You're both lucky to be alive,' he said quietly as he gestured to my wounds.

'I know,' I said, as the paramedic started to stick cotton wool to the side of my neck with a plaster.

'Annie has given us her statement,' he explained in a quiet voice. 'She told us that it was her who stabbed Stephen.'

'Yes.' I sighed. 'I'd be dead if she hadn't.' Then I looked at him. 'It's self-defence.'

'Yes,' he agreed. 'Justifiable homicide.'

'The IOPC are going to have to look at Ian Goddard and the whole Tatchell case again,' I said.

'I'll be phoning them in the morning. Bit of a mess all round.' Dewi raised an eyebrow. 'We found your shotgun. Why didn't you shoot him?'

'He came from behind me,' I explained, and then gestured to my neck. 'I wish I had shot him.'

Dewi pointed over to the outbuildings. 'Right, I need to get back in there. I'll send over a DC to take your statement if you're up to it.'

'Of course.'

'And get some rest, Frank,' he said as he turned and walked away.

'I got you a sugary tea,' said a voice.

I turned and saw Annie standing nearby. She had a blanket wrapped around her shoulders. She was carrying a mug of tea in each hand.

'How are you feeling?' I asked as I took a mug from her.

'Like I drank a bottle of Scotch and have the worst hangover of my life,' she admitted.

'Yes, chloroform will do that to you.'

The paramedic looked at me. 'Right sir, I've patched you up, but any concerns - if you're sick or dizzy - go straight to A&E.'

'Thank you,' I said gratefully.

Annie came and sat down next to me in the back of the ambulance.

We sat in silence for a few minutes. It was difficult to know what to say. What could I say?

'Twenty-four hours ago, I didn't think my life could get any worse,' she said in a virtual whisper. 'And then it just did.'

Silence.

'At the risk of being purely practical,' I eventually said, 'where will you stay?' Then I gestured. 'This lot will be here and all over your house for at least another twenty-four hours.'

Annie sighed. 'A hotel?' she said with a forlorn shrug.

'We have a spare room at our farmhouse,' I suggested. Then I looked at her. 'It'll be best for you not to be on your own in a hotel room after everything.'

'Thank you.' She blinked, now deep in thought. 'If I had to sit alone in a hotel room, I think I would go insane.'

3 days later

It was 9pm by the time I went over to check in with Sam and Caitlin. We had been waiting with baited breath for about ten minutes before Sam walked out of the bedroom. He was wearing a brand new blazer, bottle green school tie, trousers and shoes.

'What do you think, Taid?' he asked, puffing out his chest. He had such a lovely smile on his face.

'Very smart, mate,' I said with a proud grin. 'Going to be breaking some hearts very soon, aren't you?'

He looked bewildered, and glanced at Caitlin for some kind of explanation.

She laughed. 'Taid's talking about girls.'

He grimaced. 'Erm, no, it's all right thanks.'

I laughed as he walked back into the bedroom.

'Bit early for all that,' Caitlin said. 'He still thinks that girls are the enemy.'

'Not the worst attitude to have going forward,' I joked.

'Hey,' Caitlin groaned with mock offence.

'When does he start?'

'His new form tutor would like him to start after half term.'

I raised an eyebrow. 'And what does he think?'

'He says that he can't wait,' she replied. 'So fingers crossed.'

'He's going to get teased for having a London accent mind you,' I chortled.

'Yeah, that's true ... How's Annie doing?'

I shrugged. 'I don't think she can bring herself to go back there.'

'Which isn't surprising.'

'No, it's not. I've told her that she's welcome here for as long as she wants.'

Caitlin smiled. 'I caught her and Mum having a right old gossip yesterday about people they knew from the past.'

'That's good.'

'Yes, it is,' she agreed. Then she gestured to my neck. 'Those look sore.'

'They are,' I replied. 'I'm just glad that they're superficial.'

I got up from where I was sitting.

'I'm glad you're alive after all that,' she said.

I gave her a wry smile. 'Me too.' Then I pointed to the wall. 'And we need a very big telly up on that wall. I'll sort that out this week for you guys.'

'You don't need to do that, Dad.'

I gave her a meaningful look. 'Yes, I do. And you don't need to worry, okay?'

I gestured to the front door. 'I'd better go and check on the old ladies,' I joked.

Caitlin laughed. 'That's a bit rude.'

'Night, Sam,' I called.

'Night, Taid,' he called back.

I got to the door and turned to give Caitlin a hug. She had a puzzled look on her face.

'You and Annie …' she said. She didn't need to finish the question.

I took a moment to answer. Then I shook my head. 'Just platonic. I wouldn't do that to your mother.'

Caitlin looked awkward. 'Sorry, I didn't mean …'

'I can see why you asked though,' I reassured her. 'I'll see you guys in the morning then.'

COMING BACK INTO THE FARMHOUSE, I could hear that the television was burbling from the living room. I walked past the kitchen which was in darkness. Then I came down the hallway and heard the sound of canned laughter.

Taking a step into the living room, I saw that an episode of the old American sitcom *Cheers* from the 80s was playing. Annie was lounging on the sofa, but Rachel was no longer sitting in her recliner.

'Hi Frank,' Annie said with a smile. 'She went up about twenty minutes ago.'

'Is she okay?' I asked.

Annie nodded and then gestured to the television. 'It was Rachel's suggestion to watch this. She remembered everything about it. The characters, the stories.'

I nodded. 'We watched it together every Friday night back then. A bowl of crisps each. I'd have a beer and she'd have a glass of wine. It was our little Friday night treat.'

Annie sighed with a smile. 'Sounds perfect.'

'Yeah, it was perfect,' I admitted as I spotted her rubbing her arms. 'You look chilly?'

She shook her head. 'I'm fine really. Just tired.'

I put up my hand as I went over to a long wooden chest which I opened. I pulled out a big, soft, chocolate-brown blanket. 'Here we go.'

Annie gave a snort of laughter. 'You didn't need to do that.'

'Nonsense,' I said as I came over and put the blanket over her.

She gave me a twinkly smile. 'Oh, right, the full treatment is it?'

I leaned over and kissed her on the cheek. 'Night, Annie.'

We looked at each other for a second.

'Night, Frank,' she said.

I walked out of the living room, down the hallway and up the stairs.

Chapter 60

I grabbed another stone from the path and hurled it towards a line of old tin cans on the dry stone wall just down from our farmhouse. It knocked a tin can at the far end clean off with a satisfying crack.

'Hey,' Sam said in mock annoyance. He was sitting next to me holding his own stone. 'How do you keep doing that?'

'Practise,' I replied with a chortle. 'When I was your age, there wasn't a lot to do. Throwing stones at tin cans was as exciting as it got.'

He frowned at me, as if he didn't believe what I was telling him.

The mid-morning autumnal sun was bright, and the sky a beautiful clear blue. The chocolate-coloured leaves on a nearby tree glistened in the light. The wind picked up, and the tin can I'd knocked off the wall skittered along the stones before coming to rest on a patch of overgrown grass.

'Your turn,' I said to Sam.

He immediately flung the stone. It missed the line of

cans and hit the stone wall below. He looked at me deflated.

I ruffled his hair and smiled. 'Don't throw it straight. Throw it up so that it falls and then lands on a can. In an arc.'

He furrowed his brow.

I took another stone from the ones we'd collected. 'Like this,' I said, demonstrating as I hit another can off the wall. I handed him a stone. 'Here, you try.'

He closed one eye, the tip of his tongue out of his mouth in utter concentration. Then he threw the stone up. It sailed through the air and then hit the middle can with a crack.

'I got it!' he yelled in excitement.

'There you go!' I said in a thrilled voice.

We high-fived each other.

In the distance, I could hear the rumbling of an approaching vehicle. I was expecting a delivery so I got up and put my hand on Sam's shoulder.

'Come on, mate,' I said as I looked up and saw an old green Land Rover coming up the track pulling a dark blue horsebox behind.

'Who's that?' Sam asked as he squinted and put his hand up to shield his eyes from the sunshine.

'Let's go and find out, shall we?' I had butterflies of excitement in my stomach. I couldn't wait to see Sam's face.

The Land Rover turned and parked up outside the stables.

'Okay,' Sam said as we walked down the track to meet the driver.

'Frank,' said a middle-aged man with a dark black beard and weathered face. It was an old friend of mine, Tony Ellis.

'Tony,' I said with a smile. Then I pointed to the horse-box. 'How's he doing?'

'Good as gold.' Tony walked to the back of the horsebox and slid off the bolts so he could lower the tailgate.

'Is there a horse in there?' Sam asked.

'A pony,' I explained as Tony lowered the tailgate.

Inside was a beautiful white Connemara pony.

Tony went into the horsebox, took the tether and brought the pony out onto the pathway.

'Come on,' I said as I guided Sam over. I put my hand gently on the pony's nose as he sniffed. 'You want to give him a stroke?'

Sam looked tentative as he lifted up the palm of his hand.

'It's fine, mate,' I reassured him. I took his hand and guided it so that he stroked the pony's nose. The pony gave a little whinny which made Sam jump a bit.

'Don't worry,' Tony laughed. 'He's just saying hello.'

'Do you like him?' I asked Sam.

Sam nodded enthusiastically. 'Yeah. He's beautiful.'

'That's good because he's yours. If you want him?'

His eyes widened with excitement. 'Really?' he gasped.

Tony chortled. 'I'm taking that's a yes.'

'What's his name?' Sam asked, as he stroked the pony's nose with more confidence.

'His name is Lleuad, which is Welsh for moon.'

'Lleuad,' Sam said to himself, and nodded.

'In Wales, we think that a white horse is a good omen,' I told him. 'The Welsh goddess Rhiannon rode on one.'

'What do they mean?' he asked.

What is the best way of explaining it?

'They symbolise the hope of new beginnings.'

SIMON MCCLEAVE

Sam nodded, but I wasn't convinced he knew exactly what that meant.

'Hey, he's here then?' called a familiar voice. My daughter.

I looked up to see three figures approaching – Caitlin, Rachel and Annie. They were all wrapped in big coats, scarves and woolly hats.

'He's beautiful,' Rachel said under her breath as they arrived.

'He is, isn't he, Mum?' Caitlin said. She turned to Sam. 'You like him?'

Sam shook his head in amazement. 'He's beautiful.'

I gestured over to the stable. 'I've got a brand new saddle, bridle and hat in there for you.'

As he wandered away, I heard the sound of another vehicle approaching.

Rachel caught my eye. 'You expecting anyone, Frank?'

'No,' I replied with a frown.

As the vehicle turned the corner of our track, I saw that it was one of the unmarked CID cars from Dolgellau.

Then I saw that Kelly was driving it. She pulled over and parked.

That's weird, I thought, assuming that there were probably a few things from the investigation into Megan's murder and Stephen's death that needed to be clarified with Annie.

I strolled over as she got out of the car.

'Morning Kelly,' I greeted her.

'Hi Frank.'

She looks decidedly concerned.

I gestured. 'Have you come to see Annie?'

She shook her head. 'No. I need to speak to you actually.'

'Oh right,' I said. 'What is it?'

'Tom Gilmore is your daughter's partner?'

'Unfortunately he is.'

She let out a long breath. 'The CPS have downgraded the charges to aggravated assault and possession of class A drugs.'

What?

I groaned. 'I don't understand.'

'I'm afraid he was released on bail late last night.'

My heart sank at the news. 'You're kidding?'

'I wish I was.'

'But he came here to attack my daughter and my grandson! How can they let him out? It puts them in danger.'

'I'm really sorry Frank, but you know what the prisons are like. They're bursting at the seams.'

'Where is he now?'

'I don't know. A friend picked him up last night. He's on a 7pm curfew and has to report to a police station three times a week.'

'Did he say where he was going to stay, or if he was heading back to London?'

She shook her head. 'He was adamant that he was staying in North Wales. He said that's where his family is. And he said he wasn't going anywhere without his son.'

I looked over at Caitlin who gave me a quizzical look as if to ask if everything was all right.

'Taid! Taid!' Sam shouted as he came out of the stable holding his new saddle and wearing his new riding hat. He had a sparkle in his eyes and a beaming smile on his face. I was overwhelmed by emotion.

TJ wasn't coming anywhere near Caitlin or Sam.

Your FREE book is waiting for you now

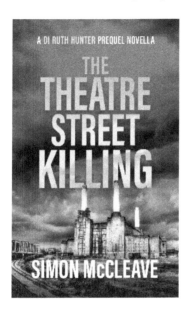

Get your FREE copy of the prequel to
the DI Ruth Hunter Series NOW
http://www.simonmccleave.com/vip-email-club
and join my VIP Email Club

DC RUTH HUNTER SERIES

London, 1997. A series of baffling murders. A web of political corruption. DC Ruth Hunter thinks she has the brutal killer in her sights, but there's one problem. He's a Serbian war criminal who died five years earlier and lies buried in Bosnia.

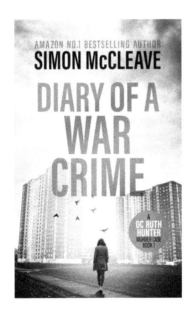

My Book
My Book

AUTHOR'S NOTE

Although this book is very much a work of fiction, it is located in Snowdonia, a spectacular area of North Wales. It is steeped in history and folklore that spans over two thousand years. It is worth mentioning that Llancastell is a fictional town on the eastern edges of Snowdonia. I have made liberal use of artistic licence, names and places have been changed to enhance the pace and substance of the story.

Acknowledgments

I will always be indebted to the people who have made this novel possible.

My mum, Pam, and my stronger half, Nicola, whose initial reaction, ideas and notes on my work I trust implicitly. Rebecca Millar for her fantastic editing. Carole Kendal for her meticulous proofreading. My designer Stuart Bache for yet another incredible cover design. My superb agent, Millie Hoskins at United Agents, and Dave Gaughran for his invaluable support and advice.